美国后现代小说论丛

丛书主编/杨仁敬

Highlighting Moral Ethos in Diasporic Space: On the Jewishness in *Cynthia Ozick's* Fiction

在流散空间凸现道德意识：论辛西娅·欧芝克小说中的犹太性

By Biao Xiao

肖飚 著

厦门大学出版社 国家一级出版社
XIAMEN UNIVERSITY PRESS 全国百佳图书出版单位

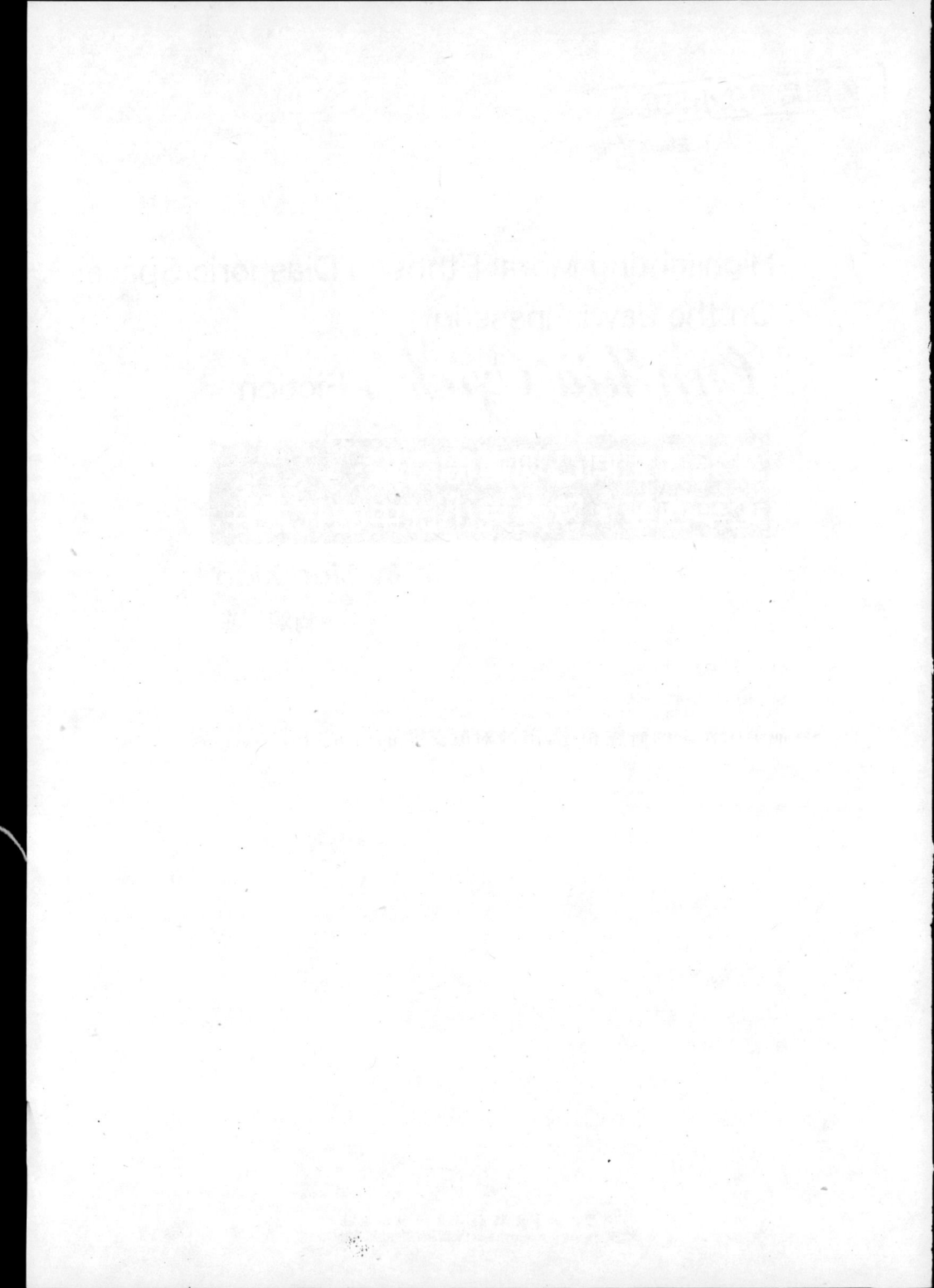

序

杨仁敬

  犹太小说是美国现当代文学重要的组成部分。它在上世纪五十年代曾经一枝独秀，轰动美国文坛。犹太作家索尔·贝娄、艾萨克·巴什维斯·辛格曾以他们独特的艺术风格，荣获了诺贝尔文学奖。伯拉德·马拉默德、菲利普·罗思、约瑟夫·海勒、诺曼·梅勒、罗纳德·苏克尼克以及埃·劳·多克托罗等犹太作家分别多次获得美国普利策奖、全国书评界奖和国家图书奖三大文学奖。他们在美国文学史上写下了光辉的一页。他们的作品受到世界各国读者的欢迎。

  辛西娅·欧芝克是美国犹太作家中的后起之秀。她大器晚成，成名时已五十七岁。她的小说中的犹太性比较浓厚，在美国犹太作家中有一定代表性，因此，她深受学界的关注。我国学界虽有人提及欧芝克，但往往泛泛带过，至今仍缺乏系统而深入的研究，鲜有专论。与其他美国作家的研究相比，国内对欧芝克的研究相对滞后。肖飚同志这部专著《在流散空间凸现道德意识：论辛西娅·欧芝克小说中的犹太性》填补了这个空白，具有重要的学术价值和现实意义。

  肖飚同志来自陕西黄土高原。早年毕业于西安外国语大学英文系，获硕士学位，后到西安建筑科技大学任教至今。她英文基础扎实，工作认真负责，任劳任怨，积极上进，曾多次陪同西安市和陕西省领导出访多个国家，担任口译，出色地完成了任务。2005年，她考入厦门大学，在我的指导下攻读美国小说史方向的博士学位。在校期间，她谦虚谨慎，团结同学，刻苦钻研，认真思考，门门功课成绩优秀，英文基本功很好，知识面较广，具有独立开展学术研究的能力和潜力。

  在确定研究欧芝克的选题时，我和她多次交谈和沟通，达成了共识。一方面，我们感到欧芝克虽大器晚成，但成果非凡，况且在世的美国犹太名作家不多了,她很值得我们研究,特别是国内欧芝克研究还是个空白,应该抓紧研究,迎头赶上;另一方面研究欧芝克的确难度很大。她的作品比较多,至今已发表7部长篇小说、4部短篇小说集、5部文学评论集,还有诗集、剧作和译文集,如何围绕论文的中心选择相关的文本,这是个难题。更难的是她作为一位美国犹太女作家,作品涉及犹太教、喀巴拉思想、米德拉什和泥人传说等等。这些是美国主流作家的小说所没有的。不过,这些困难是可以克服的。肖飚同志试读了欧芝克的名篇《披肩》和《异教徒拉比》,参阅了她的师兄师姐原先对欧芝克的评介,感到有所启发,兴趣很浓,认为欧芝克研究仍有拓展的空间。于是,她增强了信心,下定决心将选题定下来。

回到原单位后,肖飚同志立即启动学位论文的写作。她一面挤时间细读欧芝克的英文原著,然后拟定论文提纲;另一面多方委托亲朋好友帮助收集相关资料。她教学任务繁重,又担任副系主任,后来升为副院长,行政工作也很忙。她总是乐观愉快地工作,利用节假日和周末充实论文提纲。她与我多次通电话,反复修订论文提纲。为了寻找论文的切入点,她没少花时间。最后,她确定以欧芝克小说中的犹太性为中心,选用布拉的"流散空间论"来加以评析。2011年7月至8月,她利用暑期加班加点,不辞劳苦地写完了初稿。我审阅后提了一些修改意见,她又不厌其烦地多次修改补充,终于在10月底定稿,12月初正式答辩。她的博士学位论文受到校内外专家的高度评价,成绩优秀。专家们认为这是一篇优秀的博士学位论文。

这部专著就是以肖飚同志的博士学位论文为基础修订而成的。它具有下面几大特点:

第一,运用最新的"流散空间论"深刻而系统地揭示了欧芝克小说中犹太性的内涵和特色。1996年,阿弗塔・布拉提出"流散空间论",受到美国国内外学界的重视,但尚未引起我国学界关注。肖飚同志是第一位运用布拉的理论来解读欧芝克小说中犹太性的学者,其意义极不平常。她在论著中明确指出,欧芝克小说中的犹太性主要表现在四个方面:(1)在文学创作中渗透犹太观念并凸现道德意识;(2)凸现道德意识,改良正统犹太教性别观;(3)用犹太教渗透、拓展和改良正统的犹太教性别观并凸现道德意识;(4)运用后现代主义叙事策略来呈现犹太性。由此可见,欧芝克小说内涵丰富,独具特色。作者对布拉理论用得恰到好处,提出了独特的见解,对欧芝克的研究有新的突破。

第二,坚持语境、文本和理论三结合的原则,使欧芝克研究达到一定的深度和广度。作者选用了欧芝克的作品《异教徒拉比》、《披肩》、《升空》、《普特梅瑟和赞西佩》和《斯德哥尔摩的弥赛亚》等6部小说的文本来评析欧芝克的犹太性。论著从面到点逐步评述,先历史地回顾了美国犹太文学的形成及其犹太性的变迁,然后论及欧芝克小说中犹太性的表现、对犹太传统的继承和创新,结合相关理论一层一层加以剖析。论据充分,分析深刻,显得有血有肉,具体生动,令人信服。这说明作者对欧芝克的6部英文原著和相关理论有很好的理解和把握。

第三,将一些核心的犹太理念与多种文论巧妙地融合在一起,揭示了欧芝克凸现道德意识的不懈探索。作者将令人难解的一些重要的犹太理念如喀巴拉思想、米德拉什和泥人传说与后现代主义小说的侵入式叙事、零度写作、互文性等以及与女权主义、新历史主义和社会学理论密切结合,深刻地指出欧芝克彰显道德意识的途径主要表现在:反对偶像崇拜,坚持历史判断和阐释功能,用"思想的厄洛斯"改写正统的犹太教女性观等,这是很有创意的。研究美国犹太文学,不深入了解重要的犹太理念是不行的。但这绝不是一件易事。作者对喀巴拉思想、米德拉什和泥人传说等的理解和把握无疑为她顺利解读欧芝克小说中的犹太性打下了坚实的基础。这充分反映了作者刻苦钻研的精神、扎实的理论功底和独立搞科研的实力。

第四,将欧芝克的小说与她的文艺观结合起来,使评论更有客观性和准确性。欧芝克是个很有个性的犹太女作家。她对学界议论很多的"犹太性"有自己的看法。本书设专节对此加以评介,既指出她的观点,又不盲从,而是结合她的小说加以评论,指出她所强调的道德意识是基于她对流散空间中代表故园的"少数"与代表他乡的"多数"两者之间冲突的困惑和权衡。接着作者对故园的"少数"与他乡的"多数"四种具体情况作了深入浅出的分析，使评论不至于停留在欧芝克小说中犹太性的表面上，而是能够由表及里，深刻揭示它在流散空间突显道德意识的实质。这是一般评论欧芝克的文章做不到的。

这部专著用英文出版，文字简洁流畅，结构紧凑，表述清晰，资料翔实，立论公允。它将给我们带来有益的启迪。

这本专著的问世标志着肖飚同志学术研究的新开端。千里之行始于足下。漫漫学术路，艰难何所惧？肖飚同志能吃苦，善坚持，勇于探索，敢于创新，终于取得了佳绩，获得了荣誉和赞扬。这是来之不易的。但这仅是个良好的开端，任重而道远。作为她的导师，我深为她的成功感到欣慰，同时衷心地希望她再接再厉，与时俱进，再创辉煌！

美国犹太文学发展至今已有百年历史，博大精深，名家辈出，欣欣向荣，薪火相传。据说，美国至今已发表文学作品的犹太作家有两三百人。他们中间还会涌现像欧芝克一样的名作家，值得我们不断关注，并努力开创美国犹太文学研究的新局面。

2012 年 4 月 6 日于厦大西村

前 言

辛西娅·欧芝克(1928—),美国当代犹太女作家,已出版长篇小说七部、短篇小说集四部、评论文集五部,亦有诗歌、剧本和译作发表,荣获多种文学奖项:美国国家图书奖提名、布朗布里斯犹太文化遗产奖、爱德华·华伦纪念奖、美国艺术学会文学奖、国家犹太图书小说奖、犹太文学杰出贡献奖、欧·亨利奖等等。因其小说所呈现的犹太本质(Cohen 1994 180),欧芝克被称为当代犹太人及其犹太性的代言人(Yang 421),成为 20 世纪 70 年代以来美国最重要的犹太作家之一,其作品被评论家誉为当代文学的佳作(*Newsweek* 1971-5-10)。

尽管欧芝克在美国犹太文学领域享有举足轻重的地位,饱受赞誉,但在中国却鲜为人知。本书旨在通过基础性研究,以微薄之力促进中国欧芝克研究,使美国犹太小说研究走向深入。

目前国内外既无研究系统探讨欧芝克小说的犹太性,又尚未有学者在流散背景之下研究其犹太性的内涵和特色,已有的对其内在矛盾的研究只拘泥于其犹太作家身份,而忽视其女作家身份。

本书以欧芝克通过流散空间凸现道德意识从而在其小说中呈现出的犹太性为重点,关注她在流散背景下,消解其犹太人、女性和作家多重身份之间的对立的文学尝试。本书采用辩证视角,将历史、文化和理论研究与文本分析相结合,选取欧芝克的六篇小说——四篇短篇、一篇中篇、一篇长篇作为范本,代表其不同阶段、不同篇幅的小说创作。其中最早的一篇写于 1971 年,最新的一篇写于 1989 年。这六篇小说分别是:短篇小说《异教徒拉比》(1971)、《普特梅瑟:她的工作经历、家世和来生》(1982)、《普特梅瑟和赞西佩》(1982)和《升空》(1982);中篇小说《披肩》(包括《披肩》和《罗莎》)(1989);以及长篇小说《斯德哥尔摩的弥赛亚》(1987)。

本书运用阿弗塔·布拉于 1996 年提出的"流散空间"理念来阐释欧芝克小说中的犹太性。阿弗塔·布拉认为流散表现为横向、流动、多极,而非线性、固定、二元(Mishra 2006 17)。随着族裔研究主客疆域二元说的瓦解,"中点"概念应运而生——德勒兹和加塔里称其"自发形成连续不断的震动"(Deleuze and Guattari 21)。在"中点"概念的基础上,阿弗塔·布拉提出"流散空间"的概念,认为那是"一个自相矛盾的非空间,或者也可以看作⋯⋯第三空间"(Mishra 2006 83)。此外,布拉认为"流散空间"中代表故园的"少数"与代表他乡的"多数"之间的界限由多轴权力作用而决定(Brah 189)。

本书围绕权力作用即欧芝克作为犹太女作家在其小说中通过凸现冲突中的道德意识来彰显犹太观念的文学尝试展开阐述,包括作为一神教的犹太教反对偶像崇拜的本质与沦为偶像的文学呈现之间的冲突、艺术呈现包括大屠杀在内的犹太记忆过程中历史性与艺术性之间的冲突、欧芝克对犹太教的忠诚与其对正统犹太教性别歧视研判之间的冲突,及其后现代叙事服务于犹太性呈现之间的冲突。

鉴于欧芝克作品中浓厚的犹太性,本书涉及一些核心犹太概念和观点,诸如喀巴拉思想(特别是语言使用的神秘性)、米德拉什、泥人传说等。本书同时运用复调、元小说侵入式叙事、零度写作、互文性等文学概念,本质和社会建构等社会学概念,为阐释欧芝克的想象力提供必要的理论背景。

为了揭示欧芝克小说中犹太性的特点及其具体表现,本书首先回溯美国犹太文学的发展,着重考察欧芝克犹太性形成的时代背景,梳理美国 20 世纪 50 年代至 21 世纪的犹太小说,总结出其阶段性特征,即:道德意识、犹太教渗透、呈现大屠杀时坚持历史性。

本书指出,欧芝克将当代美国犹太小说所呈现的犹太性的主要特点加以叠加和拓展,从而拓展、丰富了犹太性内涵。具体表现在:首先,欧芝克叠加了道德意识和犹太教渗透;其次,欧芝克以道德意识贯穿呈现历史的过程;再次,欧芝克将犹太教渗透拓展至改良正统犹太教性别观并凸显道德意识;最后,欧芝克运用后现代主义叙事策略,以利于其犹太性的呈现。

本书进一步指出,欧芝克在流散空间通过凸现道德意识努力彰显犹太性的观点表现在三方面,即:反对偶像崇拜、坚持历史的判断及阐释功用、用"思想的厄洛斯"改写正统犹太教女性观,其犹太性体现在彰显这些观点的过程中所呈现的道德意识,而其道德意识基于她对于存在于作为"中点"的"流散空间"中代表故园的"少数"与代表他乡的"多数"两者之间冲突的困惑与权衡。正是欧芝克的文学尝试决定了故园"少数"与他乡"多数"之间的界限。实际上,源于欧芝克在流散空间建构的道德意识,故园"少数"终于融于他乡"多数"从而得以彰显。

本书界定了四种具体情形下的故园"少数"与他乡"多数"。第一,欧芝克笃定坚持拒绝偶像崇拜,其中他乡"多数"表现为沦为偶像的文学呈现手段,故园"少数"表现为作为一神教的犹太教对于偶像崇拜的抵制。第二,欧芝克坚持历史的判断及阐释功用,其中他乡"多数"表现为艺术性,故园"少数"则表现为历史性。第三,欧芝克用"思想的厄洛斯"改写正统犹太教女性观,其中他乡"多数"表现为女权主义思想,故园"少数"表现为对于犹太教的忠诚。第四,欧芝克运用后现代主义叙事策略,服务于其犹太性呈现,其中他乡"多数"表现为以"不确定性"为特征的后现代主义策略,故园"少数"表现为欧芝克明确的对于犹太性的坚持与彰显。

本书具体阐述了欧芝克小说犹太性中将故园"少数"融于他乡"多数"并将其加以弘扬彰显的道德意识。

第一,以想象力和语言作为文学呈现的典型代表,分析了欧芝克在呈现犹太教拒绝偶像崇拜与沦为偶像的文学呈现手段之间的冲突中显现出的道德意识。首先以《异教徒拉比》为例论述偶像崇拜与想象力。尽管艾萨克和申黛尔对想象力持有不同态度,且二人想象能力也不相同,但是他们都被塑造为偶像崇拜者(尽管方式不一)。因此,道德意识得以显现:因道德困境(即:想象力和犹太性之关系的困惑)而生发故事,并且赋予判断(即:关于偶像崇拜的行为与效果的判断)以道德价值。继而以《斯德哥尔摩的弥赛亚》中拉尔斯·安德曼宁的经历为例,论述欧芝克反对语言与文本崇拜的道德意识。研究指出,抵制偶像崇拜的主张最终在欧芝克的文学实践中得以弘扬,恰恰体现了流散空间故园"少数"与他乡"多数"的融合。

第二,道德意识还反映在欧芝克对于犹太记忆的艺术建构和解构以及兼顾历史性与艺术性、用米德拉什方式呈现大屠杀的文学实践。本书以露丝·普特梅瑟为例,阐释欧芝克对于犹太记忆的艺术虚构与解构。露丝·普特梅瑟是欧芝克多篇小说中反复出现的人物。在选取的《普特梅瑟:她的工作经历、家世和来生》和《普特梅瑟和赞西佩》两篇小说中,普特梅瑟在她的过往中虚构了金代尔叔叔,创造了泥人赞西佩,试图与历史建立联系。分析指出,欧芝克通过艺术虚构历史,是其强调历史价值的悖论性表征,揭示欧芝克坚持历史的判断功用。另外,本书阐述欧芝克如何在《披肩》中运用米德拉什方式,使历史性和艺术性得以相辅相成;同时探究后大屠杀困境,进一步论述欧芝克运用米德拉什方式,对真实犹太性所作的道德阐释,由此阐释大屠杀对当代美国犹太认知产生的影响,揭示欧芝克坚持历史的阐释功用。本书指出,流散空间中的故园"少数"历史性最终借由他乡"多数"艺术性得以彰显,而历史性与艺术性恰是欧芝克权衡并力图求得平衡的两个方面。

第三,欧芝克寓道德判断于犹太教渗透,从而丰富了犹太教渗透的内涵,同时在塑造犹太女性过程中倡导"思想的厄洛斯"。首先,本书说明欧芝克作为犹太女作家的矛盾主要来源于犹太性和女性主义的双重边缘化以及二者之间的对立。其次,从三个方面呈示种族和性别歧视:其一,欧芝克在求学与职业生涯中遭遇的偏见;其二,正统犹太教对女性的禁锢;其三,女性写作的消极接受。本书讨论欧芝克作品中对于犹太女性的呈现,包括表现女主人公对正统犹太性别教义的服从与反抗,以及表现大屠杀中的犹太母亲身份——犹太性和女性主义双重边缘化的缩影,继而审视欧芝克坚持的"思想的厄洛斯"——既为女主人公构建想象之旅,又对其加以道德净化。研究指出,欧芝克对于犹太教的忠诚最终是借助其对于正统犹太性别观的文学改写得以实现的,而其文学改写是欧芝克对于正统犹太教禁锢女性及其女权主义文学改写的道德权衡的结果。

第四,欧芝克使用后现代主义叙事策略服务于其犹太性呈现,其中的道德意识表现在欧芝克使用以不确定性为特征的后现代主义叙事策略,目的明确而现实,即坚持犹太性。研究首先阐述了诸如"复调"、"元小说侵入式叙事"、"零度写作"、"互文性"在欧芝克小说中的运用,继而逐一分析了它们服务于欧芝克坚持犹太性的现实功用。

作为美国犹太女作家,辛西娅·欧芝克通过权衡犹太性与沦为偶像的文学呈现手段、犹太性与历史呈现方式、犹太性与女性表征、犹太性与叙事策略四对冲突,凸现道德意识,通过文学实践,在流散空间将代表故园的"少数"与代表他乡的"多数"相融合,最终彰显了代表故园的"少数"。欧芝克浸透着道德意识的小说因其犹太本质而卓尔不群,必将因其民族性而走向世界,铸就不朽。

Contents

Introduction

An acclaimed novelist, short story writer, essayist and translator, Cynthia Ozick, an important voice in American literature, is "on anybody's list of the ten most important writers in North America today" (Bolick interview Internet). Best known as the champion for the Jews and the Jewishness in contemporary America (Yang 2008 421) with the authentically Jewish nature in her fiction (Cohen 1994 180), she is esteemed as one of America's most prominent Jewish writers since the 1970s, and her work is hailed by the critics as among the best of contemporary literary creation (*Newsweek* 1971-5-10).

I. Cynthia Ozick's Life and Literary Career

Cynthia Ozick was born in New York on April 17, 1928 to Russian-Jewish immigrant parents: William (a pharmacist) and Celia (Regelson) Ozick. She got her B. A. (cum laude) from New York University in 1949 and her M. A. from Ohio State University in 1950. She was married to Hallote Bernard, a lawyer, in 1952, and they have a daughter, Sarah Rachel. Ozick lives now in New York.

Ozick enjoys memberships in PEN, Authors League of America, American Academy of Arts and Letters, American Academy of Arts and Sciences, Dramatists Guild, Academie Universelle des Cultures (Paris, France).

Ozick's novels began with *Trust* (1966) and continued with *The Cannibal Galaxy* (1983), *The Messiah of Stockholm* (1987), *The Shawl* (1989), *The Puttermesser Papers* (1997), *Heir to the Glimmering World* (2004), and *Foreign Bodies* (2010). Her collections of short fiction are *The Pagan Rabbi and Other Stories*

(1971), *Bloodshed and Three Novellas* (1976), *Levitation: Five Fictions* (1982), and *Dictation: A Quartet* (2008). Her literary criticism and other intellectually rigorous essays have been collected in *Art and Ardor* (1983), *Metaphor and Memory* (1989), *Fame and Folly* (1996), *Quarrel and Quandary* (2000), and *The Din in the Head* (2006). Early in her career Ozick published poems, and in her later years she has written plays. (The Columbia Encyclopedia Internet) She has published translations in numerous periodicals and anthologies.

She is the recipient of numerous literary awards including the National Endowment for the Arts fellow in 1968; B'nai B'rith Jewish Heritage Award, Edward Lewis Wallant Memorial Award, and the National Book Award nomination, all in 1972, and all for *The Pagan Rabbi, and Other Stories*; Epstein Award, Jewish Book Council, in 1972, for *The Pagan Rabbi, and Other Stories*, and in 1976, for *Bloodshed and Three Novellas*; the American Academy of Arts Award for Literature in 1973; Hadassah Myrtle Wreath Award in 1974; O. Henry First Prize Award in fiction in 1975, 1981, and 1984; Pushcart Press Lamport Prize in 1980; Guggenheim fellow in 1982; the National Book Critics Circle Award nominations in 1982, 1983, and 1990; Mildred and Harold Strauss Livings grant, American Academy and Institute of Arts and Letters in 1982-87; Distinguished Service in Jewish Letters Award, Jewish Theological Seminary, in 1984; the Distinguished Alumnus Award, New York University, in 1984; PEN/ Faulkner Award nomination in 1984; Rea Award for Short Story, Dungannon Foundation, in 1986; Lucy Martin Donnelly fellow, Bryn Mawr College, in 1992; the National Jewish Book Award for Fiction, Jewish Book Council, in 1977, for *Bloodshed and Three Novellas*; O. Henry Award in 1992, for "Puttermesser Paired"; PEN/Spiegel-Diamonstein Award for the Art of the Essay in 1997; Harold Washington Literary Award in 1997, from the City of Chicago; John Cheever Award in 1999; the National Book Critics' Circle Award nomination for criticism in 2000, for *Quarrel and Quandary*.

She is a writer "whose intellect. . . is so impressive that it pervades the words she chooses, the stories she elects to tell, and every careful phrase and clause in which they are conveyed" (Ozick Gale Internet).

Her fiction, written with high intelligence, elegant incisiveness, and sharp, frequently satiric wit, is mainly concerned with facets of Jewish life and thought including the Holocaust and its legacy, the Jewish presence in contemporary life, and Jewish mysticism and legend (The Columbia Encyclopedia Internet).

Critics relegate Ozick to a group which they call "the third generation of Jewish American writers" (Bell 61). The first-generation Jewish American writers consist of those who grew up in Europe and used Yiddish as their literary language in struggling to preserve the Jewish culture which they felt had been threatened by its transplantation to an alien land. The second-generation Jewish American writers are those who were born in America to immigrant parents and who "had a fierce need to capture not only the stifling life of the ghetto but their own struggle to escape it, often into the world of radicalism" (62). The novels of these writers, therefore, served as a means of communication, which was often limited, between two incongruent worlds. But unfortunately the influence of these first and second generations of Jewish American writers in American letters has been trivial. It was not until the next generation, represented by Saul Bellow and Bernard Malamud, did Jewish writing make its way into the mainstream of American literature and the image of Jewish American writers evolved as a formidable presence. However, the definition of a "Jewish writer" has now become uncertain, for to many Jewish American writers, "Jewishness" means no more than being born of Jewish parents and having some odd Yiddish words scattered here and there in their writing. For many of them, the link with their Jewish heritage has long since rusted away, and some of them even chose to deny their Jewish identity and felt annoyed at being classified as a

"Jewish writer." For example, Philip Roth insisted that "I am not a
Jewish novelist. I am a novelist who is a Jew" (Epstein 65). Contrary
to Philip Roth and other Jewish writers who try to preserve their writing
from the label of parochialism and wish to affirm that their writing is
part of Western civilization, Cynthia Ozick has never hesitated to
acknowledge herself as a Jewish writer, who is constantly conscious of
her Jewish heritage and is obsessed with Jews and everything Jewish.
As Sarah Blacher Cohen observes, "What does concern Cynthia Ozick
is that her fiction retain an authentically Jewish nature" (180).

Before the mid-1980s, most of the writers identified as Jewish-
American were men, with Saul Bellow, Bernard Malamud, Philip
Roth, and Herbert Gold among the most influential. However, since
the second half of the 1980s, "Jewish-American writers" have
increasingly become associated with women: Grace Paley, Tillie
Olsen, Kim Chernin, Vivian Gornick, Rebecca Goldstein, Adrienne
Rich, and Cynthia Ozick. "In the twentieth century their numbers
increased significantly, and they found a new voice" (Norwood
Internet 551). Distinguished from most of these women writers who
"represent a secular Jewish tradition concerned with the social problems
that beset Jews and other minority peoples in a multicultural nation,"
and "a feminist world view that confronts the patriarchal nature of
Judaism" (Yalom 427), Cynthia Ozick, "intrigued by the creative
process and how the writer's work competes with the work of God"
(Norwood Internet 551), embraces her prime allegiance to Judaism and
has expanded the possibilities of what Jewish-American fiction can be
in that "she has changed radically the way we define Jewish-American
writing, and more important, the way Jewish-American writing defines
itself" (Pinsker 1).

Described by Elaine M. Kauvar in *Contemporary Literature* as a
"master of the meticulous sentence and champion of the moral sense of
art," Ozick writes on a variety of subjects, often mixing such elements
as fantasy, mysticism, comedy, satire, and Judaic law and history, in

a style that suggests a poet's perfectionism and a philosopher's dialectic (qtd. in Clark 17).

"Cynthia Ozick is arguably the most uncompromisingly Jewish American novelist" (Berger 223). She calls for an assimilation of a new type that reverses the normal direction. Ozick insists that "The world ought to be reassimilated into the Jewish tradition. I want gentiles in our community to say *Shavuot* and to, learn what it means" (Lowin 1988 10). (Note: Quoted from statements made by Ozick in a "dialogue" with William Berkowitz at Alice Tully Hall, Lincoln Center for the Performing Arts, New York, 13 June 1984. *Shavuot* is the Feast of Weeks, a holiday celebrating the anniversary of the giving of the Torah on Mount Sinai seven weeks after the Exodus from Egypt.)

II. Cynthia Ozick in the Critical Context

A. Cynthia Ozick Criticism in the United States

In 1974, Harold Fisch introduced Ozick in an article entitled "Introducing Cynthia Ozick" with a discussion of her first novel and earliest collection of short stories. Since then, her work has enjoyed the attention of some of Jewish literature's most notable critics, among them Harold Bloom, Louis Harap, Sanford Pinsker, Alvin Rosenfeld, and Ruth Wisse. It is the consensus of these scholars that Ozick's fiction is, at best, influenced by her Jewishness, and at worst, restricted by it. Nearly all the critics agreed that Ozick's non-fictional essays are in irreconcilable conflict with her fiction because of the idolatry paradox. However, most of the critics have contented themselves with identifying the conflict as a source of productive tension without bothering to seek an analytic resolution. For instance, Harold Bloom quipped: "her daemon tells the stories, while it cheerfully allows Ozick our rabbi and teacher to write the essays" (Bloom 5).

The first book of Cynthia Ozick criticism was edited by Harold

Bloom: Cynthia Ozick (1986), a collection of thirteen book reviews and six essays, a chronological scan of Ozick criticism since the publication of her first book in 1966 up to 1985.

Among the thirteen book reviews, there are two of *Trust* (1966), Ozick's first published book, representing opposite polarities. While David L. Stevenson in "Daughter's Reprieve" (1966) praises *Trust* for its total success and originality, Eugene Goodheart in "Trust" (1967) accuses the book of "discontinuity between language and reality or between expression and feeling" (Bloom 14).

To *The Pagan Rabbi* (1971), Ozick's first volume of stories, Johanna Kaplan and Paul Theroux present parallel responses, both commending her vigor as a story teller. While in "The Pagan Rabbi and Other Stories" (1971), Kaplan focuses on Ozick's skill at naturalistic representation, Theroux in "On The Pagan Rabbi" (1972) emphasizes her strengths of fantasy and their aesthetic limits.

Z. Knopp takes as the subject of his essay "Ozick's Jewish Stories" (1975) the complex matter of Ozick's Jewish stance as a narrator by comparing Ozick to I. B. Singer in one aspect and to Saul Bellow in another.

To *Bloodshed and Three Novellas* (1976), contrasting reactions are presented by Thomas R. Edwards and Ruth R. Wisse. Edwards expresses aesthetic doubts concerning "Usurpation (Other People's Stories)," while commending the other novellas in his "Bloodshed" (1976), however, though troubled by "Usurpation," Wisse in her essay "Ozick as Jewish American Writer" (1976) sets it and the other novellas of the volume in the context of contemporary Jewish fiction and avoids aesthetic judgment.

Leslie Epstein and A. Alvarez review *Levitation: Five Fictions* respectively in "Stories and Something Else" (1982) and "Flushed with Ideas: *Levitation*" (1982). Epstein feels uneasy at Ozick's bias against imagination. Alvarez, though admiring Ozick as stylist and humorist, expresses an uneasiness at the way in which she "bends . . . her strange imagination to the service of folk magic" (Bloom 56).

In "Covenanted to the Law" (1982), Ruth Rosenberg reviews "Usurpation" and provides the context that would help readers in making their own judgment as to the novella's success.

In "The Three Selves of Cynthia Ozick" (1983) and "Jewish Tradition and the Individual Talent"(1983), *Art & Ardor*, Ozick's first volume of essays, is brought under discussion by Katha Pollitt and by Sanford Pinsker. Pollitt divides these essays among three Ozicks: "the rabbi, the feminist, and a disciple of Henry James" (Bloom 64) who sometimes work against each other, sometimes in symbiosis. Pinsker argues that "the ardor of her Jewishness takes a fearsome toll on her discussions of Art" (Bloom 124).

Catherine Rainwater and William J. Scheick in "The Unsurprise of Surprise" (1983) present a comparison of Ozick as fiction writer to Shirley Hazzard and Anne Redmon with some contrasts between Ozick and her contemporaries both in relation to precursor figures and to language.

In the essay "The Art of Cynthia Ozick" (1983), Victor Strandberg considers her as a major figure in the American tradition of literature.

"Images of a Mind Thinking" (1983) by Edmund White, "On *The Cannibal Galaxy*" (1983) by A. Alvarez, "Wresting Life from the Void" (1983) by Max Apple and "Metaphors and Monotheism" (1984) by Margaret Wimsatt are the four reviews of *The Cannibal Galaxy*. White compares Ozick to Flannery O'Connor, each of whom has received from her religious commitment "authority, penetration and indignation." Alvarez prefers Ozick in her stories and novellas to her performance in the full-length novel, plot being not a consuming interest for her. Apple praises the book for the Blakean courage and clarity in looking "at the central mysteries of creation," whereas Wimsatt emphasizes Ozick's preference for sagacity over idolatry. (Bloom 139)

In "Ozick's Book of Creation" (1985), Elaine M. Kauvar gives a full reading to "Puttermesser and Xanthippe" and traces in it the Kabbalistic pattern. Moreover, Kauvar sees Puttermesser and the golem as initially reflecting two parts of a split personality.

Since the mid-1980s, the study on Cynthia Ozick has flourished. More scholars have approached Ozick's works from diversified perspectives, which results in some eight monographs and collections including *The Uncompromising Fictions of Cynthia Ozick* (1987) by Sanford Pinksker, *The World of Cynthia Ozick: Studies in Jewish American Literature* (1987) by Daniel Walden, *Cynthia Ozick* (1988) by Joseph Lowin, *Inevitable Exiles: Cynthia Ozick's View of the Precariousness of Jewish Existence in a Gentile Society* (1989) by Vera Emuna Kielsky, *Understanding Cynthia Ozick* (1991) by Lawrence S. Friedman, *Cynthia Ozick's Fiction: Tradition and Invention* (1993) by Elaine M. Kauvar, *Cynthia Ozick's Comic Art: From Levity to Liturgy* (1994) by Sarah Blacher Cohen, and *Greek Mind/Jewish Soul: The Conflicted Art of Cynthia Ozick* (1994) by Victor Strandbery.

Many of these book-length studies on Ozick, published in the late 1980s and early 1990s, ventured into aspects of her *oeuvre* that were not elaborated upon by the previous critics.

In *Cynthia Ozick* (1988), Joseph Lowin, a French literature scholar, apart from providing introductory and biographical information, delves into Cynthia Ozick's theme of pedagogy in *Trust*, "An Education," and "Bloodshed," her notion of a Jewish aesthetic in "The Pagan Rabbi," "Levitation," and *The Cannibal Galaxy*, her Jewish techniques of rewriting in "Usurpation (Other People's Stories)," "The Shawl," "Rosa," and *The Puttermesser Papers*, and the role of redemption in fiction as is shown in *The Messiah of Stockholm*. Lowin has squarely established Ozick in the category of Jewish writer: he discusses the idolatry paradox and offers a sprinkling of Jewish scripture to shore up his points about Ozick's "Jewish Idea."

Elaine M. Kauvar illuminates Ozick's "themes that obsess

[Ozick's] fiction" and "the dialectic existing between the tales, the storyteller's habit of doubling both within tales and between them" (xiii) in *Cynthia Ozick's Fiction: Tradition and Invention* (1993). Kauvar observes that "Endeavoring to merge the contributions of western culture with the legacy of Judaism," Ozick "seeks peace between the embattled kingdoms of artistic imagination and moral responsibility" (148). Kauvar denies the centrality of Jewishness to Ozick's fiction and appeals to regard her "not as a spokeswoman for normative Judaism, not as a redeemer of its literary efforts, not even as something of a feminist," but instead, "to arrive at the mainspring of her art," which "will establish Cynthia Ozick's centrality in contemporary American letters" (xx).

In *Cynthia Ozick's Comic Art: From Levity to Liturgy* (1994), Sarah Blacher Cohen focuses on Ozick's "Comic Art" and presents a reading that is incisive to the ironic and socially-progressive qualities of Ozick's fiction. Cohen sets Ozick in the Jewish comic tradition, and argues that "just as Ozick believes that literature must have *tachliss*, a higher purpose than art for art's sake, so she believes that the levity in Ozick's fiction must have a higher purpose than laughter's sake (168). Cohen insists that Ozick's status as comic performer is precisely because of her precarious and unstable cultural standpoint. In Cohen's vision, Ozick's humorous portrayal of certain characters "reveals that [people] are not ethereal paragons of virtue, but earth-bound, awkward creatures repeatedly committing the same mistakes ... grappling with inevitable disruptions and reversals" (3).

In *Greek Mind/Jewish Soul: The Conflicted Art of Cynthia Ozick* (1994), Victor Strandbery reads the sweeping ideas in Ozick's text as part of the process of elaboration of the two counterposed worlds of Western and Jewish Culture bridged by her writing:

> The confrontations at the center of her art emanate in turn from a profoundly conflicted mind. She hates the whole of Western civilization but takes pride in the

Jewish groundwork of that civilization. She protests the reduction of "Jewish history" to what has been done to Jews but saturates her writing with just that version of Jewish history. [...] Her fiction exemplifies the Jewish writer oxymoron, every page a blasphemy against the Second Commandment, every work a revelry of pagan enticement. (190)

Strandbery proclaims that "a proper understanding of Cynthia Ozick's art requires a grasp of its bedrock religious sensibility" (19). In particular, what he brings to the existing Ozick criticism is the "L'Chaim Principle," a commitment on the part of the characters to live "Life As It Actually Is" without sugarcoating or romanticizing (47).

According to ProQuest, since the year of 1984 up till now, there have emerged in the United States thirty-four English doctoral dissertations on Cynthia Ozick, among which six are specialized Ozick studies whereas the rest set Ozick studies either on a comparative basis or in the context of contemporary American-Jewish literature.

The latest ProQuest doctoral dissertation specialized in Cynthia Ozick study is "Cynthia Ozick's Sacral Aesthetic" (2005) by Amy Weintraub Kratka from Boston University, where the stories "The Pagan Rabbi" and "Envy; or, Yiddish in America," the novellas "Bloodshed" and "Rosa," and the novels *The Cannibal Galaxy* and *The Puttermesser Papers* are analyzed. It argues that Ozick's short stories and novels are engaged in untangling her self-styled contradiction between the creative impulse and Jewish observance. It focuses on the narrative strategies including her characterizations often featuring pious intellectuals, her midrashic narrative structures, and her frequently liturgical language, all of which point to the return to the Hebrew covenant.

In 2003, Daniela Fargione from the University of Massachusetts at Amherst, in "Cynthia Ozick and Jewish Literature: a Reader," offers a sample of Ozick's literary production as representative of both contemporary American literature and Jewish culture. Ozick's poems, short stories, and essays have been chosen to introduce the author's kaleidoscopic production as reflective of her immense variety of interests and mental acuteness. Ozick's work is also used to exemplify some of the major recent shifts in translation studies in Italy.

In 1990, "Innovation und Orthodoxie: Cynthia Ozick und der Versuch Eines Neuen Amerikanisch-Juedischen Romans" by Gislar Donnenberg from Leopold-Franzens Universitaet Innsbruck (Austria) acclaims Ozick as an important innovator of Jewish American fiction with her fusion of the orthodox-Jewish heritage and the tradition of western Anglo-American literature and culture.

In 1987, in "Cynthia Ozick, the Self-Subverting Artist," Naomi Liron from the University of California, Berkeley, applies the techniques of feminist criticism to Ozick's fiction, assessing the subversive aspects of her works. It argues that Ozick's essays provide an authoritarian basis which makes possible her fiction.

In 1985, "Inevitable Exiles: Cynthia Ozick's View of the Precariousness of Jewish Existence in a Gentile World (Short Stories)" by Vera Emuna Kielsky from Arizona State University provides an analysis of her major tales disclosing her masterly skills in description and characterization and the richness of her language and literary devices. It reflects the means by which she utilizes myth and mysticism to highlight the perturbed state of Jewish heritage in the predominately Gentile society. It emphasizes her position that the return to the God of the Fathers is the only way to solve the problem of alienation.

In addition to the five doctoral dissertations mainly on Ozick's fictional works, there is one which studies her essays, "On women and the Essay: An anthology from the Seventeenth Century to the Present" (2004) by Jenny Spinner from the University of Connecticut, which attempts to map a tradition of women essayists.

The remaining twenty-eight ProQuest doctoral dissertations fall roughly into two categories in the light of their major concerns, one of which is a comparative study and the other an exploration into Ozick and her works chiefly in the American-Jewish background.

There are three comparative studies, the first of which is "Portraying Religious Mystery in the Fiction of Malamud, Percy, Ozick, and O'Connor" (1996) by Lamar L. Nisly from University of Delaware. The dissertation aims to show that the Jewish and Catholic practices of giving structure to mystery are mirrored by four authors' use of narrative forms that lead to the non-rational and it links Bernard Malamud with Walker Percy and Cynthia Ozick with Flannery O'Connor in that the two pairs show a similarity in their narrative portrayals of religious mystery.

The second is entitled "Transcending Stereotyped Motherhood: the Social Construction of Mothers under Duress in Toni Morrison's *Beloved* and *Song of Solomon* and Cynthia Ozick's *The Shawl* and *The Cannibal Galaxy*" (2007), in which Carol A. Fishbone from Drew University primarily focuses upon the question of motherhood under the direct or indirect social traumas of slavery and the Holocaust. Sethe in Toni Morrison's *Beloved* and Rosa in Ozick's *The Shawl* are chiefly under discussion while Morrison's *Song of Solomon* and Ozick's *The Cannibal Galaxy* are subsequently analyzed for their similarities regarding the mother characters.

The third came out in 2009. In "The Pagan Writes Back: Hetero-religiosity, Heterology, and Heterogeneous Space in Four Contemporary Novels," Zhange Ni from the University of Chicago carries out a comparative study of world religions and world literature beyond the boundaries of monotheistic religions and the Western literary canon. Through reading Salman Rushdie's *Satanic Verses*, Shusaku Endo's *Deep River*, Margaret Atwood's *Handmaid's Tale* and Cynthia Ozick's *Puttermesser Papers*, it studies the confluence of hetero-religiosity and the novel as a form of heterology from the critical perspective of heterogeneous space, calling for due respect to conflictive traditions and diverse contexts.

The twenty-five ProQuest doctoral dissertations setting Ozick studies in the context of the contemporary American-Jewish canon can be further classified into five categories. The first is set in a multicultural background, the second shows efforts to define contemporary Jewish America identity with a particular concern for history and Jewish heritage, the third centers around Feminist studies, the fourth has its focus on the Holocaust, and the fifth delves into works about artists, aesthetes and the process of creation.

"Reading the Multicultural Moment: A Theory of American Literature" (2000) by Dean Joseph Franco from University of Southern California falls into the first category in that it is concerned with how ethnicity works in a multicultural background. Furthermore, it aims to discover what the history and context of one ethnic group's literature can say to that of another. Comparing Cynthia Ozick, Philip Roth, Tony Kushner, and earlier depression era Jewish writers with Chicano writers such as Alejandro Morales, Helena Maria Viramontes, Arturo Islas and Cherrie Moraga, the dissertation finds the two bodies of literature to be in fruitful conversation.

Comparatively speaking, the second group, primarily concerned with history and Jewish heritage pointing to identity construction, is of a larger size with twelve as its members including "A Craving for History: Immigrant Themes in Jewish-American Literature" (1984) by Jeffrey Saperstein from University of New Hampshire, "A Study of Jewish Literary Identity in Contemporary Writers in America: a Curriculum" (1985) by Reva Ehrlich from St. John's University (New York), "Telling Stories about God: Narrative Voice and Epistemology in the Hebrew Bible and in the Fiction of Flannery O'Connor, Graham Greene and Cynthia Ozick" (1990) by Janet M. Gallagher from Fordham University, "One and the same openness: Narrative and Tradition in Contemporary Jewish American Literature" (1995) by Tresa Lynn Grauer from University of Michigan, "In Pursuit of a Past: History and Contemporary Jewish American literature" (1997) by Sophia Badian Lehmann from State University of New York at Stony

Brook, "Surviving Lamentations: A Literary-Theological Study of the Afterlife of a Biblical Text" (1997) by Tod Linafelt from Emory University, "Jewish-American Gothic" (2000) by Stuart R. Rabinowitz from University of Colorado at Boulder, "'The Messiah Is Uptown': Jewish Literary Practice in Postwar America" (2000) by Julian Arnold Levinson from Columbia University, "Subject to Laughter: Comedy and Ethnicity in Contemporary American Fiction" (2001) by Jonna Mackin from University of Pennsylvania, "New Directions in Jewish American Fiction" (2002) by Ezra Cappell from New York University, "Jewish American Canons: Assimilation, Identity, and the Invention of Postwar Jewish American Literature" (2006) by Jeremy Shere from Indiana University, and "Magical American Jew: the Enigma of Difference in Contemporary Jewish American Short Fiction and Film" (2009) by Aaron Tillman from University of Rhode Island.

"A Craving for History: Immigrant Themes in Jewish-American Literature" (1984) is a cross-generational study of three immigrant themes in Jewish-American literature: transformation, freedom, and connection. It concerns the attempt by modern Jews to recover aspects of their tradition. It looks at a number of non-fiction memoirs as well as fictional works by Mark Helprin, Cynthia Ozick, and Hugh Nissenson, works in which both memory and imagination are enlisted in an attempt to recover "the useful past."

"A Study of Jewish Literary Identity in Contemporary Writers in America: a Curriculum" (1985) is a study of the fiction by Saul Bellow, Isaac Bashevis Singer, and Cynthia Ozick on the basis of the critical analyses of eight distinguishing qualities most often identified in Jewish-American literature from 1963 to 1983.

"Telling Stories about God: Narrative Voice and Epistemology in the Hebrew Bible and in the Fiction of Flannery O'Connor, Graham Greene and Cynthia Ozick" (1990) examines the relationship between narrative voice and epistemology in several modern religious novels: Flannery O'Connor's *The Violent Bear It Away*, Graham Greene's *The*

Heart of the Matter and *The End of the Affair*, and Cynthia Ozick's *Trust* and *The Cannibal Galaxy*.

"One and the Same Openness: Narrative and Tradition in Contemporary Jewish American Literature" (1995) argues that by transforming the Jewish legend of the golem to allow for female creation, Cynthia Ozick (in "Puttermesser and Xanthippe") and Marge Piercy (in *He, She and It*) speak to perceived gender inequities within Judaism while still maintaining that traditional narratives can fruitfully inform contemporary female identity.

"In Pursuit of a Past: History and Contemporary Jewish American Literature" (1997) contends that in Cynthia Ozick's "The Pagan Rabbi," a story based on a religious sense of Judaism, an analytic understanding of history is sought in the Torah and adjoining rabbinic commentary. It foregrounds Ozick's insistence on viewing the Holocaust as part of a historical continuum as well.

"Surviving Lamentations: A Literary-Theological Study of the Afterlife of a Biblical Text" (1997) traces the drive to supplement and thus to "keep alive" the book of Lamentations, as it is manifested in Second Isaiah, Targum Lamentations, Lamentations Rabbah, the medieval Hebrew poetry of Eliezer ben Kallir, and in Ozick's works.

In one of the three chapters of "Jewish-American Gothic" (2000), which is entitled "Transformation," the focus is on three stories by Cynthia Ozick which employ Jewish folklore and mystical tradition to establish their relation to a gothic literary tradition.

"'The Messiah Is Uptown': Jewish Literary Practice in Postwar America" (2000) examines the emergence of a "religious" sensibility in Jewish American literature in works by Alfred Kazin, Arthur A. Cohen, and Cynthia Ozick. It holds that Cynthia Ozick, while suggesting Jewish morality challenges the very assumptions of art, questions whether a literary work can mimetically reproduce the paradigms of Jewish belief.

"Subject to Laughter: Comedy and Ethnicity in Contemporary

American Fiction" (2001) focuses on comic transactions in texts that negotiate ethnic identity, in particular, how Ozick's parody of idealism destabilizes the concept of the "good Jew". It further argues that Ozick's comedy creates ambiguity regarding the Jewish ideal.

"New Directions in Jewish American Fiction" (2002) locates Liturgical Literature, which is centrally Jewish in its concerns and characterized by a midrashic mode, in the late twentieth-century works of Cynthia Ozick and Henry Roth.

"Jewish American Canons: Assimilation, Identity, and the Invention of Postwar Jewish American Literature" (2006) investigates canon-forming texts-anthologies of Jewish American writing, literary criticism focused on Jewish authors, and novels written by Jewish American authors in the postwar period-within the context of major intellectual trends and developments influenced and in some cases initiated by Jewish intellectuals. It contends that the concept of a "Jewish American Canon" took shape under the influence of two related and sometimes opposed forces: assimilation and the reinvention of Jewish identity in postwar America. Moreover, it argues that among many intellectuals and writers, Cynthia Ozick has turned to Jewish literary history as a base from which to conceive a literary Jewishness not completely at odds with modern intellectual sensibilities.

"Magical American Jew: the Enigma of Difference in Contemporary Jewish American Short Fiction and Film" (2009) studies the magical realist techniques, the employment of which sheds light on the tension that has contributed to the creation and (mis)-understanding of contemporary Jewish American identities. Ozick's short story "Levitation" is analyzed in an effort to challenge the common association between Jews and guilt and posits shame as a more discerning perspective through which to view Jewish American difference-a difference influenced by a history in which the Holocaust is a principal concern.

The third group is made up of seven feminist studies: "Mother

Images in American-Jewish Fiction (20th Century)" (1985) by Abbey Poze Kapelovitz from University of Denver, "Women's Voices, Women's Visions: Contemporary American-Jewish Women Writers (Kaplan; Schaeffer; Jong; Ozick)" (1987) by Connie Beth Saulmon Burch from Purdue University, "Confessions and Accusations: Violence and Redemption in Contemporary United States Women's Fiction" (1994) by Amy Sara Gottfried from Tufts University, "Writing Selves: Constructing American-Jewish Feminine Literary Identity" (1996) by Joan M. Moelis from University of Massachusetts at Amherst, "From Shadow to Substance: The Figure of the Mother-Artist in Contemporary American Fiction" (1999) by Nancy Faith Gerber from the State University of New Jersey, "A Woman's Legacy: Conflict in the Mother-Daughter Relationship in Contemporary American Fiction" (2007) by Jacqueline Lautin from City University of New York, and "'Whenever You Tell the Story of one Woman, Inside is Another': Mother-Daughter Relationships in Writing by Contemporary Jewish Women" (2008) by Brittany Brook Dashe from University of South Carolina.

In "Mother Images in American-Jewish Fiction (20th Century)" (1985), a close analysis is given to the works of ten writers of Jewish ancestry including Cynthia Ozick in an attempt to indicate the image of the mother in American-Jewish fiction varies according to the generation and the gender of the writer.

"Women's Voices, Women's Visions: Contemporary American-Jewish Women Writers (Kaplan; Schaeffer; Jong; Ozick)" (1987) describes several themes emerging from their works. It also points out the different sense of the world held by Jewish women than Jewish men in that the writings by Jewish women turn out to be more self-reflexive, more in search of self, and that Jewish women resemble women of other religious backgrounds in their concern for family, and for the rights and welfare of women.

From a materialist-feminist perspective, "Confessions and

Accusations: Violence and Redemption in Contemporary United States Women's Fiction" (1994) examines some contemporary United States women's novels that reclaim national and personal histories of ignored or suppressed abuse including Cynthia Ozick's *The Shawl*, where the Holocaust is condemned as violence and horror. It illustrates how her religious, political, and theoretical concerns inform the uses of both "real" and "fictional" violence in a creative act.

Drawing on feminist criticisms that emphasize both form and social context, as well as on Bakhtinian dialogism and theories of Otherness, "Writing Selves: Constructing American-Jewish Feminine Literary Identity" (1996) focuses on Cynthia Ozick, Grace Paley, and E. M. Broner who construct multiple and mutable selves rather than fully-integrated personae.

"From Shadow to Substance: The Figure of the Mother-Artist in Contemporary American Fiction" (1999) analyzes the figure of the mother-artist in such texts as *Maud Martha* (1953) by Gwendolyn Brooks, "I Stand Here Ironing" (1956) and "Tell Me a Riddle" (1960) by Tillie Olsen, *The Shawl* (1989) by Cynthia Ozick, and *Breath, Eyes, Memory* (1994) by Edwidge Danticat so as to explore the impact of race and social class on the mother-artist's development.

"A Woman's Legacy: Conflict in the Mother-Daughter Relationship in Contemporary American Fiction" (2007) intends to explore the motif of the cyclical, multi-generational mother-daughter relationship in Amy Tan's *The Joy Luck Club*, Toni Morrison's *Beloved*, Cynthia Ozick's *The Puttermesser Papers*, Jane Smiley's *A Thousand Acres*, and Edwidge Danticat's *Breath, Eyes, Memory*, where there are both the abuses of slavery and culturally sanctioned, patriarchal mistreatment by society of women, especially minority women and other marginalized groups of women.

"'Whenever You Tell the Story of one Woman, Inside is Another': Mother-Daughter Relationships in Writing by Contemporary Jewish Women" (2008) explores mother-daughter dynamics in the

context of writing by contemporary ·Jewish women including Cynthia Ozick, Marge Piercy, Tova Mirvis, Marjorie Agosin, Carmit Delman, and Farideh Goldin, focusing on the tension between a traditionally misogynistic brand of Judaism and feminism.

Three Holocaust studies comprise the fourth group.

"Ghostwriters: Remembering the Holocaust in America" (1996) by Judith Nysenholc from the University of Wisconsin situates itself in critical debates concerning the contribution of literature and the place of a revised humanism in a post-Holocaust world with an exploration into how the American literature of the Holocaust both reflects and responds to conflicting influences: popular American commodifications of history and normative discourses on the inadequacy of language to represent the horror and on the risks of aestheticizing it. In particular, Cynthia Ozick's *The Messiah of Stockholm* is analyzed in that Ozick has turned it into a palimpsest over a murdered writer's work as she struggles against simplistic forms of remembrance and with her own faith in the creative powers of literature.

"Writing the Void: the Holocaust, Representation, and American Culture" (1998) by Joshua Leonard Charlson from Northwestern University investigates the dynamics by which the Holocaust has been recalled and represented in the cultural imagination of the United States since 1945. Fundamental to the study is the notion that America's relation to the past of the Holocaust has been defined by an imposing sense of an absence or void-of geography, experience, and historical context. In one of the five chapters, the dissertation argues that Jewish-American guilt and bereavement are embodied in the character of the Holocaust survivor in realist novels by Cynthia Ozick.

"Screaming Laughing: the Functions and Varieties of Humor in American Holocaust Literature" (2000) by Frank Harry Katz from Arizona State University analyzes the functions of women's humor in Cynthia Ozick's *The Shawl*, focusing on the ways in which Ozick uses humor to attack norms and to focus on women's experiences during the

aftermath of the Holocaust.

There is a common interest in artists, aesthetes, and creation in "The Interaction of Rhetoric and Aesthetic in the Artist Tales of Contemporary American-Jewish Writers" (1992) by Ruth Anne Goldhor from the University of Texas at Austin and "Images of Absences: Nineteenth-Century British Novels as Film, History, and Autobiography" (1998) by Patricia Vigderman from Tufts University, which consist the fifth group.

"The Interaction of Rhetoric and Aesthetic in the Artist Tales of Contemporary American-Jewish Writers" (1992) studies the novels and stories about artists and aesthetes produced by Bernard Malamud and Cynthia Ozick which reveal a strong ambivalence toward art and its relevance to their Jewishness. In "Images of Absences: Nineteenth-Century British Novels as Film, History, and Autobiography" (1998), the question is raised of the reader's relationship with the absent author from the perspective of Jacques Derrida's *The Ear of the Other* and Michel Foucault's "What is an Author?" and *Technologies of the Self.* It discusses five biographies of George Eliot, and Cynthia Ozick's fictional doubling of Eliot's life in "Puttermesser Paired," and theorizes a biographical mimesis in which the reader shares an impossible identity with the author.

Of course, there is no absolute dividing line between the groups. Overlapping is not sporadic. For instance, to mention only a few, "One and the Same Openness: Narrative and Tradition in Contemporary Jewish American Literature" (1995) is at once a study deeply attached to history and Jewish heritage and a feminist study. "Confessions and Accusations: Violence and Redemption in Contemporary United States Women's Fiction" (1994) is a Holocaust study from a feminist perspective. "In Pursuit of a Past: History and Contemporary Jewish American literature" (1997) attaches its academic concerns to both the significance of history and the Holocaust impact in particular. "Magical American Jew: the Enigma of Difference in

Contemporary Jewish American Short Fiction and Film" (2009) not only focuses on the magical realist techniques and the contemporary Jewish American identities but also locates the Holocaust as a principal concern in history. "From Shadow to Substance: The Figure of the Mother-Artist in Contemporary American Fiction" (1999) and " Confessions and Accusations: Violence and Redemption in Contemporary United States Women's Fiction" (1994) are feminist studies that are concerned with artists and artistic creation. "Writing Selves: Constructing American-Jewish Feminine Literary Identity" (1996) integrates feminist and ethnic studies.

Besides the doctoral dissertations, there are three ProQuest M. A. theses on Cynthia Ozick.

In "' So What's the Joke?': Locating Jewish-American Female Authorship" (1997), Batia Boe Stolar from Concordia University (Canada) examines the fiction of three contemporary Jewish-American female writers, Grace Paley, Cynthia Ozick and Erica Jong, and locates their writing in the context of their quasi-double-marginalization—the yoking of their Jewishness and femaleness with their rewritings and inscriptions of Jewish-American femaleness on the basis of an examination of the narrative strategies that these writers utilize—oral storytelling, traditional genre paradigms, and hyperbolic satire.

There is an intention to illuminate Ozick's ethical sensibilities in "The Ethical Fiction of Cynthia Ozick" (1995) by Dean Joseph Franco from California State University. It is argued that Ozick's knowledge of man's deepest ethical dilemmas is the driving force behind her fiction, which is at once didactic, realistic, and compelling.

"Cynthia Ozick's *The Cannibal Galaxy*" (1987) by Yongshun Jin from Stephen F. Austin State University attempts to analyze its main thematic elements.

In addition to monographs, collections, doctoral dissertations and M. A. theses, there are numerous reviews and journal articles on

Ozick, which features contemporary Ozick criticism since the mid 1990s.

Of particular enlightenment to the present study are the following journal articles, which deal with the liturgical nature of Ozick's writing, the relation between religion and literature, contradictory tension between the fiction and non-fiction of Ozick, and in particular, her paradoxical wisdom.

"Fragmented Art and the Liturgical Community of the Dead in Cynthia Ozick's *The Shawl*" by Amy Gottfried, "Cynthia Ozick's Liturgical Postmodernism: *The Messiah of Stockholm*" by Elisabeth Rose focus upon the liturgical nature of Ozick's writing.

In "Cynthia Ozick as the Jewish T. S. Eliot", Mark Krupnick compares Ozick's works to the writings of T. S. Eliot, mainly in terms of "some likenesses between Ozick and Eliot" in their concerns over the relation between religion and literature.

The contradictory tension between Ozick's fiction and non-fiction has been well-documented in such journal articles as Katha Pollitt's "The Three Selves of Cynthia Ozick," Leslie Epstein's "Stories and Something Else," Ruth Rosenberg's "Covenanted to the Law," Sanford Pinsker's "Jewish Tradition and the Individual Talent," Ellen Pifer's "Invention and Orthodoxy," Louis Harap's "The Religious Art of Cynthia Ozick," and Janet Handler Burstein's "Cynthia Ozick and the Transgressions of Art."

In "Cynthia Ozick's Paradoxical Wisdom" (1996), Marilyn Yalom focuses on Ozick's recalling of "the paradoxes intrinsic to the fiction of Kafka, I. B. Singer, and the rabbinical tales of Eastern Europe" in her expressions of "the contradictory mysteries of human existence, which are always more complex than our theories about existence" (Yalom 427). As a matter of fact, the present study has been positively inspired by Marilyn Yalom's ideas in this very article, though further expansions have been made in scope to the diasporic representation of the tension Cynthia Ozick has undergone as a woman, as a writer, and as a covenanted Jew.

B. Cynthia Ozick Studies in China

While Ozick's belletristic reputation has been amply recognized in the United States, her popularity in China is still scant as very little of her production has been translated into Chinese. Compared with the Ozick scholarship abroad, research on Ozick in China is rather limited. The domestic studies are generally confined to introduction to the writer, interpretation of a few of her works, and analysis of her themes, her ethnic concerns and narrative strategies.

Chen Hong (2003), focusing on Ozick's "Toward a New Yiddish", *Bloodshed and Three Novellas,* "Innovation and Redemption: What Literature Means,*" Levitation: Five Fictions*, and *The Messiah of Stockholm,* studies Ozick's narrative strategy and her ethnic concerns.

Wang Zuyou (2004), centering around Ozick's "The Shawl" and "Puttermesser: Her Work History, Her Ancestry, Her Afterlife,*"* makes an introduction to Ozick and touches upon her postmodernist presentation in "The Postmodernist Spokesperson of the Jews: Cynthia Ozick" and "Historical Introspection in Postmodernist Texts: Views on Cynthia Ozick's Two Short Stories."

Shi Jinfang (2005), in her M. A. thesis "The Soul of Cynthia Ozick's Art," taking as samples "Suitcase," "Envy: or Yiddish in America," "The Pagan Rabbi," "Usurpation," and *Levitation: Five Fictions*, remarks the three equations in Ozick's art, namely, confrontation between Jews and gentiles, equation of idolatry and art, and fusion of reality and fantasy.

Zhang Guosheng (2008), basing his M. A. thesis "Perseverance in the Jewish Tradition: A Study of Cynthia Ozick's Novels" on the analysis of four novels, *The Cannibal Galaxy, The Messiah of Stockholm, Heir to the Glimmering World,* and *The Puttermesser Papers*, seeks for her intention of literary creation with an emphasis on her adherence to Judaism, Jewish cultural awareness, and Jewish historical consciousness based on the Holocaust.

Zhou Nanyi (2001) and Chen Xian (2008) have carried out researches on Ozick in their doctoral dissertations. In "Toward a New Utopia: a Study of the Novels by Saul Bellow, Bernard Malamud, and Cynthia Ozick," based on the analyses of *Trust* and *The Puttermesser Papers*, Zhou Nanyi argues that in Cynthia Ozick's novels, like in those of Bellow and Malamud, there is a tendency to construct an ideal society, which can be traced to both classical utopianism and modern political philosophy. Meanwhile, there is a great concern about the means to build an efficient democratic governmental system in the light of Enlightenment ideals, and furthermore, greater significance is attached to the humanistic improvement of human beings.

In "The Jewish Memory and Literary Redemption—Cynthia Ozick's 'Liturgical Literature'," Chen Xian has taken Ozick's essays, *The Cannibal Galaxy*, and *The Puttermesser Papers* into her analysis of Ozick's dominant themes, the arguments in her essays, and the narrative techniques she has employed in an attempt to explore the means in answering Ozick's call for a liturgical literature impregnated with Jewish values.

In addition, the recent ten years have witnessed Cynthia Ozick's being recognized by Chinese scholars as an important voice in Jewish American literature in their publications on the literary history of the United States and history of Jewish American literature. In *Literary History of the United States* (2002) by Prof. Liu Haiping, Prof. Wang Shouren, Prof. Zhang Chong, Prof. Yang Jincai, and Prof. Zhu Gang, Cynthia Ozick is ranked among the most important Jewish American writers. *A Concise History of American Literature* (2008) by Prof. Yang Renjing and Prof. Yang Lingyan devotes a specific discussion to Cynthia Ozick. Ozick's literary achievements and contributions are ellaborated in *Literary History of the 20ᵗʰ Century United States* (2000, 2003, 2010) by Prof. Yang Renjing. Prof. Qiao

24

Guoqiang highlights Ozick's moral power in *Jewish American Literature* (2008).

All these critical ideas of Ozick scholars provide invaluable information on understanding Ozick and further help me form my own critical perspective. So far, there has been neither exploration into Ozick's Jewishness, nor studies of Ozick in the diasporic context. Furthermore, despite the existence of studies of the tension Ozick encounters and resolves, they are confined to those stemming from her identities as a Jew and as a writer, ignoring those stemming from her identities as a Jew and as a woman, and from her identities as a woman and as a writer. The present study, an attempt to explore the Jewishness in Ozick's fiction in terms of the tension she encounters and resolves as a Jewish American woman writer in the diasporic context, then is worthwhile.

Drawing on the concept of the "diasporic space" presented by Avtar Brah in 1996, the present study is to delve into the representation of Jewishness in Cynthia Ozick's fiction in the process of her encountering and resolving the tension of being a Jewish American woman writer in Diaspora.

III. The Theoretical Framework and Structure of the Present Study

"Diaspora" is derived from *speirein*, a Greek word for "scattering" or "sowing," and it literally accounts for the botanical phenomenon of seed dispersal (Mishra 2006 vi).

When used to refer to a specific historical event, "Diaspora" refers to the "dispersion of Jews among the Gentiles after the Babylonian Exile (586 BC)" (*Britannica Concise Encyclopedia* 472).

When "diaspora" is applied to humans, "the ancient Greeks thought of ... migration and colonization" (Cohen 1997 ix). For Jews, Africans, Palestinians and Armenians there is a more sinister and brutal meaning in "diaspora," for it signifies "a collective trauma, a banishment, where one dreamed of home but lived in exile" (ix). In addition, in recent years, peoples abroad who have maintained strong collective identities have defined themselves as diasporas as well even though "they were neither active agents of colonization nor passive victims of persecution" (ix).

There are three sites in which diasporas take form: the homeland, the hostland, and the diasporan group itself (Butler 2001 195).

Sudesh Mishra holds that "the genre of diaspora criticism has, so far, witnessed three scenes of exemplification" (15). The first scene is labeled the *scene of dual territoriality*, and "the emphasis falls on divided terrains as exemplars seek to account for diasporic subjects, cultures and aesthetic effects in terms of the subjective split between the geo-psychical entities of here and there, of hostland and homeland" (16). The main contributors to this scene are Gabriel Sheffer, Walker Conner, William Safran and Robin Cohen.

The second scene is described as the *scene of situational laterality*. The participating exemplars "take issue with the idea of bounded terrains and the constitutive role play by the tensional split between homeland and hostland in diasporic subject constitution" (16). Making efforts to explain the diaspora of the black Atlantic in ways that "transcend both the structure of the nation-state and the constraints of ethnicity and national particularity" (Gilroy 19), Paul Gilroy emphasizes the "rhizomorphic, fractal structure of [this] transcultural, international formation" (4). Stuart Hall makes a case for diasporic identities based on what he terms strategic *positioning* in "Cultural Identity and Diaspora" first published in 1990. James Clifford refers to the lateral axes of dissemination as distinct from dualistic concepts for origin and return: symbolic, psychological or actual. He argues that "multi-locale diasporas are not necessarily defined by a specific geopolitical boundary" and that they betray a "principled ambivalence about physical return and attachment to land" (Clifford 1994 304-05). Vijay Mishra thinks of this ambivalence in relation to what he calls the "semantics of the hyphen" (Mishra 1996 433). Avtar Brah thinks of diasporas in terms of lateral, peripatetic and multipolar (as distinct from linear, fixed and bipolar) positionalities (Mishra 2006 17).

The third is the scene of *archival specificity*, both critiquing and enlisting the exemplars of the two previous scenes. Typical exemplars in the third scene are Martin Manalansan's work on queer Filipinos in New York, Donna Gabaccia's account of Italian dispersion over the *longue durée*, Brent Hayes Edward's work on the black Atlantic and Martin Baumann's analysis of religious identity formations among Hindu Trinidadians (Mishra 2006 18).

By 1996, "the dual territorial pillars supporting the ethno-national architrave had collapsed, leaving behind an ungrounded milieu or mid-point" (Mishra 2006 83). Deleuze and Guattari talk of the mid-point as "a continuous, self-vibrating region of intensities whose development avoids any orientation toward a culmination point or external end" (Deleuze and Guattari 21-22).

Based on the mid-point, Avtar Brah proposes the "diasporic space" in *Cartographies of Diaspora* (Brah 181). She understands the "diasporic space" to be "a paradoxical non-space, or, if you like, a ... third space" (Mishra 2006 83). According to Brah, "The concept of disapora signals process of multi-locality across geographical, cultural and psychic boundaries" (Brah 193). "In marking the joint/rupture between one space and another (or several others), the border is clearly devoid of its own space and yet indispensible to spatial categories" (Mishra 2006 83), and "one is neither absolutely one thing or another but constituted multiply in the line of fracture which, as logic would have it, is also the line of suture. ... one is never solely one thing or another, but altogether something else—a veritable third" (83). Mishra further explicates that "Brah presents us with a camouflaged version of *différance* where the pursuit of presence, of the self or its other, of location or dislocation, of fissure or fusion, of national or transnational subjects, is constantly interrupted by the supplement" (84). In particular, Brah touches upon power differentials:

> The concept of diaspora that I wish to propose ... is embedded within a multi-axial understanding of power: one that problematises the notion of "minority/ majority." A multi-axial performative conception of power highlights the ways in which a group constituted as a "minority" along one dimension of differentiation may be constructed as a "majority" along another. (Brah 189)

In Brah's opinion, the distinction between the "minority" representing the homeland and the "majority" representing the hostland relies upon the multi-axial performance of power. Brah further explains that the "majority" representing the hostland and the "minority" representing the homeland as the prevailing "mainstream" and "the marginalized" respectively.

By the 1960s, when Cynthia Ozick started her literary career, the process of assimilation has greatly changed the second generation of the American Jews. Most of them were already among American middle-class. With the rise in economic and social status, growth of political power and intermarriage rate, the majority of American Jews came to embrace the so-called "symbolic Judaism"—a minimal adherence to specific Jewish cultural values and patterns—and become sufficiently subjected to dominant American values while symbolically adhering to Judaism, Jewish cultural values and behavioral patterns. It was estimated that by the end of the 1960s, over a million American-born Jews had completely given up their Jewish heritage (Zhou 28). Most of the American Jews have come to see themselves first of all as American, and then as Jewish. As Samuel C. Heilman points out,

> It was enough to remember and stress it at certain moments of Jewish life— family passages, weddings, and funerals—or in situations when the community was under perceived attack—occasions of anti-Semitic assaults or when Israel or some other Jewish population was in distress and required ... but they were also not prepared to make too much of it. For them, neither Judaism was a religion nor

Jewish ethnic self-consciousness completely filled their cognitive and behavioral universe. Being Jewish no longer determined the way they looked at and understood the cosmos and reality, no longer very much affected the way they felt about the world, themselves, and others or that they did. (66-67)

As a result of assimilation, American Jews are relinquishing their distinctive Jewish belief and reforming their behavioral pattern. Rabbi Morris Kertzer, president of the Jewish Chaplains Organization, declared in 1952,

> the only loyalty of an American Jew is to the United States of America without any ifs, ands or buts. The state of Israel is the ancestral home of his forefathers, the birthplace of his faith. [...] But spiritual bonds and emotional ties are quite different from political loyalty. (qtd. in Heilman 17)

Judaism, and Jewishness consequently, has turned into "the minority" in the hostland from "the majority" in the homeland.

With the marginalization of Jewishness, which ends up as the "minority," concrete embodiment of Jewishness has consequently become the "minority" including the Judaic adherence to anti-idolatry, the Jewish insistence upon history as interpretation and judgment, the allegiance to Judaism, and the wish to stay Jewish.

However, as a steadfast Jewish writer who intends to be Jewish, Ozick attributes the lack of Jewish literary masters to the intention to address mankind universally and she insists on "being tribal," being Jewish:

> Why have our various Diasporas spilled out no Jewish Dante, or Shakespeare, or Tolstoy, or Yeats? Why have we not had equal powers of hugeness of vision? These visions, these powers were not hugely conceived. Dante made literature out of an urban vernacular, Shakespeare spoke to a small island people, Tolstoy brooded on upper-class Russians, Yeats was the kindling for a Dublin-confined renascence. They did not intend to address the principle of Mankind; each was, if you will allow the infamous word, tribal. Literature does not spring from the urge to Esperanto but from the tribe. (Ozick "Towards a New

Yiddish" Art & Ardor 168)

What's more, on the basis of her insistence upon the centrality of Jewishness, she claims "If we blow into the narrow end of the *shofar*, we will be heard far. But if we choose to be Mankind rather than Jewish and blow into the wider part, we will not be heard at all" (177).

It is the performance of power, specifically the performance of the literary power that Ozick, as a Jewish American woman writer in Diaspora, endows her fiction with in order to foreground Jewishness that serves as the primary interpretive tool of this book, hence the diasporic space Ozick as a writer creates in her fiction, where such "minorities" as the Judaic adherence to anti-idolatry, the Jewish insistence upon historicity and upon history as interpretation and judgment, the allegiance to Judaism, and the wish to stay Jewish are eventually foregrounded.

My focus is specifically on Ozick's literary foregrounding of Jewish visions in the moral ethos she highlights in confronting the opposing claims of Judaism as monotheism in anti-idolatry and literature as idol, in confronting the conflict between the balance of historicity and figuration in fictional representation of Jewish memories including the Holocaust, in confronting the conflict between her allegiance to Judaism and her judgment that the Orthodox Judaic gender law is prohibiting women from acting as intellectual equals to men, and in her employment of postmodernist literary narrative to stay Jewish.

This study covers six of Ozick's works: four short stories, one novella, and one novel, which represent the panoramic scene of her fiction creation in terms of both production phase and work size. The earliest was created in 1971 while the latest in 1989. These samples are as follows-four short stories: "The Pagan Rabbi" (1971), "Puttermesser: Her Work History, Her Ancestry, Her Afterlife" (1982), "Puttermesser and Xanthippe" (1982), and "Levitation"

(1982); one novella: *The Shawl* (consisting of "The Shawl" and "Rosa") (1989); and one novel: *The Messiah of Stockholm* (1987).

This book consists of five chapters plus the Introduction and the Conclusion. Chapter One traces the shaping of Jewish American literature and examines in particular the contemporary Jewish American fiction from the 1950s to the 1990s, the background in which Ozick's Jewishness is nurtured, in hopes to disclose the major characteristics and primary embodiment of the Jewishness in Ozick's fiction. Following the examination is the finding that Jewishness in contemporary Jewish American fiction is chronologically featured by moral ethos, Judaism engagement, and loyalty to fact in Holocaust representation, which stand independent respectively. Then the study turns to Cynthia Ozick and her Jewishness. To begin with, Ozick's elaboration on Jewish visions and definition of Jewishness in her essays are brought into discussion. Then on the basis of her elaboration and definition, taking into account the distinguishing features of the Jewishness in contemporary Jewish American fiction, the study argues that Ozick has expanded and thus enriched the contemporary Jewishness in that she highlights moral ethos in her mingling and expanding of the essential aspects featuring contemporary Jewishness. In addition, the study further asserts that idolatry resistance, history as judgment and interpretation, and "Eros of ideas" as the rewriting of Orthodox Jewish femininity are the primary visions that Ozick intends to foreground via attaching literary power to moral ethos in the diasporic space.

Chapter Two focuses on Ozick's primary Jewish insistence upon anti-idolatry, resulting from her moral weighing of Jewishness and "literature as idol." First of all, the "minority" representing the homeland and the "majority" representing the hostland are respectively defined in this case as Judaic monotheistic anti-idolatry and literature representation necessitated by imagination and language as idol-worshipping. Since Ozick's meditations on Jewish literary practice are informed in particular by moral imagination concerning idolatry, this chapter is to center around the relationships between idolatry and imagination, and between idolatry and language worship.

The first part of the chapter, on idolatry and imagination, takes "The Pagan Rabbi" as its sample. Despite their difference in attitude to and capability of imagination, Isaac and Sheindel are both characterized as having committed idolatry, though in distinct ways, hence the significance of moral imagination: both in inspiring the story with the moral dilemma, namely, the puzzling meditations on the relationship between imagination and Jewishness, and in imbuing imagination with the moral values concerning idolatry in its practice and effect.

The second part of the chapter, on idolatry and language worship, takes *The Messiah of Stockholm* as its sample. Having found his lack of ancestry in a world without a past, Lars claims that his father was Bruno Schulz, the Polish writer who was gunned down in 1942 by Nazis on the street of a tiny Polish town. Above all, for Lars, Schulz's writing serves as the answer to his enigmatic identity and he attempts to establish continuity with the past by tracing the threads of the texts to himself. The analysis consists of four parts: language's meaningfulness, language's peril and destructiveness, Ozick's corona, and Lars's redemption. Ozick's call to read in a non-idolatrous manner is highlighted.

Chapter Three centers around Ozick's adherence to historicity resulting from her moral weighing of Jewishness and history representation. Firstly, the "minority" representing the homeland and the "majority" representing the hostland are respectively defined in this case as historicity and figuration. Secondly, since the study of Ozick's fictional construction of Jewish memories is based on the presentation of the Jewish cultural crisis of which she has a keen sense, the three embodiments of the crisis are analyzed. Thirdly, Ozick's fictional construction and deconstruction of Jewish memories are exemplified in Ruth Puttermesser, a character to whom Ozick has returned in several of her stories. The works chosen are "Puttermesser: Her Work History, Her Ancestry, Her Afterlife," and "Puttermesser and Xanthippe," where Puttermesser recreates her past as having Uncle Zindel, and Puttermesser creates her golem, Xanthippe, both attempting to get connected with the past. The analysis points out that Ozick paradoxically asserts the significance of the past through inventing the past as fantastic. Fourthly, Ozick's Midrashic representation of the Holocaust is elaborated with *The Shawl* as a sample, focusing upon Ozick's dovetailing historicity and figuration and upon the exploration of the post-Holocaust dilemmas as extensions of Ozick's moral interpretations of Jewish authenticity in the Midrashic mode.

Chapter Four explores Ozick's feminist mending of the Orthodox Judaic gender law which prohibits Jewish women from acting as intellectual equals to men, resulting from her moral weighing of Jewishness and feminine representation. First, the "minority" representing the homeland and the "majority" representing the hostland are respectively defined in this case as allegiance to Judaism and feminist views challenging the Orthodox Judaic gender law. Then, the study explores Ozick's literary representation of Jewish femininity, which consists of the representation of female protagonists as both acquiescent to and rebellious against Orthodox Judaic gender law, and the representation of Jewish mothering in the Holocaust which epitomizes the dual marginality of Jewishness and femininity. Lucy Feingold in "Levitation" and Ruth Puttermesser in "Puttermesser and Xanthippe" are studied as bearers of both feminist and Jewish traces in the diasporic space while Rosa's mothering in "The Shawl" is analyzed as a result of the oppression and racism in the Holocaust and its aftermath. The focus is on the social construction of mothering, the dismantling of mothering stereotypes, and the way in which the racial tragedy and survival define a Jewish mother's role, and by extension, Jewish feminine identity in Ozick's diasporic space. Finally, Ozick's attempts in both conjuring and purifying flights of imagination for these female protagonists are analyzed, focusing upon Ozick's efforts in creating "Eros of ideas," a feminist mending of the Orthodox Judaic gender law in shifting the role of women from sexual objects and domestic servants to active intellectual equals.

Chapter Five tries to disclose Ozick's employment of postmodernist literary narrative to serve her needs to stay authentically Jewish. First, the "minority" representing the homeland and the "majority" representing the hostland are respectively defined in this case as Ozick's determinate aim to be Jewish and postmodernism featured by "indeterminacy." Second, the employment of such postmodernist literary narrative as "polyphonic narrative," "metafictional intrusion narrative," "writing degree zero," and "intertextuality" is elaborated. Third, the realistic significance these postmodernist literary narratives function is respectively analyzed.

In Conclusion, observations based on the study are outlined. Cynthia Ozick, as a Jewish American woman writer in Diaspora, has managed to give her literary power to highlight moral ethos in the diasporic space where the "minority" representing the homeland, should it be anti-idolatry, historicity with history as interpretation and judgment in history representation, "Eros of ideas" as a feminist mending of Orthodox Judaic gender law, or postmodernist narratives for realistic needs to stay Jewish, is merged with the "majority" representing the hostland and is eventually foregrounded. It is Ozick's literary power elevating the essentially ethnical that ushers in universal and timeless significance.

Chapter One

Contemporary Jewish American Fiction and Jewishness

As part of American literature, Jewish American literature has played a crucial role in the American literary climate. Jewish American writers have made great contributions to contemporary American literature.

Cynthia Ozick, as "the acknowledged leader" of the "second act" in Jewish American writing (Kremer 1993 572), distinguishes herself with the authentically Jewish nature in her fiction (Cohen 1994 180).

The examination of the Jewishness in Ozick's fiction is to be based on the overview of Jewish American literature in contemporary American literature in general and the attempt to delineate Jewishness as displayed chronologically from the 1950s to the 1990s in the examination of Jewish American fiction.

I. Jewish American Literature as Part of Contemporary American Literature

Jewish American literature has taken its shape in the American multicultural context. It stems from Jewish immigration onto the American soil and is nurtured in the ensuing interaction with both the Jewish heritage and the American value.

A. Jews and Jewish Culture in Multicultural America

As a "melting pot," the United States is featured by its

multicultural context. Jews and Jewish culture have been playing a significant role in the enrichment of the American multicultural aroma and the shaping of American culture as a result of the successive waves of Jewish immigrants.

There were three waves of Jewish immigrants coming from Europe into what was first colonial America and then the United States, which brought with them the Jewish heritage.

The first wave was of the Jewish immigrants from Spain and Portugal during the century and a half between the 1630s and the American Revolution in 1776. Many of these immigrants did not come straight from Spain and Portugal. Rather, they came by way of Brazil, Holland, and England, where Jews had fled after their expulsion from Spain in 1492 and Portugal in 1497. Despite their small number, "they made real contributions to the life and thought of their times, and to the story of the American Revolution" (Brownstone 2).

The second wave of the Jewish immigrants was mostly from Germany and other German-speaking European countries, numbering approximately 250,000-300,000 in all. They arrived from the 1830s through the early 1880s. "German Jews played important roles in the settlement of the American West, during the Civil War, and as industrial America began to develop after the war" (Brownstone 2).

The third wave was a huge Jewish immigration numbering 2,500,000 from Russia and Eastern Europe in flight from intolerable oppression between the early 1880s and the mid-1920s. It was the restrictive immigration laws the U. S. Congress passed in the early 1920s that made further mass immigration from these areas impossible. Eventually this wave of the Jewish immigrants mixed and partially merged with the German-speaking and Spanish-Portuguese Jews who had arrived before, hence the Jewish ethnic group and the Jewish-American heritage. Some additional tens of thousands of Russian Jews and small numbers of Israeli Jews have in recent years become Jewish-Americans (Brownstone 4).

Out of thousands of years of history, from many lands and from distinct kinds of situations, Jews brought to multicultural America Jewish heritage. As is argued by David M. Brownstone, apart from "a thirst for freedom," "strength," "pride," "the ability to hope," "a strong feeling for family and community," Jews brought "skills and talents" as well (Brownstone 4-5).

From the ancient times, Jews have worked as scientists, physicians, philosophers, translators, mapmakers, and teachers, playing a leading role in these and every other branch of human knowledge. Jews have been among the greatest traders and merchants due to their strong banking and other financial skills.

Jews are of great talents as well. In Spain, in Germany, in Russia, in all the lands from which Jews came to America, there were a lot of Jewish painters, sculptors, writers, and performers of all kinds. "For significant periods they dominated comedy, and were of critical importance in the comic strip and comic book industries" (Norwood xiii). The imprint of Jews on American art and music has been far-reaching. Jews are noticeable for their impact on "such fields as psychoanalysis and psychology; the physical sciences and economics, in which Jewish American Nobelists have figured prominently; anthropology and sociology" (Norwood xiii). Their talents, together with their skills, are part of the Jewish heritage.

As is argued by Wirth-Nesher and Kramer, "landmarks of modern and contemporary American culture are products of Jewish American experience" (Wirth-Nesher and Kramer 2), with telling examples in various artistic representation: in fiction, Gertrude Stein's *Three Lives*, Bellow's *Herzog*, Philip Roth's *Goodbye, Columbus*, Nathanael West's *Miss Lonely Hearts*, the stories of Cynthia Ozick and Grace Paley, and Paul Auster's *New York Trilogy*; in poetry, Allen Geinsberg's *Howl* and Adrienne Rich's "Diving into the Wreck"; in drama, Arthur Miller's *Death of a Salesman*, Lillian Hellman's *The Children's Hour*, David Mamet's *American Buffalo*; in addition, in film, Woody Allen's *Annie Hall* and Steven Spielberg's *E. T.*; in American musical theater, *Porgy and Bess* (George and Ira Gershwin), *My Fair Lady* (Lerner and Lowe), *West Side Story* (Bernstein, Sondheim, Laurents, and Robbins); in American song, Irving Berlin's "God Bless America" and Bob Dylan's "Blowin' in the Wind. "

Despite the marginalization and even ignorance of American historians and textbooks, "Jews have profoundly influenced American society" and "significantly shaped American culture" with their "major impact on American literature, theater, film, and television" (Norwood xiii). It is worthwhile taking into consideration the shaping of Jewish American literature in particular.

B. The Shaping of Jewish American Literature

The literary remains of the earliest Jewish settlers are mainly petitions addressed to the Dutch West India Company protesting the exclusionary policies of the governor and demanding economic and political rights.

The first Jewish-authored literary texts were published in the eighteenth century. In general, the literary state of the Jewish community at that time was undeveloped. Despite the skepticism held by some scholars of the authorship, the publication of the volume of conversionist discourses, *The Truth, The Whole Truth, and Nothing But the Truth,* under the name of Judah Monis (1683-1764), an Italian Jew probably of Portuguese descent, made him the first Jewish author in America (Norwood 538). The next significant Jewish-authored publications in America were translations. In 1766 was published *Prayers for Shabbath, Rosh-Hashanah, and Kippur* by Isaac Pinto (1720-91) who noted that Hebrew was "imperfectly understood by many, by some, not at all" and took it as his mission "to translate our Prayers, in the Language of the Country wherein it hath pleased the divine Providence to appoint our Lot" (qtd. in Norwood 538).

In the early decades of the nineteenth century, while Samuel B. H. Judah (1799-1876), Jonas B. Philips (1805-69), Isaac Hardy (1788-1828) produced "what they believed could and should be a distinctly American literature," Mordecai Manuel Noah (1785-1851) "wrote frequently on Jewish themes, often marked by his penchant for the unusual and the flamboyant" (Norwood 540) as a self-appointed, outspoken champion of Jewish causes and was considered as the most prominent Jew in antebellum America.

In the second quarter of the nineteenth century, the Jewish literary scene changed substantively with the second wave of Jewish immigration. The audience for Jewish-themed literature grew, and in the ensuing decades the amount of literature produced and read by American Jews rose considerably. In addition, the character and range changed significantly, chiefly due to Isaac Mayer Wise (1819-1900) and to others such as Isaac Leeser (1806-68) who were pioneers of the Jewish press in America: Leeser established *The Occident and American Jewish Advocate* in 1843 and Wise founded *American Israelite* in 1854. Nathan Mayer (1838-1912) was esteemed as the most accomplished of the early Jewish American novelists who also wrote music and drama criticism and verse. Emma Lazarus (1849-1887) was considered as the most talented and literate, the most successful in addressing both Jewish and non-Jewish audiences (Norwood 544).

The twentieth century saw the development of Jewish American literature. In 1912, Mary Antin published her autobiography *The Promised Land*, which describes her assimilation into American culture. In 1917, *The Rise of David Levinsky* by Abraham Cahan reveals the advantages and disadvantages of assimilation for Jews in New York in light of Orthodox Judaic values: the secular rise in wealth accumulation is at the expense of spiritual fall. In 1930, Michael Gold (1894-1967) published *Jews Without Money* which tells of what it meant to be Jewish, poor, and the child of immigrants on Manhattan's

East Side in the years before the First World War, intending to awaken the Jews to their rights for justice. Henry Roth's *Call It Sleep* which came out in 1934 is considered as the best of those novels which, from the perspective of the thirties, looked back on the ghetto life and the immigrant Jewish community of several decades before. In *Miss Lonelyhearts* (1933) and *The Day of the Locust* (1939), Nathanael West (1903-40) "showed uncommon perceptiveness in sensing a closeness between the New England and the Jewish character. This is a significant fact which has been mainly forgotten by Gentile and Jew alike" (Brooks 2354).

The 1950s witnessed the rise and maturity of Jewish American literature (Yang 2003 508), with Bernard Malamud (1914-86), Saul Bellow (1915-2005), Isaac Bashevis Singer (1904-91), and Philip Roth (1933-) as its prominent representatives.

Well aware of the social problems of his day: rootlessness, infidelity, abuse, divorce, and more, Bernard Malamud touches lightly upon mythic elements and explores themes like isolation, class, and the conflict between bourgeois and artistic values in his fiction and he also depicts love as redemptive and sacrifice as uplifting. In "Picture of Malamud," in *The New York Times*, Philip Roth calls Malamud "A man of stern morality," who was driven by "the need to consider long and seriously every last demand of an overtaxed, overtaxing conscience tortuously exacerbated by the pathos of human need unabated" (Roth 1986a). In 1959 and 1967, Malamud was awarded the National Book Award respectively for *The Magic Barrel* and *The Fixer*. In 1967, *The Fixer* won the Pulitzer Prize for Fiction. The 1969 O. Henry Award went to Malamud's "Man in the Drawer."

Seeing the flaws in modern civilization, its ability to foster madness, materialism and misleading knowledge, Saul Bellow in his works speaks to the disorienting nature of modern civilization, and the countervailing ability of humans to overcome their frailty and achieve greatness (or at least awareness). Principal characters in Bellow's fiction have heroic potential, and many times they stand in contrast to the negative forces of society. These characters are often Jewish and have a sense of alienation or otherness.

In spite of Bellow's bristling at being called a "Jewish writer", a major theme in his work is Jewish life and identity while there is a great appreciation of America, and a fascination with the uniqueness and vibrancy of the American experience.

Propelled by the success of *Humboldt's Gift*, Bellow won the Nobel Prize for Literature in 1976. In addition, Bellow was awarded the National Book Award, the Pulitzer Prize, and the National Medal of Arts. He is the only writer to have won the National Book Award three times, and the only writer to have been nominated for it six times.

As the most famous Yiddish writer of the twentieth century, Isaac Bashevis Singer depicts the annihilated Jewish world of Eastern Europe, reflecting the fears, longings, and ambivalence of the Jewish immigrants. Drawing on folk memories and mystical traditions, his work dramatically moves from the realistic to the fantastic. His characters are often Holocaust survivors haunted by their immediate past and disoriented by American reality.

Philip Roth gained fame with the 1959 novella *Goodbye, Columbus*, an irreverent and humorous portrait of Jewish-American life that earned him a National Book Award. In 1969, with the publication of the controversial *Portnoy's Complaint*, he became a major celebrity. He has been awarded the National Book Award twice, and the PEN/ Faulkner Award three times. He received a Pulitzer Prize for his 1997 novel, *American Pastoral*. His 2001 novel *The Human Stain* was awarded the United Kingdom's WH Smith Literary Award for the best book of the year. His fiction is known for its philosophically and formally blurring the distinction between reality and fiction and for its provocative explorations of Jewish and American identity.

As a matter of fact, contemporary Jewish American fiction has burgeoned into a prominent body of work in the twentieth century after a series of transformations, during which its Jewishness has taken shape.

II. Contemporary Jewish American Fiction and Jewishness

As both "the product of and a reaction to American culture" (Berger 221), Jewish American fiction has been featured by a duality resulting from the conflict between the demands of Jewish tradition and the expectations of American culture. Before burgeoning into a prominent body of work in the twentieth century, Jewish American fiction has undergone a series of transformations. The transformations have primarily centered around the interweaving of American and Jewish traditions, the emphasis shifting from Jewish to American to a mingling of the two.

In the fifties, the critical issue became the success of assimilation and the exploration of America, usually expressed in the voice of the children of immigrants, whose connections with the prior generation were increasingly tenuous: Augie March in Saul Bellow's novel of the same name, the children of the aging couple in Tillie Olsen's "Tell Me a Riddle," the assortment of ethnic characters who interact in the stories of Grace Paley and Bernard Malamud.

In the sixties and early seventies, the conflict was frequently resolved in favor of the expectations of American culture, though with mixed feelings. The novels by Saul Bellow, Bernard Malamud, and Philip Roth amply illustrated this phenomenon (Berger 221). Reviewed regularly and often lauded in the critical press, their works were popular with the reading public.

Critical works including John Clayton's *Saul Bellow: In Defense of Man* (1967), Max Schulz's *Radical Sophistication: Studies in Contemporary Jewish-American Novelists* (1969), Sanford Pinsker's *The Schlemiel as Metaphor* (1971), and Ruth Wisse's *The Schlemiel as Modern Hero* (1971) tended to name the trio of Saul Bellow, Bernard

Malamud, and Philip Roth as "principal exemplars of a distinctive literary mode" that evinced "an overall cultural ethos associated with post-immigrant Jews in American cities in the 1940s and the 1950s, an emphatically moral ethos, affirming the nobility of the embattled individual, the so-called schlemiel, who stands alone against the impersonal forces of the modern world" (Levinson 3).

The primarily secular and "schlemiel" mode, an emphatically moral ethos, in fiction by Saul Bellow, Bernard Malamud, and Philip Roth coincides with Max Schultz's revelation that "The best of the contemporary Jewish American novelists... explore the theme of the man of heart in a mass-produced civilization"(6), which is "particularly Jewish," a legacy of a past religious tradition and of a specific set of historical experiences (Levinson 3).

Despite the centrality of Jewish subjects to their fiction, Bellow, Malamud, and Roth denied that they were "Jewish writers" and generally preferred instead the epithet of "American writer." In various interviews, they have each made statements to this effect. The conflict between the presence of Jewishness in their works and their rejection of the epithet of "Jewish writer" is related to the marginalization of Jewishness in the 1960s.

Some critics anticipated the end of the Jewish American fiction, for instance, in 1977, Irving Howe claimed that "Jewish fiction has probably moved past its highpoint," insofar as it is dependent upon the immigrant experience (16). There are Jewish writers who have managed to assimilate into the American mainstream, with Norman Mailer (1923-2007) as the most outstanding representative.

A novelist, journalist, essayist, poet, playwright, screenwriter, and film director, Norman Mailer (1923-2007) has been a towering figure in American literature for nearly 60 years. Born to a well-known Jewish family in Long Branch, New Jersey, with a maternal grandfather who is an unofficial rabbi, Mailer, however, gives no representation of Jewishness at all in the eleven novels he published over a 59-year span.

In 1948, Mailer published *The Naked and the Dead*, based on his military service in World War II. A *New York Times* bestseller for 62 weeks, it was hailed by many as one of the best American wartime novels and named one of the "one hundred best novels in English language" by the Modern Library. In 1980, *The Executioner's Song* — Mailer's novelization of the life and death of murderer Gary Gilmore— won the Pulitzer Prize for fiction. In 1992, Mailer received the annual Peggy V. Helmerich Distinguished Author Award presented by the Tulsa Library Trust. In 2005, he won the Medal for Distinguished Contribution to American Letters from the National Book Foundation.

Besides, Mailer is considered an innovator of creative nonfiction, a genre sometimes called New Journalism, which superimposes the style and devices of literary fiction onto fact-based journalism and combines actual events, autobiography, and political commentary with the richness of the novel. He is praised by Robert Lowell as "the best journalist in America."

Mailer's works are best known for their stylish nonconformity and his controversial views of American life. With his high literary reputation and no single touch of Jewishness at all in his works, Norman Mailer serves as the best example in assimilating into the American mainstream, totally ignoring Jewishness in his literary creation.

However, Jewishness as "the minority" was turned into "the majority" in the seventies, which witnessed the emergence of a Jewish American fiction by such writers as Arthur A. Cohen, Hugh Nissenson, and Cynthia Ozick who advocate the norms of the Jewish tradition as its standard. Their novels, with "a distinctively Jewish literary cadence, theological concern, and ritual awareness" (Berger 221), were termed by Ruth Wisse "Act two" of Jewish American fiction (41).

Wisse observes that Jewish American writers are building on the legacies of the older generation, "Having no longer to defend themselves from real or imagined charges of parochialism, the new Jewish writers ... are freer to explore the 'tribal' and particularistic aspects of Judaism" (41). While Saul Bellow, Bernard Malamud, and Philip Roth only occasionally placed Jewish literary influences and Jewish history in the forefront of their fiction, "Jewish thought, literary precursors, and history are often at the center of a fictional universe" (Kremer 1993 571) in the "second act" of Jewish American writing. As a result, there emerged "pervasive treatment of Jewish subjects and values, reference to Judaic texts, and introduction of the midrashic narrative mode," which herald a Jewish-American literary renaissance and leave a profound mark on American thought and literature.

Gone was the primarily secular, humanist outlook of such established writers as Saul Bellow, Bernard Malamud, and Philip Roth—writers who, according to Morris Dickstein, "brought Jews into modern American literature but left Judaism out" (34). According to Wisse, the interest of the emerging Jewish writers was not in "the sociological or even the psychological legacy of a Jewish background, but in the national design and religious destiny of Judaism, in its workable myths" (40).

Therefore, the "second act" of Jewish American writing is featured not only by the sheer quantity of new works featuring Jewish characters or a Jewish milieu, but also by the angle of vision of these works: an engagement with religious matters. Vestigial Jewishness in the primarily secular and "schlemiel" mode was replaced by "a more religiously inflected type of work" (Levinson 4), engaging Judaism in literary texts. As S. Lillian Kremer points out, "A significant portion of contemporary Jewish-American fiction is pervasively Jewish in its moral insistence and its reference to Judaic texts" (1993 571).

However, the "second act" of Jewish American writing is not unified. There are multiple ways of engaging Judaism in a literary text. Among others, Alfred Kazin and Arthur A. Cohen present two distinct modes due to their respective understanding of the identity of the "Jewish writer. "

Alfred Kazin dismisses the notion of secular Jewishness as "a sentimental tradition that developed as an American product. " In its place, Kazin proposed what he terms "Hebrew culture, " namely the religious stance epitomized by the prophets of the Hebrew scriptures. In his autobiographical text *A Walker in the City* (1951), he writes himself into this tradition, representing himself as an inspired boy directly encountering the Jewish God through prayer in translation. Kazin's engagement with Judaism is imbued with the Romanticism that he championed in his critical writings about Emerson and Whitman, which is based on private, visionary experience. Signaling the allegiance to the canon of Jewish texts, Kazin also proclaims an antinomian independence from any tradition. In short, Kazin, the romantic Jewish writer, attests to a broken covenant with God, acquiescing in feelings of awe and wonder in place of confident faith (Levinson 7).

Arthur A. Cohen presents a model of Jewish literary practice that differs from Kazin's romantic approach. Beginning as a self-professed "Jewish theologian, " Cohen turns subsequently to novel writing and finally to "an idiosyncratic genre between the theological and the literary" (Levinson 8). Rejecting Howe's premise that an authentic Jewish identity requires the ethnic space of the *shtetl* or the Lower East Side, Cohen holds that the Jew is a figure with both a supernatural destiny and a natural fate. He "entrusts literature with the task of representing the specific paradigms for Jewish religious life" (Levinson 8). The most distinguishing amongst these paradigms is that of "Exile" or *Galut*, the meanings and possibilities of which he represents in *In the Days of Simon Stern* (1973). To sum up, Cohen, the theological Jewish writer, creates a myth that embodies his conception of Exile as the metaphysical basis of Jewish existence (Levinson 7-8).

In brief, on the basis of their distinct understanding of the identity of the "Jewish writer," Kazin and Cohen engage Judaism in their texts in the romantic and theological mode respectively.

According to Alan L Berger, "The decade of the eighties ... constitutes nothing less than a third act" (221).

First, there are such established novelists as Hugh Nissenson, Cynthia Ozick, Chaim Potok, Tova Reich, and Anne Roiphe, whose Jewishness is reflected in their increasingly turning to the traditional Jewish figures and classical texts in telling their contemporary tales—"Abraham and the Bible, Akiva and the Talmud surpass and judge Protestantism and the American way. A midrashic feel for the complexity of Jewish history and a compelling sense of the theological implications of Jewish survival stand in stead of concerns about 'what the Christians will think'" (Berger 222).

Second, there are emerging writers as well: Thomas Friedmann, Allegra Goodman, Rhoda Lerman, and Steve Stern, who are distinguished by their determination in "imagining with the materials of Jewish myth and mysticism" (Berger 222).

Third, Jewish American fiction in the eighties is characterized by concern for the Holocaust, one of the two critical events of the twentieth-century Jewish history, the other being the establishment of the Israeli State.

Until the late 1960s, the Holocaust was relatively absent as a theme in much Jewish-American fiction, Edward Wallant's *The Pawnbroker* (1961) being a significant exception. Since that time, a number of works have appeared explicitly incorporating the Holocaust and generating intriguing questions about historical and cultural memory. Such works range from Bellow's *Mr. Sammler's Planet* to Philip Roth's *The Ghost Writer* to Art Spiegelman's *Maus*. While critical works attending directly to the Holocaust have no doubt raised important questions about the uses and abuses of Jewish memory and about the limits of representation, the focus on literary response has tended to obscure the dynamics of literary creation. The Jewish writer has been positioned above all as a spokesperson for collective trauma, a "witness," to use Kremer's term.

As far as the Jewishness in representing the Holocaust is concerned, "American Jews have adapted documentary material to the fictional universe, incorporating historic figures and relying heavily on evidentiary matter to create a fictional Holocaust universe" (Kremer 1993 576). For instance, Susan Fromberg Schaeffer based her presentation of the Vilna ghetto and Kaiserwald labor camp in *Anya* on the numerous interviews she had conducted with the survivors. Norma Rosen incorporated in *Touching Evil* the documentary materials from the Eichmann trial. Leslie Epstein based *King of the Jews* upon historical documents of the Lodz ghetto. Marge Piercy set an example of the research novel that covers multiple civilian and military fronts in her epic war novel *Gone to Soldiers*. In general, "primary loyalty is to fact presented through the prism of fiction" (Kremer 1993 577).

Ever since the nineties, younger Jewish writers such as Allegra Goodman, Steve Stern, and Myra Goldberg have been "seeking an identity in a Judaism that their literary and familial forebears had abandoned" (Levinson 2), as on the cover of the November 1997 edition of *Tikkun*, the editors of the magazine welcomed what they called the "Jewish literary revival" (Levinson 1).

In the 21st century, Jewishness is tainted by the synthesis of what is traditionally Jewish and innovations of various kinds. There are such Jewish writers who question and reject the conventions of traditional fiction-writing as Ronald Sukenick (1932-2004), who, after Roland Barthes announced the "death of the author," extends the metaphor even further toward "the death of the novel." To Sukenick, the list of what is missing contains: reality, time or personality. There are Jewish writers including Paul Auster (1947-   ), who "synthesized postmodernist literary devices, existentialist theories and a fluid, readable writing style" (Li i) in the fictional world which is governed by chance and absurdity. Haunted by the Jewish themes such as "father and son," "sacrifice and redemption," Auster is likewise concerned with the Jewish attitude toward writing: "to witness, to remember, to play divine and utterly serious textual games" (Finkeisten, 1995 49 qtd. in Li 23). There are Jewish writers like E. L Doctorow (1931-) whose realistic representation of the postmodern world defines the literary appeal.

To summarize, in the sixties and the early seventies, Jewish American fiction is featured by the Jewishness that is in a primarily secular and "schlemiel" mode, an emphatically moral ethos. In the seventies, the Jewishness is embodied in the emergence of "a more religiously inflected type of work," though in distinct modes. In the eighties, the Jewishness in Jewish American fiction is represented in turning to traditional figures and classical texts, in imagining with the materials of Jewish myth and mysticism, and in sticking to historicity by adapting documentary material for the Holocaust representation. From the nineties on, there emerges the resurgence of Jewish writing as Judaism is re-exploited for a quest of Jewish identity. In the 21st century, Jewishness is featured by innovations of distinct kinds.

In general, there are three points that feature contemporary Jewishness chronologically, namely, moral ethos, Judaism engagement, and loyalty to fact in Holocaust representation, which stand independent respectively.

Cynthia Ozick, "the acknowledged leader" of the "second act" in Jewish American writing, "a revitalized Jewish-American literary movement" (Kremer 1993 572), self-consciously defines herself as a Jewish writer. The authentically Jewish nature in her fiction serves as the distinguishing feature of her creation.

III. Jewishness in Cynthia Ozick's Fiction

Struggling with the tension she confronts as a Jew, a woman and a writer in Diaspora, Ozick morally weighs the conflicts and insists on merging the "minority" representing the homeland with the "majority" representing the hostland in the diasporic space and attempts to foreground the "minority" as a result in her literary endeavor, wherein her Jewishness emerges.

The conflicts Ozick morally weighs mainly stem from the tension she encounters in Diaspora as a Jew and a writer, and those she encounters as a Jewish woman writer, both of which are consequent on Jewishness that is marginalized as the minority in Diaspora.

While Judaism and Jewishness in America have no longer "determined" or "affected" the "cognitive and behavioral universe" of most of the Jews, Ozick insists on the Jewishness of Jewish-American literature and claims that no fiction produced by Jews in the Diaspora has had lasting value except that which is "centrally Jewish" (Ozick *Art & Ardor* 155). Likewise she insists on the centrality of Judaism to Jewish identity.

Ozick elaborates on the Jewish visions as she attempts to define Jewishness in her essays, distinguishing herself from many Jewish American writers, to whom Jewishness was "a condition of being that did not demand special efforts either to deny or to define" (Chen Internet 49).

A. Ozick's Definition of Jewishness

Though "the only consensus on the problem of how to define Jewishness is that there is no consensus" (Brauner 3), Ozick has defined Jewishness in five aspects as "originating in the covenant (*Art & Ardor* 123), history, the avoidance of idolatry, the ability to make distinctions, and study (*Metaphor & Memory* 224)" (Cooper 181).

a. Originating in the Covenant

In one of her early essays, "Bech, Passing," which was published in *Commentary*, Nov. 1970, Ozick rebukes John Updike for having created a "Jewish" protagonist who is "theologically hollow" (*Art & Ardor* 113). In Ozick's judgment, Updike is a "crypto-Christian, a reverse Marrano celebrating the Body of Jesus while hidden inside a bathing suit" (115), who himself is short of the imagination of what a sacral Jew might be, and hence the protagonist lacking the essence of Jewish identity:

> Emancipated Jewish writers like Bech (I know one myself) have gone through Russia without once suspecting the landscape of old pogroms, without once smelling another Jew...[But Bech's] phrase "peasant Jews" among the Slavs is an imbecilic contradiction—peasants work the land, Jews were kept from working it. ... If there had been "peasant Jews" there might have been no Zionism, no State of Israel ... ah Bech! ... despite your Jewish nose and hair, you are—as Jew—an imbecile to the core. (117)

Ozick further attributes Updike's "failure of invention" (169) to his imbecility without grasping the essential of being a Jew:

> Being a Jew is something more than being an alienated marginal sensibility with kinky hair. Simply: to be a Jew is to be covenanted; or, if not committed so far, to be at least aware of the possibility of becoming covenanted; or, at the very minimum, to be aware of the Covenant itself. ... If to be a Jew is to become covenanted, then to write of Jews without taking this into account is to miss the deepest point of all. (123)

Therefore, the core, the deepest point of Jewishness, in Ozick's opinion, is to be covenanted, to obey, or to be faithful to the covenant made with God so as to maintain an integral Jewish identity.

b. History

In her later essay "Bialik's Hint," Ozick touches upon Jewishness in showing her dismay on seeing many Jewish American writers pursuing a prominence in the American mainstream at the cost of Jewish historical memory and Jewish civilization:

> To be a Jew is to be old in history, but not only that; to be a Jew is to be a member of a distinct civilization expressed through an oceanic culture in possession of a group of essential concepts and a multitude of texts and attitudes

elucidating those concepts. Next to the density of such a condition—or possibility—how gossamer are the stories of those writers "of Jewish extraction" whose characters are pale indifferent echoes of whatever lies at hand. (*Metaphor and Memory* 224)

While some of the Jewish American writers are in pursuit of an ethnic exoticism that is of current appeal to American readers, what they have lost is a full-blown Jewish identity in Ozick's point of view (Powers 1995 379). Ozick attaches great importance to history, within the realm of which Jewishness is posited. In her eyes, history is "judgment and interpretation" (Ozick *Bloodshed* 6) while identity is crucially related to history.

c. Anti-idolatry

In Ozick's vision, the central precept of the Judaic ethos, featured by monotheism, is the taboo against idolatry that has distinguished Judaism from other religions since the time of Abraham (Strandberg 22). Correspondingly, the Jews must abide by the Second Commandment and resist idolatry. She further clarifies her thought in "Literature as Idol: Harold Bloom,"

> The single most useful, and possibly the most usefully succinct, description of a Jew—as defined "theologically"—can best be rendered negatively: a Jew is someone who shuns idols, who least of all would wish to become like Terach, the maker of idols. (Ozick *Art & Ardor* 188)

In addition, as a fiction writer, Ozick sees it as a mission to shun idols in insisting that "The commandment against idols, it seems to me, is overwhelmingly pertinent to the position on the Jewish fiction writer in America today" (Ozick "Toward a New Yiddish" *Art and Ardor* 165).

Anti-idolatry, in turn, results in distinction-making, one of the five aspects of Jewishness as Ozick defines.

d. Distinction-making

Ozick considers distinction-making as one of the two momentous standards which characterize the Jewish Idea. In her opinion, "The first, the standard of anti-idolatry, led to the second, the standard of distinction-making—the understanding that the properties of one proposition are not the properties of another proposition" (Ozick "Bialik's Hint" *Metaphor & Memory* 224).

e. Study

To Ozick, study serves as an effective means to delve into the essence of Jewishness. The Jewish emphasis on study and articulation as means of cultural transmission has long historical roots. The ubiquitousness of the educational enterprises is expressed in the biblical Shema Yisrael (Hear, O Israel), adapted since ancient times as, the central prayer of Jewish liturgy (Chen Internet 52).

In terms of Ozick's personal experience, "My reading has become more and more urgent, though in narrower and narrower channels. [. . .] I read mainly to find out [. . .] What it is to *think* as a Jew" (Ozick "Toward a New Yiddish" *Art and Ardor* 157).

As a matter of fact, the emphasis on study is, by extension, an emphasis on intellectual significance, continuity of the heritage, and on the capacity of making distinction, hence it is rather an assurance to stay Jewish.

To sum up, Ozick has defined Jewishness as "being covenanted," "anti-idolatry," "history," "distinction-making," and "study." Her definition is nevertheless somewhat overlapping. While "being covenanted" serves as the guideline, "anti-idolatry" and "history" are more potential concrete practice to observe, and "distinction-making" and "study" act as the means for the assurance of staying Jewish.

B. Jewishness in Ozick's Fiction

Ozick distinguishes herself from her contemporaries in her emphasis on the Jewishness of Jewish American literature and her overt acknowledgement of being a Jewish writer. Furthermore, in the diasporic context, more than any other Jewish American writers, Ozick explores the relationship between Judaism and imaginative writing. Her works well reflect her efforts in constructing Jewishness as the majority in resolving the tensions she has encountered and struggled against in achieving unity as an observant Jew, a woman, and a writer in America, the three basic ingredients of the composition of her own identity in the diasporic context.

Specifically speaking, as a Jewish writer, she has struggled between her respect for the Jewish tradition with the injunction not to be idolaters, the commitment to serve God as is covenanted, the Jewish insistence on parenthood and historicity, and her veneration of literature as creative art. She is engaged in "what both the fact and idea of creation mean to the Jew who would also write imaginative literature" (Parrish 440). As a Jewish woman writer, while rejecting the differences between men and women in imagination which she claims as genderless, she attempts to create "Eros of ideas" for a feminist mending of the prohibiting Orthodox Judaic gender law.

As is argued in the previous analysis, contemporary Jewishness in Jewish American fiction is featured by three points, namely, moral ethos, Judaism engagement, and loyalty to fact in Holocaust representation.

Ozick has mingled and expanded the essential aspects featuring contemporary Jewishness and therefore enriched it. The Jewishness in her fiction is characterized by the moral ethos that she has highlighted in the diasporic space, where the "minority" representing the homeland is merged with the "majority" representing the hostland and is eventually foregrounded as a result of the literary power Ozick endows with her fiction imbuing with moral weighing of the conflicts between the insistence upon Jewishness and "literature as idol," history representation, feminine representation, and literary narrative.

Above all, contemplating upon writing, she mingles moral ethos with Judaism engagement in her primary Jewish insistence upon anti-idolatry in resolving the conflict between Judaic monotheism and literature as idol, and foregrounds idolatry resistance in her literary practice.

Moreover, she foregrounds moral ethos in constructing and deconstructing Jewish memories as well as the moral ethos in her insistence on the balance between historicity and figuration and in her advocacy of Jewish authenticity in Post-Holocaust Midrashic representation of the Holocaust, pointing to her Jewish vision that history is judgment and interpretation.

In addition, she enriches Judaism engagement with moral judgment that she makes of the prohibiting Orthodox Judaic gender law that results in her representation of Jewish femininity, highlighting the "Eros of ideas."

Last but not least, she endows postmodernist literary narrative with realistic significance to serve her needs to stay authentically Jewish.

In short, the Jewishness in Ozick's fiction is distinguished by her highlighting the moral ethos in her literary struggle to merge the "minority" representing the homeland with the "majority" representing the hostland in the diasporic space. The ensuing analysis is to center around the characteristics and embodiment of the Jewishness in Ozick's fiction which find expression in the relationships between Jewishness and "literature as idol," Jewishness and history representation, Jewishness and feminine representation, and Jewishness and literary narrative.

Chapter Two

Jewishness and "Literature as Idol"

Ozick has mingled and expanded the essential aspects featuring contemporary Jewishness and therefore enriched it. Above all, she mingles moral ethos with Judaism engagement in her primary Jewish insistence upon anti-idolatry in resolving the conflict between Judaic monotheism and literature as idol, and foregrounds idolatry resistance in her literary practice.

Ozick distinguishes herself from Alfred Kazin and Arthur A. Cohen in Judaism engagement. While Kazin's engagement with Judaism is influenced by Romanticism and Cohen is known as a "Jewish theologian," Ozick brings Judaism and literature into an explicit conflict.

Ozick insists that a religious sensibility is always at work in significant literary production. Indeed, she goes so far as to say that "The secular Jew is a figment; when a Jew becomes a secular person he is no longer a Jew. This is especially true for makers of literature" (Ozick "Towards a New Yiddish" *Art & Ardor* 169). In her fictional practice, she intends to work in the service of God, instead of violating and transgressing God's commandments.

"There are profoundly definable Jewish ideas that cannot be duplicated outside of Jewish received tradition," Ozick stated in an interview in 1993, "[one] centrally defining idea is anti-idolatry" (Kauvar interview 1993 378). About fifteen years before the interview, the same point had been emphasized in her essay, "The single most useful, and possibly the most usefully succinct, description of a Jew—as defined 'theologically,'" she holds, "can be rendered negatively: a Jew is someone who shuns idols" (Ozick "Literature as Idol: Harold Bloom" *Art & Ardor* 188).

In Ozick's insistence upon anti-idolatry in her literary practice, the "majority" is her vision of literature as idol and the "minority" is her allegiance to Judaism as monotheism which is in nature anti-idolatrous. The moral ethos emerges from Ozick's self-positioned paradoxical dilemma resultant from her understanding of what a Jew is and what a writer is in Diaspora, the contradiction she has perceived between the Jewish observance and creative impulse.

Ozick is as committed to her faith as she is to her craft, and consequently she has positioned herself in the paradox: on one hand, she is serious in writing, carving out perfection in every single "comely and muscular" sentence (Ozick *Metaphor & Memory* 109). On the other hand, she is an observant Jew who sacredly takes seriously her commitment to God. The particular commandment that Ozick, as a writer, thinks to violate is the second commandment against idolatry.

Idolatry is among the worst sins in the Bible. It is recorded that during the Exodus, Moses led the Hebrews from Egypt to Mount Sinai, where he received from God the Law, which was later called "Torah", in which were the Ten Commandments. The second reads: "You shall not make for yourself a graven image, or any likeness of anything that is in heaven above, or that is in the earth beneath, or that is in the water under the earth; you shall not bow down to them or serve them" (Exodus 20: 4). As a matter of fact, the covenant between Moses and God, by extension, between Israelites and God, requires idolatry be shunned.

Then, as Ozick says of Harold Bloom, she herself "is a struggler between Terach and Abraham," knowing "what Abraham knows," but wanting "what Terach wants" (Ozick *Art & Ardor* 195). For Ozick, who is "a worshiper of literature" (Ozick *Art & Ardor* 294) and an observant Jew at once, there is "the clash of monotheism with image-making" (Kauvar interview 1985 380). The essence of the paradox is how a writer can presume to create something that is new and whole with the knowledge that only one Being is capable of this sort of creation.

I. "A Jewish Writer": an Oxymoron

In her non-fiction essays, Ozick implicates herself in the paradox of writing as a Jew. To her, "the phrase 'Jewish writer' may be what rhetoricians call an 'oxymoron'—a pointed contradiction, in which one arm of the phrase clashes so profoundly with the other as to annihilate it" (Ozick "Literature as Idol: Harold Bloom" *Art & Ardor* 178). On one hand, to Ozick, "to be a Jew is to be covenanted; or, if not committed so far, to be at least aware of the possibility of becoming covenanted; or, at the very minimum, to be aware of the Covenant itself" (Ozick "Bech, Passing" *Art & Ardor* 123). She further observes that "The commandment against idols... is overwhelmingly pertinent to the position of the Jewish fiction writer in America today" (Ozick "Towards a New Yiddish" *Art & Ardor* 165). On the other hand, to her, "literature, one should have the courage to reflect, is an idol" (Ozick "Literature as Idol: Harold Bloom" *Art & Ardor* 196), for idol worship is the worship of anything other than the monotheistic God, and idols come in many different forms—they can be made of ideas, words, spoken syllables; they can be stories.

In concluding "Literature as Idol: Harold Bloom," the essay in which Ozick's most sustained explicit discussion of idolatry takes place, she observes:

> If there can be such a chimera as a "Jewish writer," it must be the kind of sphinx or gryphon (part one thing, part another)..., sometimes purifying like Abraham, more often conjuring like Terach, and always knowing that the two are icily, elegiacally, at war. (Ozick "Literature as Idol: Harold Bloom" *Art & Ardor* 198)

For Ozick, the "Jewish writer" must dialectically shift between "conjuring" and "purifying." The fundamental "conjuring" force stems from imagination and language representation while the primary "purifying" results from the moral ethos the writer foregrounds in the literary practice. Then the key issue is to what degree and in what manner the "conjuring" imagination and language representation can be "purified" and employed by a Jewish writer to serve Jewish needs.

Insisting on the co-existence of "purifying" Abraham and "conjuring" Terach in literary creation, Ozick attempts to weave the Judaic anti-idolatry, the "minority" representing the Judaic homeland, into the literary representation, the "majority" representing the American diasporic hostland. Therefore, her fiction turns out to be a forum in which she stages a confrontation between what she conceives as the conflicting claims of Jewishness and literature with imagination and language representation as its primary means. There naturally emerges Ozick's moral ethos pertinent to the conflict between Jewishness and imagination as idol and language worship as idol.

While "dread[ing] the cannibal touch of story-making," Ozick cannot help "lust[ing] after stories more and more and more." Moral ethos concerning idolatry informs Ozick's conception of Jewish literary practice and as a result concerns with idolatry serve as the focal point of her meditations over the category of " Jewish writer," from imagination, "the blood and flesh" of literary creation, to literary acceptance, the reading of texts.

The ensuing analysis is to take "The Pagan Rabbi" and *The Messiah of Stockholm* as samples to detect the moral ethos Ozick highlights in her resistance against imagination as idol and language and text worship as idol.

II. Idolatry and Imagination

The confrontation between what Ozick thinks of as the conflicting claims of Judaism and art is well shown in "The Pagan Rabbi" (1966), one of her earliest stories. "The title of 'The Pagan Rabbi' reveals the primary tensions of the story, the divisions between holy and pagan, nature and study, Pan and Moses" (Cooper 183).

As Ruth Wisse has observed, the late nineteenth and the early twentieth century Hebrew and Yiddish works frequently feature a rabbinical student who is drawn away from study, towards the sensual pleasures of "natural" life (Wisse 41). In poems and stories by figures such as S. Y. Abramovitch, Chaim Bialik, and Saul Tchernikhovsky, Wisse contends, "the physical world of sun, storm, trees, and rivers provides a model of freedom counterposed to the self-denial of *Shtetl* culture" (41). "The Pagan Rabbi" is no doubt a modern version of this theme, narrating the life of a brilliant Talmudic student, a rabbi who suddenly becomes enthralled and seduced by the beauty of nature with a focus on the inner conflict of the protagonist.

In the story, Isaac Kornfeld, a famous author of "remarkable" collections of responsa and Professor of Mishnaic History, finds himself inextricably drawn to nature, a practice typically denounced as "Idolatry" in Judaic Law. Venturing into urban parks—hiking, collecting berries, and imploring the powers of nature to respond to him, he abandons his life of Talmudic scholarship in order to commune with nature. Eventually, Isaac achieves a coupling with the dryad Iripomonoeia and experiences "marvels, blisses, and transports no man has slaked himself with since Father Adam pressed out the forbidden chlorophyll of Eden" (32). Furthermore, his soul, greedy to possess Iripomonoeia, escapes and attaches itself to her. However, his nature-spurning, Torah-reading soul horrifies Isaac in revealing to him "The dryad, who does not exist, lies," "all that has no real existence lies" and "If you had not contrived to be rid of me, I would have stayed with you till the end" (36). Moreover, as a result of his successful attempt in the separation between his body and his soul, he will lie in his grave alone and his soul will forever "walk here alone ... in my garden" (36). Desperately, Isaac calls to Iripomonoeia, his nature dryad, for assistance, for it is to her that he has forsaken his soul, however, it is on deaf ears that his cries fall. "In an effort to integrate the sacred with nature, Isaac loses both" (Cooper 188). Distraught, Isaac commits suicide by hanging himself from a tree with his prayer shawl. Ironically, nature and religion have joined in a paradoxical attempt to destroy his Jewish self and to merge with nature or to bring an end to his struggle between the two.

However, the story features itself with its polyphonic features both in its presentation of diversities of discourse and its polyphonic narrative mode, which point to Ozick's meditation on the relationship between "imagination" and "Jewishness" in her formative years, an impetus for and an embodiment of moral imagination and liturgical literature which have secured her prominence in contemporary Jewish American writing.

A. Heteroglossia in "The Pagan Rabbi"

The phenomenon of diversities of discourse, termed "heteroglossia" or "heteroglot" in Bakhtin's theory of dialogism, refers to a diversity of individual voices artistically presented. Bakhtin describes this kind of plurality of discourse as,

> The internal stratification of any single national language into social dialects, characteristic group behavior, professional jargons, generic languages, languages of generations and age groups, tendentious languages, languages of the authorities, of various circles and of passing fashions [...] The novel is the expression of a Galiean perception of language, one that denies the absolutism of a single and unitary language. (Bakhtin *Dialogic Imagination* 366)

In "The Pagan Rabbi, " there are three characters who are all Jews— Isaac Kornfeld, the protagonist; his friend, the unnamed narrator of the story; and Sheindel, Isaac's widow. The story is an artistic orchestration of a diversity of their discourses. Not one of their individual voices is privileged. Each authorizes itself.

Having withdrawn in his second year from the rabbinical seminary where he had been classmates with Isaac, the narrator is doing business first in fur and then in running a bookstore. Born in a concentration camp, Sheindel survived the Holocaust. Being thrown to the electrified fence "when an army mobbed the gate; the current vanished from the terrible wires," she has "a mark on her cheek like an asterisk, cut by a barb" from the fence (Ozick "The Pagan Rabbi" 7).

It is Sheindel's firm belief that there is a fence between what is Jewish and what is pagan with no intermediate space in between. She interprets Jewish law as a fence (Lyons 19). Sticking to Jewish requirement of female etiquette, Sheindel "wore a dark thick woolen hat" "that covered every part of her hair" when "it was July" (Ozick "The Pagan Rabbi" 6). When men were talking, "Sheindel was sitting perfectly still; the babies, female infants in long stockings, were asleep in her arms" (6). What's more, "she had no mother to show, she had no father to show, but she had, extraordinarily, God to show—she was known to be, for her age and sex, astonishingly learned" (7).

The metaphor of a fence reveals Sheindel's familiarity with *Mishnaic* literature, such as *Pirke Avot (Chapters of the Fathers)*, which repeatedly employs the metaphor of a fence to explicate the importance of God's word and the corresponding necessity of measures designed to protect it (Levinson 170).

Mishnaic literature provides not only a metaphor for Sheindel, but also an epigraph for the story. Taken from *Pirke Avot* (3:7), the epigraph reads, "Rabbi Jacob said: 'He who is walking along and studying, but then breaks off to remark, "How lovely is that tree!" or "How beautiful is that fallow field!"'—Scripture regards such a one as having hurt his own being'" (Ozick "The Pagan Rabbi" 3). With the employment of such an epigraph, Ozick has prepared the reader to come to the realization of the greater error Isaac has committed than Rabbi Jacob warns against in "having hurt his own being," for he has gone much farther than the complimentary remark on the loveliness of a tree. Moreover, with the employment of such an epigraph, Ozick has prepared a moral anchor on which judgment between imagination and Jewishness is to be made.

It is to Jewishness that Sheindel adheres. She is inside the fence, to use her metaphor of the fence. In contrast, the narrator is outside the fence, having distanced from Jewishness in withdrawing from the seminary, in being brought to atheism, and in marrying a Gentile girl. The central tension of the story is whether Isaac Kornfeld is a rabbi or a pagan as "he scaled the Fence of the Law" (24).

The letter of Isaac, a suicide note and a love letter to nature at once, keeps a record of his encounters and his eventual demise. Despite Isaac's absence, his voice is brought into the presentation with his letter, which is read aloud successively by Sheindel and the narrator, who interpret and make judgments respectively. Embracing Jewishness, Sheindel is antithetical to the narrator, who distances from it. Isaac stands in between. The collision between the interpretations and judgments acts as the crucially framing element in the narrative.

B. Polyphonic Narrative in "The Pagan Rabbi"

The narrative point of view in "The Pagan Rabbi" is first person limited omniscient. It is through the perspective of the narrator that Ozick's meditations on the relationship between imagination and Jewishness are presented in a polyphonic mode. Sheindel reads the first half of Isaac's letter and the narrator the second half. While listening and reading, the narrator has access to all the voices presented, each constituting a dialogue with the narrator. Consequently the polyphonic narrative includes Isaac's voice through his letter, Sheindel's interpretations and judgments, and those of the narrator's. The unfolding of the story is as a matter of fact a process in which the narrator comes to the understanding of and doubts against, agreement and disagreement with other voices. Collision and tension prevail in the story, which is suggestive of Ozick's struggle over the paradox she has positioned herself into, the relationship between imagination and Jewishness, and furthermore, imagination and idolatry.

Isaac tells the narrator that "A man should have a livelihood" (6). He himself commits suicide with his prayer shawl and "sin[s] against his own life" (5) whereas at the same time he puts into practice the Jewish doctrine that "A Jew is buried in his prayer shawl" (5). His words and deeds compete against each other in the narrator's recollection of the past.

More often Isaac's voice is rendered present in his letter, which is marked by his struggles and his contradictory perceptions. The contradiction is likewise reflected in his description of his coupling with the dryad Iripomonoeia: "I began to weep because I was certain I had been ravished by some sinewy animal," and believed "I was defiled" (29), and "Meanwhile, ... every tissue of my flesh was gratified in its inmost awareness, a marvelous voluptuousness did not leave my body; sensual exultations of a wholly supreme and paradisal order" (29), "In me were linked... appetite and fulfillment, delicacy and power, mastery and submissiveness, and other paradoxes of entirely remarkable emotional import" (30). With frankness, he reveals agony resulting from such perceptions: "I moved from clarity to doubt and back again. I had no trust in my conclusions because all my experiences were evanescent. Everything certain I attributed to some other cause less certain" (25-26). He calls for pity. He calls in despair to the dryad Iripomonoeia: "For pity of me, come, come" (36).

The agonizing struggles of Isaac are but Ozick's in her formative years in self-creating and disrupting the paradoxical oppositions between her personae as a Jew and as a writer. The root of agony is the collision between imagination, represented by Isaac, and Jewishness, represented by Sheindel.

Difference in attitude to and capability of imagination is what differentiates Isaac and Sheindel, hence the source of the primary tension of the story. In the narrator's eyes, Isaac's imagination "was so remarkable" (4) while Sheindel "was one of those born to dread imagination" (14). The narrator's judgment on their Jewishness, just like the narrator's cup over which Sheindel and the narrator read Isaac's letter, is "in the neutral zone" (10).

Isaac is characterized with his remarkable imagination. In the bedtime stories he told his daughters, there are "mice that danced," "a speaking cloud," "a turtle that married a blade of withered grass," "stones [that] had tears for their leglessness," "a tree that turned into a girl," and " a pig [that] has a soul" (13). All of these are called "dark invention" (14) by Sheindel while they remind the narrator with envy of his "terrible childhood" when "My own father used to drill me every night in sacred recitation" (13). When it comes to Isaac's writing, Sheindel commented "What he wrote was only fairy tales," "full of sprites, nymphs, gods" while "I was marveling at her hatred" (14).

Serving as the focal point in the polyphonic narrative mode, the narrator further presents the antithesis and collision between the oppositions represented by Isaac and Sheindel in their attitude to and capability of imagination. Furthermore, the narrator's response reveals the narrator's judgment.

Isaac's remarkable imagination is shown in his classification of soul and his self-indulgent historical invention. To him, "Earth displays two categories of soul: the free and the indwelling" (21), and "it is our tragedy: our soul is included in us, it inhabits us, we contain it" (21), whereas "The soul of the plant does not reside in the chlorophyll, it may roam if it wishes, it may choose whatever form or shape it pleases" (21). The narrator's response at this point is to ask Sheindel to stop reading the letter, not to "look at this thing again, tear it to pieces," so as not to "destroy a dead man's honor" (22). The response reveals his objection to Isaac's practice. However, when Sheindel insists that "I don't destroy his honor. He had none" and claims "He was a pagan" (22), the narrator can not help challenging, "My God, ... Wasn't he a teacher? Wasn't he a scholar?" (22)

Isaac embraces "the wholly plausible position of ... animism within the concept of the One God" and "a historical illumination of its continuous but covert expression even within the Fence of the Law" (20). He holds that "in God's fecundating Creation there is no possibility of Idolatry, and therefore no possibility of committing this so-called abomination" (21). Attempting to turn his animistic view idolatry-free, Isaac claims that "It is false history, false philosophy, and false religion which declare to us human ones that we live among Things... There is nothing that is dead. There is no Non-life" and he invents the biblical history,

> It was not out of ignorance that Moses failed to teach about those souls that are free.... it was God's will that our ancestors should no longer be slaves. Yet our ancestors, being stiff-necked, would not have abandoned their slavery in Egypt had they been taught of the free souls. They would have said: "Let us stay, our bodies will remain enslaved in Egypt, but our souls will wander at their pleasure in Zion." (22)

Therefore, the crux of the matter turns out to be what is imagined and what it is imagined for. Isaac's imagination is related to history, however, it is invention of history. It is to serve Isaac's personal need to worship nature and to render the obviously idolatrous practice idolatry-free.

After all, while idolatry has the effect of "rooting out human pity" (Ozick "Literature as Idol: Harold Bloom" *Art & Ardor* 190), moral judgment is expected to take into account the confusion and puzzlement inherent in human nature and pay due understanding. When Isaac "considered how a man's body is no better than a clay pot, a fact which none of our sages has ever contradicted, it seemed to me [Isaac] then that an indwelling soul by its own nature would be obliged to cling to its bit of pottery until the last crumb and grain had vanished into

earth" (26). He was "grieving and swollen with self-pity" (26) and
came up with "An extraordinary thought" that "was luminous,
profound, and practical" (27)—"if only I could couple with one of the
free souls, the strength of the connection would likely wrest my own
soul from my body—seize it, as if by a tongs, draw it out, ... to its
own freedom" (28). Isaac "stumbled... for the support of solid
verticality"(28). To the narrator, Isaac "was a student, he sat and he
thought, he was a Jew," "A scholar. A rabbi. A remarkable Jew!"
while Sheindel "spilled a furious laugh" (12) and thought "he was
never a Jew" (23).

The meditations on the relationship between imagination and
Jewishness are furthered with the narrator's changing attitude to Isaac
and Sheindel as a result of the narrator's moral judgment.

The first time the narrator saw Sheindel, "I loved her at once" (5)
and "envied him [Isaac] his Sheindel" (6), however, after the death
of Isaac, when the narrator came to her, "Her voice contained an irony
that surprised me" and she even asked "Did you dig in the ground" out
of "The impulse of a detective"? (10). The narrator figured "it's a
stupidity that I came here" (11) and he had to remind her, "Rebbetzin
Isaac, your husband was a rabbi!" (11) "But she was more mocking
than distraught" (18).

Having read Isaac's notebook, the narrator returned to Sheindel
"with a single idea: I meant to marry Isaac's widow when enough time
had passed to make it seemly" (19). To his disappointment, her voice
in reading the letter "reminded me of my father's: it was unforgiving"
(21).

Listening to Isaac's belief in the existence of free souls and his
invention of the biblical history, the narrator felt "In an instant a
sensation broke in me—it was entirely obscure" (23). Then the
narrator recalled "the crisis of insight" in childhood and saw "that he
was on the side of possibility: he was both sane and inspired. His
intention was not to accumulate mystery but to dispel it" (23), which

coincides with what Sheindel describes of her experience: "The more piety, the more skepticism" (25), the narrator burst out: "All that part is brilliant", "The man was a genius" and "I snatched the crowded page" (24) and started to read it aloud.

When the narrator asked Sheindel to stop reading the letter, he felt ashamed of Isaac for his idolatrous practice. When the narrator snatched the letter and read it voluntarily, he came to respect Isaac's pious skepticism and understand his struggling in the gleamless panic. Isaac is but practicing what Sheindel says of hacking away the "choking vine on the Fence of the Law" "to make freedom for purity". It is for purity of the Law that he struggles, which coincides with Ozick's efforts in meditating upon and disrupting the opposition between imagination and Jewishness.

In contrast to the narrator's coming close to Isaac, he comes to distance himself from Sheindel (37). "I noticed that he read everything" (9), "a man half-sotted with print" (10), however, after his death at his home "There was no physical relic of Isaac: not even a book" (10). The narrator kept asking Sheindel "You don't pity him? You don't pity him at all?" only to be answered "Let the world pity me" (37). Seeing her helpless pitilessness, "I gave what amounted to a little bow of regret" in response to her inquiry "You won't come back?" and advised her "Only the pitiless are illusory. Go back to that park, Rebbetzin, " "Your husband's soul is in that park. Consult it" (37).

It seems that in the narrator's judgment, Isaac with his remarkable imagination, when worshipping nature and inventing the biblical history to serve his needs, is committing idolatry and distancing himself from Jewishness and becomes a pagan whereas Isaac with his pious skepticism, when continually hacking away the choking vine on the Fence of Law to make freedom for purity (25), is putting Jewish doctrine into practice and therefore acts as a rabbi. In contrast, Sheindel, with her adherence to Jewish doctrines and in particular her constant efforts to fight against all forms of superstition, which she explains "climb like a choking vine on the Fence of the Law" (25), is an observant Jew. However, it is her lack of pity that incurs in the narrator's judgment doubts over her observance. It is the realization of her pitilessness that triggers the narrator's distancing from her. Pitilessness is in nature a symptom of lack of pity, resulting from the incapability of imagination, the failure to sympathize and empathize. Therefore, as the focal point of the polyphonic narrative mode, the narrator's judgment of Jewishness on the basis of imagination is ambivalent. To Isaac, with his remarkable imagination pointing to idolatrous practice, "I felt ashamed for him" (17) while the narrator pities him in his panic struggles and admires his pious skepticism. To the narrator, Isaac is a pagan and a Jew at once, "He was always an astonishing man" (37).

In addition to the meditations on the relationship between imagination and Jewishness, there is a judgment made of idolatry: nature worship as idolatry, and lack of pity as one effect of idolatry, for Ozick argues, idolatry has the effect of "rooting out human pity" (Ozick "Literature as Idol: Harold Bloom" *Art & Ardor* 190).

While the narrator of "The Pagan Rabbi" observes Sheindel as "one of those born to dread imagination" (14), he sees Isaac as talented with an imagination "so remarkable he could concoct holiness out of the fine line of a serif" (4). While Sheindel struggles against the "choking vine on the Fence of the Law" and commits herself to the fence, Isaac shuns Jewish Law in indulging himself in nature worshipping and claims to perceive "Holy life ... even in the stone, even in the bones of dead dogs and dead men" (21). Therefore, it is their different attitudes to and capability of imagination that differentiate Sheindel and Isaac.

Provided that it is the morally outrageous widow, Sheindel, who has made the judgment of Isaac as "pagan," Ozick's attitude toward Sheindel and Isaac becomes crucial in locating and understanding her endeavor in the moral ethos.

While the sympathies in most of the late nineteenth and early twentieth century Hebrew and Yiddish works are with the protagonist who imagines the natural world as a beautiful and loving alternative to the life of Jewish learning, Ozick remains equivocal to Isaac as she is equivocal to Sheindel.

As a matter of fact, dread of imagination is a recurring dread to Ozick when it comes to artistic creation as it finds its way into the preface to a later collection of short stories, *Bloodshed and Three Novellas* (1972), where she describes a story contained in the collection, entitled "Usurpation," about a writer who encounters the ghost of Hebrew poet Tchernikhovsky, and she asserts that its purpose is to encourage "the dread of idols; the dread of the magic that kills. The dread of imagination" (12).

It is apparent that Ozick sides along with Sheindel in view of imagination as a dubious force and an agent of moral perdition. For Ozick, "the central teaching of Judaism is that idols must be shunned, and that the Jews are bearers of this moral truth" (Levinson 178) and she "emphasizes how one ought to act in the world (i. e. to shun idols)" (179). To Ozick as to Sheindel, imagination is to be dreaded, for it has the capacity to ascribe ultimate reality to the created world rather than the creator. This is but the sin committed by Isaac, the "pagan rabbi," who not only claims "Holy life . . . even in the stone, even in the bones of dead dogs and dead men" (Ozick "The Pagan Rabbi" 21) but eventually indulges himself in the copulation with the dryad of an oak tree. Ozick associates his animistic view of the world with idolatry.

Furthermore, Isaac's lust for nature causes him to remain in the park until dawn for months, neglecting his responsibilities to the synagogue and to his family. His practice is an embodiment of what Ozick distinguishes as idolatry—"The chief characteristic of any idol is that it is a system sufficient in itself. It is indifferent to the world and to humanity" (Ozick "Literature as Idol: Harold Bloom" *Art & Ardor* 189).

While Ozick apparently objects to Isaac's idolatrous practice, she is likewise equivocal to Sheindel.

For Ozick, idolatry violates the Second Commandment and has the effect of "rooting out human pity" (Ozick "Literature as Idol: Harold Bloom" *Art & Ardor* 190). It is pity that is eliminated by idolatry. Sheindel's lack of pity to Isaac's struggles serves as the very motive for the narrator to become critical of her.

In addition, an idol, to Ozick, is "anything that is allowed to come between ourselves and God. Anything that is *instead of* God" (Ozick "The Riddle of the Ordinary" *Art & Ardor* 207). "Sheindel's commitment to fences, then, seems to have become so unwavering that her moral sense has been jeopardized, as though she has transformed the fence around the Torah into an idol" (Levinson 178). If Sheindel had worshipped the essence, God, instead of "the fence around the Torah," the signification, her pity couldn't have been rooted out and consequently she should have presumably played a positive part in casting her influence upon Isaac in hopefully preventing him from becoming a "pagan rabbi." Their moral sense has been jeopardized respectively in that Isaac voluntarily shuns Jewish Law and betrays both his own faith and Sheindel's while Sheindel fails to be an observant Jew in the proper sense with her false worship which in effect results in pity-depriving idolatry.

Therefore, both Sheindel and Isaac have committed idolatry, though in different ways. While Isaac has straightforwardly violated the Second Commandment with his animistic view of the universe, Sheindel has made an idol of the sacred Jewish teaching with her substitute of signification for the essence itself.

Now that both Sheindel and Isaac act as idolaters, the narrator, who listens to Sheindel's reading of Isaac's letter and reads it himself, which constitutes the backbone of the narrative, functions in weighing the perspectives presented in the story and therefore serves as the closest vehicle of Ozick's interpretation and judgment. Having internalized Sheindel's fear of nature-worship, he remains critical of Sheindel's pitilessness and wary of her transformation of Jewish teaching itself into a kind of idol. He builds his own fence around the Torah in "dropping three green plants down the toilet" (37), ensuring that he will not follow Isaac's suit. It can be convincingly argued that the narrator is equivocal to both Sheindel and Isaac and he chooses to side with neither of them, for Sheindel and Isaac, in Ozick's judgment, have both committed idolatry, which is chiefly based on her moral ethos.

Ozick's is among the many voices present in the story and it is represented in their collision. The fact that each voice, including Ozick's voice, authorizes itself and none of these voices is privileged indicates that the many voices, in particular their collision which characterizes the story, represent the component oppositions in Ozick's meditations on the relationship between imagination and Jewishness. The frame design of the story, specifically the polyphonic oppositions, reveals that the very inspiration of the story stems from moral judgment between imagination and Jewishness. It is morality, in particular the moral judgment between what is Jewish and what is pagan and the moral dilemma as a result of the puzzling meditations on the relationship between imagination and Jewishness, that has inspired the imagination.

To sum up, the imagination that has served as the blood and flesh of "The Pagan Rabbi" is inspired by a moral dilemma, the puzzling meditations on the relationship between imagination and Jewishness and in the meanwhile the imagination is imbued with moral values concerning idolatry in its practice and effect.

While "The Pagan Rabbi" is concerned with anti-idolatry chiefly in terms of imagination, which is "the blood and flesh" of literary creation, *The Messiah of Stockholm* (1987) is related to anti-idolatry in terms of literary acceptance, more specifically, of the relations between memory, moral responsibility, and the reading of texts. "The Pagan Rabbi" objects to nature worshipping whereas *The Messiah of Stockholm* is opposed to text worshipping.

III Idolatry and Language Worship

The Messiah of Stockholm is about Lars Andemening, a once-a-week book-reviewer for a newspaper in Stockholm, who almost lives in isolation from the outside world and has literature as his obsession. He sleeps during the day, rarely communicates with anybody, and writes cryptic reviews of high-brow Central European writers at night. He imbues with literature the sanctity of a religion: "He had long ago thrown himself on the altar of literature" (Ozick *The Messiah of Stockholm* 7).

While "The Pagan Rabbi" touches upon Isaac's invention of the biblical history, a collective history, *The Messiah of Stockholm* centers around an individual one. Having found his lack of ancestry in a world without a past, Lars believes himself "to be an arrested soul" (Ozick *The Messiah of Stockholm* 4) and claims that his father was Bruno Schulz, the Polish writer who was gunned down in 1942 by Nazis on the street of a tiny Polish town called Drogobych. This "father had become his craze" (4). Focusing almost all his energies on learning as much about Schulz as possible and studying Polish, "He read ... in pursuit of his father's tales" (5).

Above all, for Lars, Schulz's writing serves as the answer to his enigmatic identity and he attempts to establish continuity with the past by tracing the threads of the texts to himself. Among the instances that abound, Lars is always ready to insist that it is he that Schulz is invoking either when Schulz writes that he "would like to lay ... burden on someone else's shoulder for a moment" (36) or when Schulz says "The partner in discovery is the next generation" (37). Lars claims for himself the role in declaring "I'm the one he means..."

(37).

Moreover, because of his indulgence in the fantasized relevance with Schulz, Lars maintains a hope in the retrieval of Schulz's final manuscript, a novel entitled "The Messiah, " which was believed to have been carried for safekeeping to a friend and "both friend and manuscript were swallowed up by the sacrificial fires of the Europe of 1942" (Ozick "The Phantasmagoria of Bruno Schulz" *Art & Ardor* 225). Lars is curious about his past and believes in its relevance with the present.

Ozick presents language's meaningfulness and at the same time reveals its peril and destructiveness in Lars's experience, calls on a non-idolatrous reading manner, and allows for Lars's redemption.

A. Language's Meaningfulness

By the time that *The Messiah of Stockholm* was written, Ozick had come to the reconciliation in the opposition between the Second Commandment and imagination: she has come to see that monotheism must be coupled with a powerful imagination in order to rise to the idea of noncorporeal God in saying "I now see... that you cannot be a monotheist without a very deeply developed imagination: because you have to imagine, you have to envision and imagine that which there is no evidence for whatever" (Kauvar interview 1985 394-95). The attitude accords with her knowledge of Kabbalah and Gershom Scholem, the twentieth century pioneer of Jewish mysticism, who teaches in *Major Trends in Jewish Mysticism* that the mystical way to God is an understanding of the stages of the creative process. He argues that according to the Kabbalists, language has "mystical value, " it "reaches God because it comes from God, " and it "reflects the creative language of God" (Scholem 1946 17).

According to the Kabbalah, language can be used mystically in a number of ways including allegorical and symbolic ones (26-27). While allegory is "an infinite network of meanings and correlations in which everything can become a representation of everything else, but all within the limits of language and expression, " the mystical symbol represents "a hidden and inexpressible reality, " something beyond the reach of human communication.

Cynthia Ozick insists that *"What literature means is meaning"* (Ozick "Innovation and Redemption: What Literature Means" *Art & Ardor* 247, Ozick's italics) and that "of the stories and novels that mean to be literature, one expects a certain corona of moral purpose: not outright in the grain of the fiction itself, but in the form of a faintly incandescent envelope around it" (245), and she further explicates what the "corona" means is "interpretation, implicitness, the nimbus of *meaning* that envelops story" (246). The corona is "an illumination, a didactic contribution to the clarification of human judgment, [. . .], an invisible moral imperative which realizes the tale" (Rose 95).

Ozick's idea of corona is similar to Kabbalistic symbol in that both of them result from transcendence, corona being transcendence of literary composition and Kabbalistic symbol being transcendence of expressibility. Furthermore, both of them are invisible and indispensable in contributing their shares to the respective system where they reside.

However, Ozick scoffs at sheer allegory. In her judgment, those who claim fiction is only about language and artistic presentation "have snuffed the corona. . . [and] willingly sit in the dark" (Ozick "Innovation and Redemption: What Literature Means" *Art & Ardor* 246), for they have denied the meaningfulness of language and likewise the "mystical value" of language, its sacredness held by Kabbalists in reaching God.

As is argued by Alvin Rosenfeld, the pursuit of meaningfulness is part of the Jewish Idea: what is "to be avoided is illusion about experience; what is to be found out and insisted upon. . . is signification; the truth that whatever is, *means*" (77 Rosenfeld's italics). In addition, to Ozick, signification is the "pulse and purpose of literature" (Ozick "Innovation and Redemption: What Literature Means" *Art & Ardor* 248). Making part of a novel's suspense, which Ozick thinks "emerges from the writer's conviction of social or cosmic principle" (241), signification has a communal purpose and it ignites the novel's corona and sheds light on the reader's interpretation of the world to the effect that "we can make distinctions; we can see. . . that not everything is the same" (248).

The qualities of Kabbalistic allegory in *The Messiah of Stockholm* are shown in the fact that "each object represents. . . every other object, allowing for the possibility of an infinity of meaning to attach to each representation" (Rose 96). The most frequent burning imagery "multiplies by association the significance of each item it catches" (Rose 96) including the "burning fat" in Lars's writing (Ozick *The Messiah of Stockholm* 8) and the chimney of his armpits (18), Dr. Eklund cremated (22), the "smoldering cultishness" of Bruno Schulz's tales (33), a corpse in an oven (38), the smell of burning angel's wings (57), the bookshop key burning Lars's thigh (59), the roast-meat smell of Dr. Eklund's pipe (92), etc. (Rose 96-97). These images, though varied, are unified by the signification of burning: the Holocaust (39), "a word of Greek origin meaning 'sacrifice by fire'" (Holocaust Encyclopedia Internet), and furthermore, Jewish history and the ambiguity of Jewish identity in the post-war Diaspora and exile.

As Scholem contends, "The most terrible fate that could befall any soul—far more ghastly than the torments of hell—was to be 'outcast' or 'naked,'. . . Such absolute exile was the worst nightmare of the soul" and he refers to the "Absolute homelessness" as "the sinister symbol of absolute Godlessness, of utter moral and spiritual degradation" (Scholem 1946 250).

Part of the novel's corona is ignited by the signification of the burning imagery, which helps with the reader's interpretation of Lars's identity fabrication. It is the Holocaust that has filled Ozick's

Stockholm with images of burning and refugees who have their own stories (Ozick *The Messiah of Stockholm* 24): "fabricators" all of them (26). Being an orphan, Lars has no community and when he was sixteen his foster mother's remark that he did not look Swedish "made him run away" (69). Abandoned by two wives and alienated from his colleagues, Lars has an arrested soul because he feels he belongs elsewhere (4). He chooses Bruno Schulz as his father and God, fabricating connections between his own life and Schulz's.

Like all other refugees, Lars is bereft of "a nurturing and sustaining culture" and is "almost forced into the procedures of self-invention" (Rosenfeld 79). It is exile that necessitates self-invention. In Rosenfeld's view, self-invention embodies the Jewish Idea of signification by showing what exists in the absence of meaning: panic, emptiness, falseness and peril (81). In Lars's case, while "panic" and "emptiness" are more related to the post-Holocaust climate in which Jewish identity became precarious, "falseness and peril" are pointing to his exposure to the abasement of idolatry in his self-fabrication, which points to language's peril and its destructiveness.

B. Language's Peril and Destructiveness

Lars's name has been self-chosen from a dictionary with a meaning in Swedish, "spirit, inward sense, a dimension beyond the literal and visible" (Walden 1987 171). He worships Schulz through language—he "felt he resembled his father: all the tales were about men shrinking more and more into the phantasmagoria of the mind" (Ozick *The Messiah of Stockholm* 5). His own face resembles the detailed description of Schulz's face in the books. He even detects in his daughter's paintings the talent of Schulz: "how certain phantomlike lines ... out from fierce little fist: the power of genes" (46). It is from words that his self-chosen name and identity come. It is from words that his linkage to the ancestry is established.

He suffers from "illusion about experience" which is "to be

avoided" in the Jewish Idea (Rosenfeld 77). To him, language is reality. He is swept away and consumed by reading (8). He meditates like a "dervish" over the printed word and "a greased beak tore him off his accustomed ledge and brought him to a high place beyond his control" (Ozick *The Messiah of Stockholm* 8). It is his belief that all bookstore copies of Schulz's work are his "by inheritance" (23) while his ex-mother-in-law reveals that as an orphan, he has no idea of what it is to inherit anything (46). Having "long ago thrown himself on the altar of literature" (7), he sacrifices himself; "his lids clicked open like a marionette's and he *saw* ... a vessel, curved, polished, hollowed out [and in it]... his father's murdered eye" (8 Ozick's italics). The "nucleus of his origin" is Schulz's eye (31) instead of God.

Lars's insistence that reality is words is epitomized in his reason in denying Adela as the daughter of Schulz. He receives a call from Mrs. Elkund telling him Adela, a woman who calls herself Schulz's daughter, has arrived in Stockholm and is in search of a translator for Schulz's original manuscript that is in her possession. Meeting Adela, the purported daughter of Schulz (also the name of one of the main characters in Schulz's *The Street of Crocodiles*), Lars refuses to share his parentage and refuses to believe that she is Schulz's daughter because he sees "no room in the story for another child. It's not feasible. ... There's only me" (53). He believes that "experience is language and language experience" and for him, "language is the object of his daily experiences and of his piety, part of his selfhood" (Rose 101).

All Lars sees in the world is but literature, but Ozick thinks otherwise in her view that literature is not the All of the world. Her goal is to interrelate literature, religion, and communal service with the primal monotheistic insight (Ozick "Literature as Idol: Harold Bloom" *Art & Ardor* 194). Therefore *The Messiah of Stockholm* is rooted in presenting language's meaningfulness and at the same time in reprimanding the practice of being willingly seduced by a story and putting language before God, as Rose points out, "To write and read voraciously makes a Jew an idol-maker and an idolator, a modern Terach, a maker of bloody-mawed Molochs" (Rose 94).

C. Ozick's Corona: Reading in a Non-idolatrous Manner

Ozick sets the relation to Schulz's texts as part of the corona, invites the reader to the distinction between a textual Messiah and a genuine one, and issues a call to read in a non-idolatrous manner.

In 1977, Philip Roth, general editor of the Penguin paperback series, reissued a translation of Bruno Schulz's collection of stories, *The Street of Crocodiles* in "Writers from the Other Europe" in hopes to retrieve literary works from Central and Eastern Europe that were unknown in America and England. Ozick wrote a review of *The Street of Crocodiles* for the *New York Times* in which she compared Schulz with Kafka, I. B. Singer, and Isaac Babel. She hailed Schulz as "one of the most original literary imaginations of modern Europe" (Ozick "The Phantasmagoria of Bruno Schulz" *Art & Ardor* 224). What she most emphasizes is his fascination with animism and she claims that Schulz's fiction invents its own religion: "the brute splendors of rite, gesture, phantasmagoric transfigurations, sacrifice, elevation, degradation, mortification, repugnance, terror, cult" (227). Schulz was introduced as a kind of pagan rabbi, a Jewish conjuror of imagined worlds.

Ten years after her *New York Times* review of *The Street of Crocodiles*, Ozick wrote *The Messiah of Stockholm*, which she herself calls "a book about an imaginary book" (Ozick "Cynthia Ozick" 34).

Her call to read in a non-idolatrous manner is based on the revelation of meaning-subversion. "The thin novel repeatedly alludes to itself as voluminous, overlapping, encyclopedic, disorderly and therefore untrustworthy, meaningless" (Rose 97). There is reason to become suspicious about the historicity of Schulz's life as presented, and in particular about *Messiah*, which is apparently Ozickian fabrication. Furthermore, what is clear to the reader is what is not real, for instance, while Lars's Polish teacher knows she is not a princess, she simply says she is (30). The didactic purpose in revealing meaning-subversion lies in the stricture against language as reality.

Ozick's call to read in a non-idolatrous manner is further based on language's peril and destructiveness. Lars has been refashioning Schulz's texts as a species of idol, a kind of heirloom to sate his craving for ancestry. It is through language that Lars worships Schulz and turns himself into both an idol-maker and an idolator. Lars meditates, he sees Schulz's dead eye and sees through it. It is his imagination that has created the eye and he worships his own creation. What dominates the novel is Lars's search and research into Schulz's life, and the mystical consolations of high art diminish his humanity. (Kakutani 18) Above all, Lars's connection with Schulz in his cosmos has all the four characteristics of an idol Ozick defines in *Art & Ardor*.

The chief characteristic of an idol is that it is a self-sufficient system in which "dead matter rules the quick" (Ozick "Literature as Idol: Harold Bloom" *Art & Ardor* 189). It is apparent that Lars pays homage to Schulz's murdered eye. The dead man serves as the ruling force in Lars's endeavor to copy, as Heidi accuses him, "You want to *be* him. ... Mimicry. Posing in a mirror" (Ozick *The Messiah of Stockholm* 41).

"A second important characteristic of any idol is that it is always assumed to pre-exist the worshiper" (Ozick "Literature as Idol: Harold Bloom" *Art & Ardor* 189) while every idolator absorbs old news to refurbish for his instant needs (190). Drawn to the ancestor and precursor, Lars indulges in collecting Schulz's old letters and tries to retrieve an American review of Schulz's work in a trash barrel.

Thirdly, "an idol, which cannot generate history, can be altered by it: from-the-sublime-to-the-ridiculous is the rule of every idol"

(190). In Adela's version of history, when Schulz was an art teacher in a high school, he impregnated one of his pupils, who "modeled for his drawings" (Ozick *The Messiah of Stockholm* 80). Given her version, Schulz, Lars's idol as a sublime genius and martyr, is threatened to become ridiculous. Consequently, Lars burst, "The truth! ... Malice, it's malice! ... As if such a man—*such* a man—would copulate with a child!" (102).

A fourth characteristic of any idol is that the power of the idol "can root out human pity" (190) because of the ancient practice of sacrificing infants to the god Moloch. Distancing himself from the memories of his wives and daughter, Lars is like a marionette and sees others as "waxwork men" (68).

Playing on the title of Schulz's lost work, Ozick invites the reader to the examination of the relationship between a textual and a real Messiah. Invented history through language is fantasy in nature and is not justified. Lars is tacitly criticized by the novel for misappropriating an invented past through language. With the idolatrous indulgence in his fantasized bridge to Schulz and to the past, Lars's life is closed off from others and he has blurred the distinction between Schulz's textual Messiah and a real Messiah.

Lars has been fantasizing and refashioning Schulz and his texts as an idol for him to satisfy his craving for ancestry. His reading of the text, together with all his engagement with the fantasized link with Schulz the author of the text, is an idolatrous practice in nature. He has taken away from contemplation of the idol what his psychological hunger requires.

In Lars's reading of the assumed manuscript of Schulz, "Nothing detained him, nothing slowed him down. The terrible speed of his hunger, chewing through hook and blade, tongue and voice, of the true *Messiah*! Rapacity, gluttony!" (105) Ozick's employment of metaphors concerning eating serves to code Lars's relationship to the text as a species of idolatry. Furthermore, "He had swallowed it down like a priest," Ozick writes, "the priest of some passionate sect, for whom scripture is subordinate to the hour of sacral access" (117). Rather than reading the text, Lars seeks "sacral access" over "scripture" and as a result it is safe to say he is not engaged in what might be considered a hermeneutical relation to the text, but instead, he simply clings to the text in order to fulfill his desired need. Schulz's textual Messiah is regarded by him as a real Messiah.

At last, he comes to suspect that he is being masterminded by Mrs. Eklund and her husband, to pass off a forged document as Schulz's original, and "it occurred to him that the woman in the white beret, in the morning's white brilliance, carrying a featherweight *Messiah* in a white bag, was, if she wasn't an angel, a lie" (56). Therefore, in using a fiction to nurture his sense of himself, Lars ends up with the suspicion which at last turns into conviction that he is being in someone else's fiction. He eventually comes to the realization that the Eklunds, who "want to be in competition with God", "hooked" him "from the start" (128), and above all, to the realization that language is perilous and destructive if it is not duely rendered as meaningful.

The revelation of language's peril and destructiveness points to the stricture against language for its own sake and that against worship of language instead of God. There is a communal purpose. Lars burns the manuscript, stops turning his reviews into near-theology and becomes an "ordinary reviewer" (131), marking the end of his idolatrous practice, whose price is the ordinary, which Ozick deems as "equal to the earth's provisions; it grants us life, continuity, the leisure to recognize who and what we are, and who and what our fellows are" (Ozick "The Riddle of the Ordinary" *Art &Ardor* 201). Lars's deed at the same time indicates that language-for-its-own-sake ends in smoke. In exposing the reader to this truth, the communal purpose is fulfilled.

Apart from the communal purpose, there is a liturgical purpose which has been fulfilled as well, specifically, Lars's redemption.

D. Lars's Redemption

In Ozick's view, redemption should not be understood

> on the guaranteed promise of redemption, and not on goodness, kindness, decency, all the usual virtues. Redemption has almost nothing to do with virtue, especially when the call to virtue is prescriptive or coercive; rather, it is the singular idea that is the opposite of the Greek belief in fate: the idea that insists on the freedom to change one's life. ("Innovation and Redemption: What Literature Means" *Art & Ardor* 245)

Lars changes his life, and it is pity, empathy resulting from pity, and an eye for the ordinary that have allowed Lars to change. Being finished "with all those grotesqueries," "He was taking the reviewing business seriously" (Ozick *The Messiah of Stockholm* 132). He is "like a man... who has resumed his normal rounds" (132). He has "taken on a touch of fame" (131) and "The very routine... seems extraordinary" (132).

He pities Gunnar Hemlig and Anders Fiskyngel, his fellow reviewers and feels "a tenderness... for their wax faces, wax eyes with... wax tears of pain or reproach or deprivation. ... Their terrible helplessness" (68). He pities Heidi, the bookstore owner for her straining old age (40). He pities himself, who "has belles-lettres on the brain day and night" (11), for the loss of his "ordinary bourgeois predicament" and for his life as a "transmigration of an impassioned soul" (120).

His pities, however, are not toward individuals, but rather to the signification of the individuals: reviewing, circulating, and in general, reading of literature due to the meaningfulness and destructiveness of language.

His pity and empathy are based on the revelation attained in his experience from worshiping language to coming to the realization of its peril and destructiveness in idolatrous fabrication. The corona, which realizes the fiction, reminds that "every cognition of God starts from a private revelation between God and His creature, from a manifestation of God in something else, in all that exists" (Scholem 1946 11), including language and the ordinary. It is through language, and through the ordinary, that the name of God is revealed (17).

The corona well reflects Ozick's objectives in serving the monotheistic God rather than the literary muses, who "like the idols. . . have no moral substance" (Ozick "Literature as Idol: Harold Bloom" *Art & Ardor* 191), hence an interrelation between literature, religion, and communal service.

When Ozick is struggling between idolatry and imagination, between idolatry and language worshiping, she finds the very notion of fiction-making anathema to Jewish Law and she believes Jewish morality challenges the very assumptions of art. What is at work is her moral ethos in weighing the opposing claims of literature and Judaism and she chooses to serve the monotheistic God with her literary creation. As a writer who is a Jew, Ozick eventually foregrounds her insistence on idolatry resistance by means of both imagination and language representation, merging the "minority" with the "majority" in the diasporic space.

Chapter Three

Jewishness and History Representation

Apart from idolatry resistance, what is central to Ozick's moral ethos is the balance between historicity and figuration in history representation pointing to history as interpretation and judgment in historical memory, which echoes the Judaic emphasis on memory and on continuity of tradition.

Emphasis on history and historicity is made clear in the Fifth Commandment, which exhorts Jews to honor their fathers and mothers. As Philip Roth says in *The Counterlife*, "Jews... are to history what Eskimos are to snow" (Roth 1986 368).

However, in Diaspora, where the American enthrallment with novelty and future progress dominates as the "majority," the Judaic emphasis on memory and the Jewish insistence on history reduces as the "minority" whereas "the excessive representation of the Holocaust in literary theory, popular culture, politics, and religion" that "has compounded the sense of extrahistoricity often attributed to the Holocaust" (Lehmann 1997 iv) acts as the prevailing trend, the "majority," and the Jewish adherence to historicity is marginalized as the "minority."

Ozick's moral ethos in history representation finds its way into her fictional construction and deconstruction of Jewish memories, highlighting the significance of history and the inadequacy of figuration, and her Midrashic representation of the Holocaust concerning its historicity and figuration.

I. Fictional Construction and Deconstruction of Jewish Memories

Invention of history is recurring in Ozick's works. In "The Pagan Rabbi," Isaac Kornfeld "reconstructs the biblical history to explain the origin of the rootedness of men's souls and the commandment against Idolatry" (Cooper 184) in an attempt to alleviate the incompatibility between Pan and Moses. In *The Messiah of Stockholm*, Lars Andemening fabricates connections between his own life and that of Bruno Schulz for a linkage to his ancestry. In *The Shawl*, Rosa Lublin invents the history of Magda's father.

Ozick's adherence to the Jewish historical memory has resulted from her commitment to the central traditions of Jewish religious thought and practice. However, Jewish memory has faced great threats in contemporary culture. Her attempts to recreate Jewish memories through fiction are based upon her keen sense of Jewish cultural crisis.

A. Jewish Cultural Crisis

There are three embodiments of the Jewish cultural crisis: the predominance that Jewish writers gained in the 1950s and 1960s at the expense of what is historically Jewish, the Enlightenment which has reconstructed Judaism, and the disbelief that Jewish memory can expect to be healed or rejuvenated.

First, invention of history is related to the fact of Americanized assimilation and Ozick's resistence against it, and moreover to her insistence on what is historically Jewish, which she considers as a sacrifice that the predominant Jewish writers paid in the 1950s and 1960s.

Ozick considers the predominance of Jewish writers, paradoxically, as a more profound failure. In her estimation, the literary success of Jewish writers in the 1950s and 1960s is "at the price of an idolatry by which they eschew that which is historically Jewish in favor of the ephemera of Jewish ethnicity" (Powers 1995 79), a loss of a full-blown Jewish identity:

> To be a Jew is to be old in history, but not only that; to be a Jew is to be a member of a distinct civilization expressed through an oceanic culture in possession of a group of essential concepts and a multitude of texts and attitudes elucidating those concepts. Next to the density of such a condition—or possibility—how gossamer are the stories of those writers "of Jewish extraction" whose characters are pale indifferent echoes of whatever lies at hand.... (Ozick *Metaphor & Memory* 224)

For her, for the success in the American mainstream, what Jewish-American writers have eschewed is the density of Jewish civilization and memory, which indicates a failure of specifically Jewish religious and ethical ideals and the loss of Jewish memory as an effective cultural force in the present.

Second, according to Arthur Cohen, the Enlightenment has reconstructed Judaism as a private matter of belief and the reconstruction serves as an ideological structure that allowed that a Jew could be a Jew at home and a man in the streets (12-14). Consequently, Judaism was displaced as the central and necessary feature of Jewish life with the loss of specific Jewish memories, beliefs and practices. Arthur Cohen further suggests that

> In the last fifty years, the uninformed, the religiously illiterate, and the socially assimilated have succeeded in affecting, if not shaping, the religion offered by the synagogue. Judaism is more than ever a reaction to the disinterest and embarrassment of the already secularized Jewish majority.... [The] Jew has become, in matters Jewish, doggedly and uncritically American. (191)

Cohen's basic thesis was affirmed by many other scholars. According to Arthur Hertzberg, with the Jewish "conquest of the suburbs" in the 1950s, there emerges a trivialization of Jewish religious life. In Hertzberg's evaluation, about 70% of all American Jews maintained a general belief in God, but synagogue life reflected the religiosity of mainline American Protestantism in the 1950s (327-30). Nathan Glazer holds that "Few Jews would know what the principles of the Jewish faith are" (132). Peter Kerry Powers observes that "*haskalah,* the Jewish term for the Enlightenment,*" "* in practice... reduced the comprehensive character of Judaism to a privatism that had little traction on daily life" (Powers 1995 81), Ozick presents a summary of what the Enlightenment has done to the tone and content of post-war Jewish-American scholarship in saying "An understanding of the unique content of Jewish genius has been forfeited by the great majority of modern Jews. It is the Enlightenment that has made us forfeit the understanding and forget the content" (Ozick *Metaphor & Memory* 232).

Third, many people embrace a headstrong disbelief in Jewish memory's healing and rejuvenation. For example, Yosef Hayim Yerushalmi, a historiographer, holds that Jewish memory cannot be "healed" or "rejuvenated" in claiming that

> The collective memories of the Jewish people were a function of the shared faith, cohesiveness, and will of the group itself.... The decline of Jewish collective memory in modern times is only a symptom of the unraveling of that common network of belief and praxis through whose mechanisms... the past was once made present. Therein lies the root of the malady. (94)

Hence a significant problem in Ozick's call for an aesthetics of memory rooted in Jewish tradition when those memories are indeed broken and fragmentary, and even worse, when there is no hope to heal or rejuvenate them. In order to alleviate and resolve the strain of evoking memory where memories are scant, Ozick manages to recreate the past as invention. The problems with loss of memory and the possibilities and/or the impossibilities of repairing the loss are paradoxically foregrounded. In the following analysis, Ruth Puttermesser, a character to whom Ozick has returned in several of her stories, is to be taken as a sample.

B. Construction and Deconstruction of the Past in Ruth Puttermesser

In "Puttermesser: Her Work History, Her Ancestry, Her Afterlife," Ruth Puttermesser, a thirty-four year old intellectually ambitious lawyer who lives alone in the Bronx, is starkly a solitary. As the only Jewish woman in the law firm which she leaves at last, she is cut off from the male Jewish lawyers and their male activities. She beguiles her free time playing chess against herself or completing crossword puzzles from the *New York Times*. With parents who have retired to Florida and without friends worth mentioning, "she is without connection, and specially without connection to a living Jewish community or memory" (Powers 1995 82). She is in search of history in order to satisfy her need of a living connection to the past that will give her life meaning beyond her mundane efforts in a civic bureaucracy.

Puttermesser's conscious efforts to connect herself to Jewish history culminate when she recalls learning Hebrew from a character identified as "Uncle Zindel," who is described as "a former shammes in a shul that had been torn down" (12). (Note: The term "shammes" is frequently translated as "beadle.") An unassimilated Jew in a largely assimilated family, Uncle Zindel is "a teacher, a man in touch with the laws, practices, and traditions of normative Judaism" (Powers 1995 83), which constitutes a great appeal to the intellectually ambitious protagonist. However, the narrative is abruptly interrupted by a voice that takes issue with "Puttermesser's biographer," a metafictional device to question Puttermesser's reliance on her invention of the connection,

> Stop. Stop, stop! Puttermesser's biographer, stop! Disengage, please. Though it is true that biographies are invented, not recorded, here you invent too much. A symbol is allowed, but not a whole scene: do not accommodate too

obsequiously to Puttermesser's romance. (Ozick " Puttermesser: Her Work History, Her Ancestry, Her Afterlife" 16)

This reproachful voice—which coincides with the one from Ozick of the *Bloodshed* preface and Sheindel, who dreads imagination—reminds the biographer that Puttermesser never in fact had a chance to know this uncle, and that "Uncle Zindel lies under the earth of Staten Island. Puttermesser has never had a conversation with him; he died four years before her birth. He is all legend" (36). The biographer is accused of excessive fabrication. The biographer explains that Puttermesser has fabricated Uncle Zindel because "poor Puttermesser has found herself in the world without a past" (36). Her parents are assimilated American Jews ("her father is nearly a Yankee") and she "demands connection" (36). The biographer further explains that in order to alleviate her isolation, she has elaborated a fantasy from a shred of family lore and from "old photographs of the Jewish East Side" (37), in which she has claimed for herself membership through imagination so as to forge a Jewish past of her own.

However, the metafictional voice insists that the biographer distinguish between Puttermesser's fantasy and her life, otherwise Puttermesser's yearnings would be indulged. It poses a challenge and a critique to the mythology of a seamless Jewish past. The critic of Puttermesser's biographer makes explicit that Puttermesser's connection to the Jewish past is merely imagined.

Revealing Puttermesser is an imagined descendent of Lower East Side Jews, the metafictional voice further proposes a moral imperative to the reader:

> The scene with Uncle Zindel did not occur. It could not occur because, though Puttermesser dares to posit her ancestry, we may not. Puttermesser is not to be examined as an artifact but as an essence. Who made her? No one cares. Puttermesser is henceforth to be presented as given. (38)

The resistance against temptation to "posit ancestry" is called for. Puttermesser's invention of Lower East Side origins, as is true with Kornfeld's reinvention of the biblical history and Lars's reinvention of his personal history, results from Ozick's imagination and her fictional construction, is paradoxically instructed to be regarded as the protagonist's own fantasy and is therefore destructed as a result.

Ozick returns to Puttermesser in "Puttermesser and Xanthippe," where Puttermesser is as disconnected from a tradition or people as ever. Her fantasy highlights her isolation from Jewish memory and tradition when she dreams of

> an ideal Civil Service: devotion to policy, the citizen's sweet love of the citizenry, the light rule of reason and common sense, the City as a miniature country crowded with Patriots—not fools and jingoists, but patriots true and serene: humorous affections for the idiosyncrasies of one's distinctive little homeland, each borough itself another little homeland, joy in the Bronx, elation in Queens, O happy Richmond! Children on roller skates, and over the Brooklyn Bridge the long patch-work-colored line of joggers, breathing hard above the homeland hugging green waters. (Ozick "Puttermesser: Her Work History, Her Ancestry, Her Afterlife" 85)

Puttermesser's utopia is based on the rule of "reason and common sense," the very values that feature the Enlightenment, the Jewish *haskalah*. Her fantasy of homeland is at most a secularized version of the promised land that is detached from Jewish history and covenant, for "the possibility of a 'homeland' in New York suggests for Judaism the abandonment of the promise of the homeland, the promised land, which is a primary feature of the covenant's promise for the future" (Powers 1995 85). It is safe to say that Puttermesser is disconnected from Jewish history.

Her attempt to get connected with the past is epitomized by the golem legend. However, different from Rabbi Judah Loew of Prague, who in creating his golem "sought inner purity and sanctification by means of prayer and ritual immersion" (101), Puttermesser creates her golem, Xanthippe, by accident. While Rabbi Judah Loew created the golem to save the Jews from a pogrom conducted by Christians in an anti-Jewish hysteria, Puttermesser's golem is brought into being, if anything, by her desire for a daughter, whom she fantasizes: "It was self-love: all these daughters were Puttermesser as a child. She imagined a daughter in fourth grade, then in seventh grade, then in second-year high school. Puttermesser herself had gone to Hunter College High School and studied Latin" (Ozick "Puttermesser: Her Work History, Her Ancestry, Her Afterlife" 91).

However, self-love, in Ozick's judgment, is destructive even in the name of the civic good. Although Xanthippe temporarily helps materialize Puttermesser's vision of an urban utopia, she is also complicit in its destruction. Imaging Puttermesser's desire for self-affirmation, Xanthippe represents appetite. Feeding her growing lust for food and sex, she is to fulfill her immediate desires. "She grows and grows, until she is finally too large to rise from the bed. She takes man after man to bed, until, at last, her prolific sexuality undermines the very heaven she helped create" (Powers 1995 86). What Xanthippe does ultimately threatens the well-being of Puttermesser and leads to the destruction of the golem itself. What's more, as appetite embodied, Xanthippe is unable to comprehend consequences and she lives exclusively in the present. Therefore, the golem, the employment of which intends to establish a kind of link to Jewish folklore and Jewish history, "serves to emphasize the distance that Puttermesser has traveled from the historical presence of Judaism" (Powers 1995 86).

Entirely aware of historical discontinuity, Ozick calls urgently for historicity. It is embodied by the bizarre and nearly fantastic connection with the past prevailing in Ozick's fiction, which is populated largely by people without a past. These people are brought into contact, however briefly, with embodiments of Jewish history and memory. However, Ozick paradoxically asserts the significance of the past through the past as fantastic invention.

When it comes to the significance of Jewish memory, it is inevitable to take into account the Holocaust and its consequences. In presenting the "murder of approximately six million Jews by the Nazi regime and its collaborators" (Holocaust Encyclopedia Internet), the biggest problem that has troubled writers is "how authoritative can the imagined life of a fictional creation be about historical events" (Alexander xiii), which is related to the incommunicability of man's suffering.

There are basically three stages in the Holocaust representation in Jewish American fiction. In the 1940s and 1950s, there were few Holocaust representations, with Saul Bellow's *The Victim* as the pioneer. The early 1960s witnessed the booming of literary representation of the Holocaust as a result of the trials of the Nazis, the emergence of the memories and interviews of the Holocaust survivors. Since the mid-1980s, there have come into being representations of the Holocaust impact on the offspring of the survivors.

There is direct delineation of the Holocaust as in Gerald Green's *The Holocaust* (1978); representation of its aftermath as in Isaac Bashevis Singer's *Enemies: A Love Story* (1972); representation of the memories of the survivors as in Edward Lewis Wallant's *The Pawnbroker* (1961), Elie Wiesel's *Night* (1956) and Saul Bellow's *Mr. Sammler's Planet* (1970); there is honor paid to the assistance for Jews' survival as in Saul Bellow's *The Bellarosa Connection* (1989) and Cynthia Ozick's *The Cannibal Galaxy* (1983); representation of the Nazi trials as in Philip Roth's *Operation Shylock* (1993) and Norma Rosen's *Touching Evil* (1969); representation of the rage and redemption of the survivors' offspring as in Thane Rosenbaum's *Second Hand Smoke* (1999); and postmodernist rewriting of the classical Holocaust texts as in Philip Roth's *The Ghost Writer* (1979), in which *The Diary of Anne Frank* (1947) serves as the intertext (Liu 221-33).

Ozick distinguishes herself in her Holocaust representation with the

Midrashic mode in an attempt to bring historicity and figuration to a balance, in her advocacy of authentic Jewishness, and in her insistence that history is judgment and interpretation.

The Holocaust has been a recurrent subject in Ozick's writing. *Trust*, her first published novel, dramatizes predicaments posed by the Holocaust and its consequences. *The Cannibal Galaxy* is centered around survivors' recollections. *The Messiah of Stockholm* touches upon imagined evocations. And there are numerous engagements with Holocaust and post-Holocaust themes in her short fiction.

Nevertheless, despite the actual recurrent subject in her literary practice and her reputation as one of America's most accomplished novelists of the Holocaust, Ozick is "not in favor of making fiction of the data, or of mythologizing or poeticizing it" (Ozick "Roundtable Discussion" 284). Morally sensitive to the potential of fiction to corrupt or trivialize the Holocaust, she asserts "I believe with all my soul that [the Holocaust] ought to remain exclusively attached to document and history. ... If the Holocaust becomes commensurate with the literary imagination, then what of those recrudescent Nazis, the so-called revisionists, who claim the events themselves are nothing but imaginings?" (Kauvar interview 1985 390) She asserts that "the subject is corrupted by fiction and that fiction in general corrupts history" (Kremer 1999 149).

She prefers not "to tamper or invent, or imagine [the Holocaust], yet... [she has] done it. ... It comes; it invades" (Ozick's interview with Tom Teicholz 185). As a result, despite Theodor Adorno's famous pronouncement that to write poetry after Auschwitz is barbaric, Ozick finally confesses that she "cannot *not* write about it. It rises up and claims [her] furies... [because her] brother's blood cries out from the ground" (Ozick "Roundtable Discussion" 284). Ozick urges Jewish writers to "retrieve the Holocaust freight car by freight car, town by town, road by road, document by document. The task is to save it from becoming literature" (Ozick "The Uses of Legend: Elie

Wiesel as Tsaddik" 19), literature that is "self-enamored, self-absorbed with its own aesthetic genius" (Kremer 1999 174).

Like Art Spiegelman and Philip Roth, Ozick insists on viewing the Holocaust as part of a historical continuum and therefore as directly connected with the later time at which their own stories are set. She is against the misappropriation of the Holocaust in the literary realm and scientific projects. She is not in favor of the excessive representation of the Holocaust in popular culture, politics, and religion, which has compounded the sense of extrahistoricity. This is primarily based on her steadfast adherence to Jewish authenticity.

The most salient Jewish trait is an emphasis on the historical past which counterbalances the American emphasis on the future. Murray Baumgarten has so far established a useful distinction between "free thinkers" who jettison the past and "critical thinkers" who confront it and negotiate the crisis of dual allegiances between past and present, Jewish culture and surrounding culture (Baumgarten 26). Attentive to Jewish history and values, Ozick is a critical thinker who distinguishes herself with an imagination imbued with historic and moral values in her fictional writing of the Holocaust for a negotiation between past and present, between what is Jewish and non-Jewish.

In the following analysis, *The Shawl* will be taken as a sample to elaborate on Ozick's use of the Midrashic mode not only to offer a memorial to the Jews slaughtered in the Holocaust but also to present religious, political and psychological meditations on the tragic event, and above all, to interpret the effect of the Holocaust on the present American Jewish understanding.

II. Midrashic Representation of the Holocaust

A. Midrashic Mode, a Nonoppositional Approach

Midrash is a traditional form of Jewish literary and religious inquiry. The root of the word "Midrash" means "to search" or "to inquire" (Hartman and Budick 363). "In general the Midrash is focused on either Halakhic (legal) or Aggadic (non-legal and chiefly homiletical) subject matter. Both kinds of Midrashim were at first preserved only orally, but their writing down commenced in the 2nd century" (Midrash Internet). Midrash halakha are the works in which the sources in the Tanakh (Hebrew Bible) of the traditionally received laws are identified, having to do with Jewish law and ritual. Midrashim that embrace the interpretation of the non-legal portions of the Hebrew Bible are referred to as *aggadah* or *haggadah*, meaning allegory, exhortation, legend—in short, figurative expression (Hartman and Budick 363) in classical rabbinic literature. "Midrash is usually in some way interpretation of Torah, whether it is direct exegesis, homily, or the more creative narrative. The Midrashists' project was to create a body of texts that could guide the Diaspora after the destruction of the Temple in 70 C. E. " While "interpretation of Torah" turned out to be "a chorus of rabbinical voices debating, raising questions, " Midrash is "a practice in which fantasy and figuration are inseparable from context, history, and morality" (Rosenberg 114), a nonoppositional approach essential to dovetail faithfulness to historicity and artistic freedom based on moral ethos in approaching the subject of the Holocaust.

In her essay "Bialik's Hint" Ozick interprets a statement of Chaim Bialik and entertains Midrash as a way to create a new Jewish literature, pointing out Midrash is nonoppositional, for Halachah and Aggadah, the two components of Midrash, are fused together:

"The value of Aggadah, " he asserts, "is that it issues in Halachah. Aggadah that does not bring Halachah in its train is ineffective. " If we pause to translate Aggadah as tale and lore, and Halachah as consensus and law, or Aggadah as the realm of the fancy, and Halachah as the court of duty, then what Bialik proposes next is astonishing. Contrariwise, he says, Halachah can bring Aggadah in its train. Restraint the begetter of poetry? " Is she not"—and now Bialik is speaking of the Sabbath—"a source of life and holiness to a whole nation, and a fountain of inspiration to its singers and poets?" (Ozick "Bialik's Hint" 228)

Ozick believes that imagination can be inspired by law and morality. Like the rabbis composing Midrashim, Ozick uses the Midrashic mode and allows for disruption of the opposition between the figurative representation and historical representation in fictionally approaching the subject of the Holocaust without forgetting its historicity. What genuinely functions is her moral insistence on Jewish authenticity.

Midrash primarily concerns itself with the exegesis of sacred texts, and in describing Midrashic exegesis, Daniel Boyarin comments, "The biblical narrative is gapped and dialogical. The role of the Midrash is to fill in the gaps" (Boyarin 17). Despite its primary concerns with the sacred textual gaps, Joseph Alkana argues "Midrashic activity frequently takes the form of fiction, especially didactic fiction." He further contends the focus on textual gaps may be regarded in two ways. As textual exegesis, Midrash attempts to render "comprehensible fissured or otherwise perplexing biblical passages." In addition, Midrash serves another function in bringing about "interpretations consistent with contemporary religious beliefs and circumstances," which is defined by Alkana as "moralistic aspects of Midrash work to cast contemporary intellectual and ethical dilemmas as extensions of tradition" (Alkana 969).

There have been a few insightful Midrashic studies of *The Shawl* consisting of "The Shawl" and "Rosa." Focusing upon the Midrashic function of filling textual gaps, Joseph Lowin reads "Rosa" as a Midrashic commentary on "The Shawl." He contends, with elaborations and explanations of "The Shawl" which provides little more than the most essential information for the construction of a narrative, "Rosa" complements the omissions in "The Shawl" (Lowin 109). Joseph Alkana reads "The Shawl" as a female version of the Akedah, the story of Abraham's near-sacrifice of Isaac in the Bible (Alkana 963-90). While Lowin is concerned with the first type of

Midrashic commentary, Alkana is keenly interested in the second type, which seeks to reconcile the Bible with recent history.

Despite the significance of these readings in expanding our understanding of Ozick's text and the post-Holocaust fiction, however, as Ozick has pointed out, Midrash alone is not enough when it comes to creating a contemporary Jewish literature, for Midrash usually means "a literature of parable" and it is confined by its "dependence on a single form" (Ozick "Bialik's Hint" *Metaphor & Memory* 238). Meisha Rosenberg proposes that Midrash might be looked at "not as a single limiting form that demands we read texts as literal Midrashim or as parables, but rather as a mode, a way into a Jewish literature that thrives on dialectics" (Rosenberg 117).

One of the primary dialectics in *The Shawl* is the tension between historic representation and figurative representation of the Holocaust, "which must be regarded as a historical as well as a philosophical and a personal cataclysm" (117). It is Midrash as a mode rather than a literary form that Ozick uses in her attempts to figuratively represent the Holocaust while keeping to its historicity.

It was in 1977 that Ozick completed *The Shawl* and it came out in 1989. Ozick said it was her fear of making art out of the Holocaust that prevented her from an immediate publication (Heron, *New York Times Book Review*, September 10, 1989). Ozick's predicament is the balance between historicity and figuration, which becomes the central tension in *The Shawl*. It is on the tension between historicity and figuration that Ozick's moral ethos works with an adherence to Jewish authenticity.

Ozick stays true to the historical facts and brings to light historical reality. Her writing of *The Shawl* is based upon her reading of a historical work, William Shirer's *Rise and Fall of the Third Reich*, which described the Nazi practice of hurling babies against electrified fences, which becomes the culminated horror in "The Shawl". Another source of *The Shawl*'s writing is a discussion with Jerzy Kozinski, in which the two writers touched upon the reality of those assimilated Jews who were not "shtetl Jews" but suffered the same fate. Therefore her figuration stems from the historicity she adheres to.

In addition, the two stories are set chronologically, "The Shawl" in the Holocaust, and "Rosa" in contemporary Miami. The arrangement evidences Ozick's emphasis on historicity and creates at the same time tension with Rosa's post-Holocaust fantasies with Magda, her retreat from the normal society, her rejection of Simon Persky, her refusal to play a part in Dr. Tree's misappropriation of the Holocaust, and her redemptive reentry into the Jewish community.

However, the fact that Ozick draws on historical references and her emphasis on historicity in the chronological arrangement of the novella doesn't necessarily point to her preference of historicity to figuration. "For me," says Ozick, deconstructing the opposition between morality and imagination, "literature *is* the moral life" (Ozick "Innovation and Redemption: What Literature Means" *Art & Ardor* 245). In dovetailing historicity and figuration, Ozick explores the post-Holocaust dilemmas as extensions of her interpretations to Jewish authenticity in the Midrashic mode, which finds its origins in "to search" and "to inquire."

B. Midrashic Representation of Historicity and Figuration in *The Shawl*

There are two deeply interrelated stories in historical sequence in the seventy-page novella *The Shawl*, the brief seven-page title piece "The Shawl," set during World War II, and the relatively lengthier one, "Rosa," set in post-war 1977. "The Shawl" is a powerful story of unspeakable horrors with its description of the captivity of Rosa, Magda (Rosa's infant daughter), and Stella (Rosa's adolescent niece) in a concentration camp, "a place without pity" during World War II. The "horror" is epitomized when Rosa witnessed the death of Magda, the infant's being hurled to the electric fence by a Nazi solider. "Rosa" continues the story and portrays the title character at fifty-eight, some four decades after the events recounted in "The Shawl." Rosa Lublin and Stella live in the United States, with Rosa just having moved to Florida after demolishing her used-furniture store in Brooklyn. The story tells of how she feels radically isolated and remains preoccupied with her murdered daughter and continues to suffer from the trauma, the lingering impact of the Holocaust. Moreover, apart from the wounded postwar psyche of Rosa, the story also explores her prewar life and her redemptive reentry into the Jewish community.

The fact that "only a tenth of the novella occurs during the Holocaust" in "The Shawl" and "the rest concern what follows" in "Rosa" (Lehmann 1998 35) reveals that Ozick focuses on "the consequences of interpretation," namely, the responses to interpretation and its influence on later events (Young 4).

Meisha Rosenberg argues for a paradoxical judgment of the two stories in terms of their historicity and figuration. She holds that "The Shawl" can stand for historicity in that its narrative style is spare, its use of language is minimalist and that it deems with details while "Rosa" can stand for figuration in that there is a more colorful array of characters, places, fantasy, and allusions. And she further suggests that "the two stories are too intertwined for such a simplistic assignment," for it can be conversely argued that "Rosa" stands for historical representation because it takes place in "an identifiable time and culture" while "The Shawl" stands for figurative representation "with its abbreviated structure and poetically informed disruptive tropes" (Rosenberg 124).

One of the reasons for the paradoxical judgments is that the two stories are so intertwined that each contains the other within its center. It is until the end of "Rosa", the second story, that Rosa admits to herself what has actually happened in "The Shawl," the first story, Magda was murdered. The existence of the narrative circle in the two stories, which inform each other, indicates the history presented is not linear and evolutionary. As a result, at the end of the novella, the readers are not left with "Rosa," but instead, with the "The Shawl" and in particular with the Holocaust, highlighted as a result of the figurative representation, pointing at last to its historicity. The reading experience echoes the prerequisite that the Holocaust, while it must first and foremost be remembered as history, must also allow for figuration.

Irving Halperin commented in *Commonweal*, "In a time when the memory of the Holocaust is being trivialized by slick fiction, talk shows, and TV 'documentaries,' and when some social 'scientists' (necrophiliacs, Rosa would call them) are doing 'research projects,' written in atrocious psychobabble, on the 'survivor,' Ms. Ozick's volume is a particularly welcome achievement of the moral imagination" (Halperin Internet).

Taking into account the potential collision between her steadfast adherence to Jewish values and the social reality in the post-Holocaust American Jewish context, Ozick's moral ethos concerning the post-Holocaust dilemmas, as is shown in *The Shawl*, ranges from her emphasis on historicity to her insistence on appropriate figuration. Her emphasis on historicity is shown in the moral injunction to remember, the criticism of the public disinterest in the Holocaust testimony, the objection to repress the traumatic memory so as to deny the history, and the misappropriation of the Holocaust. Her insistence on appropriate figuration is epitomized with her view of figuration as against idolatry, the removal of history from its historical continuum due to an idolatrous practice.

a. The Insistence on Historicity

The insistence on historicity embraces the necessity to remember the Holocaust and entails at the same time criticism of its opposite and that of the failure to maintain its historicity. The opposite of remembering includes to stay contented with the indifference to an assumingly communal event of public consequences, and to repress the miserable memory so as to deny the history. The failure to maintain the historicity of a memory can result from a misappropriation as a distortion of historicity. The corresponding moralistic judgments are projected in either the characterization or the deployment of the plot.

1. To Remember the Jewish History

The commitment to remembering Jewish history is a fundamental conviction in Ozick's vision. In juxtaposition, Rosa is characterized as a critical thinker who confronts the past, traumatic as it is, and negotiates between past and present in the end for a normalcy which will usher in a future whereas Stella is characterized as a free thinker who jettisons the past.

The juxtaposition of Rosa and Stella as antithetical characters reveals the importance that Ozick attaches to history despite all its agonies and its memory in that Rosa is characterized as the protagonist with her agonizing experience and the interpretation of its responses as the focal concern while Stella is characterized as Rosa's "psychological foil" (Kremer 1999 157).

Rosa's strong fixation on the past somewhat evidences Ozick's fear of the Holocaust being forgotten in the contemporary American Jewish context, for the Judaic historical paradigm differs from that of the American. The central contrast lies in the distinction between the Judaic emphasis on memory and on continuity of tradition and the American enthrallment with novelty and future progress.

Existing in the present, Rosa is mired in the past and lives in the past. Noting a key distinction between the Miami retirees and herself in terms of the separation from family, Rosa laments that they are detached, but "they had detached themselves" (29) by their own social planning while hers is an abrupt and violent separation externally imposed. Like Eliezer in Elie Wiesel's *Night Dawn Day*, who comes to the realization that "I think if I were able to forget I would hate myself" (Wiesel 303), Rosa lives in the past, as is reflected in her comment to Persky: "Without a life, a person lives where they can. If all they got is thoughts, that's where they live" (Ozick *The Shawl* 27-28).

Human experience in Rosa's vision falls into three ages: "The life before, the life during, the life after. . . . The life after is now. The life before is our *real* life, at home, where we were born" (58). "The life during", though no life to speak of, refers to the Holocaust which characterizes the Hitler epoch. Separated from her prewar halcyon days with the family she loved, the culture she loved, and the language she loved, Rosa views life as nothing but a series of dismal encounters. She tells of her bitter survival, "Once I thought the worst was the worst, after that nothing could be the worst. But now I see, even after the worst there's still more" (14).

Rosa's failure to have a life in the present is partially due to her perpetual mourning of the loss of her child, and her overwhelming obsession with the lingering nightmare of the Holocaust, which results in her unwillingness and inability to forge emotional connections, however, it is partially due to the public disinterest in her Holocaust witness, a primary cause for her failed communication and interpersonal contact as well.

2. The Public Disinterest in the Holocaust

The public disinterest in the Holocaust witness stems from the American historical paradigm which may generally bring about "free thinkers" who jettison the past. The inclination to jettison the past well accounts for the American reluctance to confront the horrors of the Holocaust. As a result of the world's indifference to her Holocaust testimony, with no one willing to listen to her Holocaust experience, a symbol of the world's acquiescence to the murder of her child, Rosa destroys her New York shop and withdraws into the hell of Holocaust memory, her only brief solace being lamentation and reveries of imagined lives for her deceased daughter. Furthermore, it is those who evade her Holocaust witness and their indifference Rosa met with when she felt willing to share her Holocaust experience that have made her rebuff Persky, a willing auditor, and reject his invitation to "unload" in saying, "Whatever I would say, you would be deaf" (27).

The public indifference has made Rosa more skeptical of audience response to her witness, which results in her retreat from normalcy of the ordinary society. For instance, feeling historically and socially alienated from Miami Jews, Rosa is withdrawn from them and further assumes their perception of her must be as one-dimensional as a refugee, "like a number-counted apart from the ordinary swarm. Blue digits on the arm" (36).

In addition to the moral judgment made on American Holocaust indifference, in *The Shawl*, Ozick presents another form in jettisoning the past, namely, the denial of history with attempts to wipe out tragic memories in her characterization of Stella.

3. The Denial of History

Stella is kept offstage and readers have no access to her thoughts and dreams. Her postwar adjustment is made known through her letters to Rosa and Rosa's commentary. She functions as "the psychological foil" of Rosa (Kremer 1999 157).

In juxtaposition to Rosa who remains strongly fixated on the past in her perpetual mourning, Stella tries to suppress the tragedy and pursues to enjoy life. Their antithetical responses to the Holocaust are where Ozick's moral imagination rests upon.

When talking of the camp captivity, Eliezer in Elie Wiesel's *Night Dawn Day* comments, "Anyone who has been there has brought back some of humanity's madness" (Wiesel 303). Rosa and Stella, characterized as antithetical survivors, brought back from their Holocaust experience distinct madness, and each of them perceives the other as mentally ill. Destroying her store in New York, Rosa is reported as "a madwoman" and Stella threatens, "One more public outburst puts you in the bughouse" (Ozick *The Shawl* 32-33). In objecting to Stella's repression of the memory, Rosa says, "A devil climbs into you and ties up your soul and you don't even know it" (15). In Rosa's view, "Stella is self-indulgent. She wants to wipe out memory" (58), and "Every vestige of former existence is an insult to her" (41). Stella's madness, in Ozick's judgment via Rosa, is her repression of the Holocaust memory, and denial of the history by extension, for history as a storehouse of culture, ritual, and religious belief includes both glories and traumas, both of which are treasures that cannot be overlooked or forsaken.

Stella plays no dramatic role in the narrative of the second story, yet her presence and influence are reinforced with the verbal echoes. The first story opens with the delineation of "Stella, cold, cold, the coldness of hell" (3) while in the sequel "Rosa," Stella, in Rosa's contemplation, is primarily linked to references to cold: "She was always cold. The cold went into her heart" (6-7), and she is referred to as a cold and heartless "Angel of Death" (15). Furthermore, in the first story, it is Stella's effort to warm herself with the shawl that leads to Magda's death and in the second story, Rosa indulges her hatred in "cannibal dreams about Stella," and she "was boiling her tongue, her ears, her right hand, such a fat hand with plump fingers" (15). The cannibal dreams remind the reader of the cannibal reference in Rosa's assumption that "Stella was waiting for Magda to die so that she could put her teeth into the little thighs" (5). Both the cannibal dreams and reference reflect Rosa's judgment of Stella as accomplice to Magda's murder, the verdict of which is confirmed in a letter to Magda, accusing that Stella "was always jealous of you. She has no heart" (44). The coalescence of cold and heart, together with the employment of the present tense in the judgment "She has no heart", establishes a causal link between her "tragic transgression and her postwar moral failures" (Kremer 1999 156).

Unsympathetic to Rosa's trauma, Stella fails to understand her prolonged mourning formed of memory. Determined to pursue a life that will diminish the lingering destructive impact of the Holocaust on her postwar life, Stella turns a blind eye and a deaf ear while Ozick "cannot *not* write about it. It rises up and claims [her] furies... [because her] brother's blood cries out from the ground" (Ozick "Roundtable Discussion," *Writing and the Holocaust* 284).

In addition, as Irving Greenberg says, "To be a Jew is to hear stories and claim them as one's own... to keep telling them to someone else" (Greenberg 12). Similar views are with Amy Gottfried who holds that "One of the strongest injunctions in Judaism is to bear witness" (Gottfried 40). With the characterization of Stella, Ozick bemoans the repression of the Holocaust testimony and the indifference of posterity, both of which will result in the loss of historicity with the dwindling of the survivors in the first place, and the bleak prospect in its figuration in the second.

Denial of the Holocaust dishonors the victims, so does misappropriation. What Rosa, together with Ozick of course, insists on is the authentic and appropriate transmission of the Holocaust history.

4. Misappropriation: A Threat to Historicity

In terms of the effect of the Holocaust on American Jewish understandings of the influence of history on the present, there inevitably arises the appropriation of history to benefit the present. The encounter between Rosa and Dr. Tree in *The Shawl* touches upon the theme of Holocaust transmission and misappropriation. Dr. Tree, a researcher who studies the behavior of Holocaust survivors, writes a jargon-strewn letter to Rosa in which he seeks her cooperation in his project "to observe survivor syndroming within the natural setting" (Ozick *The Shawl* 38). Dr. Tree boasts his interest in Rosa's camp experience for use in his study on repressed animation and calls Rosa's attention to his chapter, "Defensive Group Formation: The Way of the Baboons." Coming to the awareness that to Dr. Tree she is but a lab specimen, a figure with "blue digits on the arm," she recognizes him as a parasite who intends to capitalize on the Holocaust. Rosa condemns Dr. Tree's misappropriation, which is ill-suited to the challenge of appropriate Holocaust transmission. At last, Rosa hurls the manuscript of Dr. Tree's at the ceiling and flushes his letter down the toilet, a gesture of her refusal to act as accomplice to the misappropriation of the Holocaust.

The manipulation of the encounter between Rosa and Dr. Tree is based on the fact that in the 1960s, the Holocaust received an astounding amount of attention from Jewish American writers, in a manner which often eclipses all other facets of Jewish history and culture. Consequently, as the Holocaust itself becomes more removed, the range and number of its representations seem to proliferate. It is important to distinguish between the Holocaust itself and the "rhetorical, cultural, political, and religious uses to which the disaster has been put since then" (Lopate 90). Ozick insists that it is the Holocaust and the historicity represented in the Holocaust that are to be remembered. What Ozick objects to is the false importance attached to the misappropriation of the Holocaust as a failure for the Holocaust transmission.

Despite Rosa's refusal to be a partner to Dr. Tree in the misappropriation of the Holocaust, she herself has been mired in an unconscious misappropriation, her idolatrous transmission of the Holocaust particularly in her obsession with the shawl and her fantasies about Magda, which is, to Ozick, a figuration deprived of Jewish authenticity.

b. Idolatrous Fantasies: a non-Jewish Figuration

While Ozick adheres to the historicity of the Holocaust, she is engaged in its figuration. It is her fear that the Holocaust may be forgotten, and may be made into an idol, a practice of non-Jewish figuration.

To remember the Holocaust does not necessarily mean too overwhelming an obsession with the past which results in a sacrifice of the normalcy of a present and a future. Furthermore, Ozick is concerned with the interrelation of fantasy and idolatry, and depicts the fantasies of Rosa as "an affliction that characterizes the scarred thinking of a survivor." In Ozick's moral judgment, the Holocaust is removed from history through idolatry, for the historicity of the Holocaust is removed from the continuum of history, "frozen in time, and thus made an object of worship" (Lehmann 1998 36).

What makes Rosa guilty of idol worship is specifically her obsession with the shawl and her fantasies about Magda. Enfolding and protecting Magda, the shawl is a symbol of divine and maternal care in the camp captivity, however, in postwar America, when Rosa's worship of Magda's shawl becomes the sole tangible remainder of her daughter, when the memories of Magda creep into and are recollected in every fiber of the reality of the shawl, when the indulgence and the obsession result in a disregard of other human beings and a disruption of present normalcy, it turns into an idol because "The chief characteristic of any idol is that it is a system sufficient in itself. It is indifferent to the world and to humanity" (Ozick "Literature as Idol: Harold Bloom" 189). As Stella writes in the letter telling of the mailing of the shawl to Rosa, "Your idol is on its way. Go on your knees to it if you want. You're like those people in the Middle Ages who worshipped a piece of the True Cross, a splinter from some old outhouse as far as anybody knew" (Ozick *The Shawl* 31).

Too dreadful is Rosa's memory of Magda's torture murder for her to repress or dismiss it and "get on with life" as others urge. Withdrawing from the ordinary society with her diminished interest in life, Rosa indulges herself in writing to Magda in Polish. Magda is addressed as "my Gold, my Wealth, my Treasure, my Hidden Sesame, my Paradise, my Yellow Flower, my Magda: Queen of Bloom and Blossom" (Ozick *The Shawl* 66), indicating Magda has become God to Rosa, however, "the terms are applicable not to God, but to the golden calf or a Greek nature spirit" (Lehmann 1998 37).

The idolatrous obsession defies temporal progression and freezes the indulgence in time, which is exemplified by Rosa's insistence that the Holocaust is the only "real" time, as she explains, "Before is a dream. After is a joke. Only during stays" (Ozick *The Shawl* 58). The intensity of the trauma and the public indifference to her Holocaust testimony account for Rosa's refusal to forge emotional connection and her attempts to reserve Magda's life in her imagination, which accords with psychiatric theory that contends that when survivors are unable to complete the process of mourning the loss of a child, "various forms of denial, idealization, and ... 'walling of' become necessary" (Krystal 125).

In addition to Rosa's postwar denial of Magda's torture death, she invents idealized adult lives for Magda as a psychological and imaginative restoration of her maternal loss. There are three reveries typical of a mother's idealization: Magda visualized as a lovely young girl of sixteen at the threshold of adulthood; Magda fantasied at thirty-one, a physician married to a physician living in a large house in a New York suburb; and Magda imagined as "a professor of Greek philosophy at Columbia University" (Ozick *The Shawl* 39).

All these fantasies appear to be sympathy-provoking, for Rosa's letters to an imaginary Magda begin as an attempt to communicate. Nevertheless, they soon turn out to be fantasies to idolize "the During" and transform it into where the fantasies can linger at ease. In one of the letters, Rosa tells Magda of her father, "Our families had status. Your father was the son of my mother's closest friend. She was a converted Jew married to a Gentile: you can be a Jew if you like, or a Gentile, it's up to you. You have a legacy of choice, and they say choice is the only true freedom" (43). Rosa's invention of Magda's paternity strikingly contrasts readers' assumed knowledge that, far from having an "aristocratic" Gentile father, Magda is the result of Nazi rape (65). It is obvious that Rosa is reinventing history in self-indulgent terms. The historicity of the Holocaust is denied to the point of not acknowledging the way in which it threatened all Jews. It is idolatrous to falsify and fictionalize history with a self-indulgent imagination. However unconsciously and inevitably, Rosa has committed idolatry, which points to her Jewish inauthenticity.

c. Rosa's Jewish Inauthenticity

Rosa's Jewish inauthenticity is simultaneously reflected in her lack of historic connection to Jewry and her lack of communal and ethnical concerns in grieving only for her personal loss.

While Ozick sides with Rosa in remembering the history, Ozick has a different attitude toward her in distancing from her aversion to her Jewish identity, the fact that Rosa has allowed the prevailing anti-Semitism of her society to alienate her from the Jewish cultural heritage. Rosa has been delineated as a morally flawed character based upon the postwar adherence to her parents' prejudice against observant Jews and Jewish culture, as is shown in her postwar prejudice against Persky. Rosa is accused of "certain contempt" for Jews, whom she considers as "primitive" (52).

In a speech cast in anti-Semitic tone, Rosa asks, "Can you imagine a family like us— [...] confining *us* with teeming Mockowiczes and Rabinowiczes and Perskys and Finkelsteins, [...] walking up and down, and bowing, and shaking and quaking over old rags of prayer books, [...] we were furious because we had to be billeted with such a class, with these old Jew peasants worn out from their rituals and superstitions, phylacteries on their foreheads sticking up so stupidly, like unicorn horns, every morning" (66-67). It is with fury stemming from contempt that Rosa recollects the humiliation and dishonor in being confined with what she calls a class of stupidity. But she has failed to realize that her family, assimilated as it is, is Jewish at root. Embracing anti-Semitism, the Lublins have estranged themselves from their Jewish cultural grounding and become infatuated with Polish culture as a result. Living in Warsaw during the prime golden age of

Yiddish literature, the Lublins' library privileges most other European languages and literatures while intentionally excluding Yiddish writing, their national writing. It is their denigration of Yiddish and in particular their preference for Polish that distinguish them from most Polish Jews.

They are "self-hating Jews, products of Polish anti-Semitism," and "models of radical assimilation" (Kremer 1999 164). Rosa recalls with arrogant pride that her father identified himself as a "Pole by right" (Ozick *The Shawl* 40), and that "there was not a particle of ghetto left in him, not a grain of rot" (21).

The parental pre-Nazi anti-Semitism nurtures Rosa's estrangement from Jewry and Judaism, as is reflected in her antipathy toward Jewish Warsaw, which she describes as a "bitter ancient alley, dense with . . . signs in jargoned Yiddish" (20), her postwar chagrin that Americans mistake her for a parochial eastern Jew of Persky's ilk, and her postwar prejudice against Persky, to whose appeal to their common Polish origin she responds, "My Warsaw isn't your Warsaw" (19).

Advocating Jewish cultural particularity, Ozick explicitly exposes Jewish self-hatred as a legacy of anti-Semitism and implicitly rebukes Jews who cater for the favor of the gentile society at the expense of diminishing their Jewish cultural heritage, hence the moral message pointing to Ozick's skepticism of the merits of assimilation and her resistance to total assimilation. On the contrary, she insists that "The world ought to be reassimilated into the Jewish tradition" (Lowin 1988 10).

A central concern in *The Shawl* is the possibility of the post-Holocaust normalization which is primarily pertinent to the balance between memory and healing, and the feasibly functional elements in the process of normalization. There arises the moral judgment on what is functional and what is dysfunctional.

d. Memory and Redemptive Healing

According to Dan Bar-On, a professor of behavioral science, the

Holocaust survivors' wish for normalization can either turn out to be functional or end up as dysfunctional. The attempted normalization could become dysfunctional when "the survivors avoided a psychological mourning process, thereby becoming inwardly committed to the past they did not work through" (Bar-On 104).

A psychological mourning process seems to play an indispensable role in the post-Holocaust normalization. Rosa has abundantly experienced the psychological mourning process, traces of which have been made available in both her interior monologue and the letters she writes, whereas it is toward the end of the story that she is just starting to show her willingness to get normalized. For Stella, who seems to have become normalized, there is neither the presence nor the absence of her avoidance of a psychological mourning process. Then it is safe to say, to Ozick, it is important to undergo a psychological mourning process, however, the decisively functional element must be what has brought Rosa to her willingness to change, and in particular, in what way she has changed.

Eager to share her Holocaust testimony with others only to be frustrated with an unexpected indifference, Rosa withdraws into the hell of Holocaust memories. Abused by Stella as mentally insane and isolated from the everyday life of an ordinary society, Rosa is enthralled with idolatrous fantasies.

Coming to the awareness that her Holocaust experience could be misappropriated by bogus scholars like Dr. Tree, she decides not to act as a partner in the misappropriation. Befriended by Persky, a pre-Holocaust Jewish immigrant, Rosa comes to the willingness to change. She starts to relate part of her Holocaust experience to him, whom she misjudged and scorned. She reconnects the telephone, and calls Stella telling her about her intention to return to New York, both gestures revealing her new interest in communication. Consequently, when Persky arrives, "Magda was away" (Ozick *The Shawl* 70).

Her decision not to contribute her Holocaust history to Dr. Tree, an exploiter, is based on an ethnical judgment, a great leap from her personal mourning and transcendence from a maternal grief over a personal loss. What she is worried about is instead the communal consequence of such ethnic misappropriation, which will dishonor the victims as an ethnic whole. What she insists on is an appropriate transmission of Holocaust history.

Rosa's decision not to partake in Dr. Tree's misappropriation parallels her objection to Stella's denial of Holocaust memory, a practice of avoiding "a psychological mourning process" in that denial dishonors the victims likewise. What she appeals to is an authentic transmission of Holocaust history.

Accepting Persky who is Yiddish-speaking, Rosa distances herself from her adherence to the parental anti-Semitism and self-hatred and comes to acknowledge the Jewish identity they denied.

The healing of Rosa's trauma is under way. It is not the passage of time that heals. It is not "a psychological mourning process" that heals. It is her insistence on authentic and appropriate transmission of Holocaust history that constitutes a redemptive step toward her recovery from her idolatrous practice, from her traumatic history, and from her prejudice against Jews and Jewish culture, which ushers in hopes for her return to the Jewish community.

In short, Ozick turns to the Jewish tradition and uses Midrash as a mode, focusing upon its function in bringing about "interpretations consistent with contemporary religious beliefs and circumstances," to approach the figurative representation of the Holocaust while keeping to its historicity for a negotiation between past and present, between Jewish authenticity and Jewish inauthenticity.

Insisting on the significance of historicity, Ozick bases her creation on the historical reality. Setting the two stories in *The Shawl* chronologically without leaving the readers a linear and evolutionary history, she intertwines the two stories and makes each contain the other within its center. The two stories, as a result, can be regarded either as historical representation or figurative representation respectively, which establishes the premise that the Holocaust, while its historicity is of primary importance, must allow for figuration as well.

Ozick imbues her imagination with moral as well as historical values and uses the Midrashic mode, a nonoppositional approach essential to dovetail historicity and figuration with moral judgment made in the tension between the adherence to Jewish values and the American post-Holocaust reality, hence her moral ethos.

Specifically, the insistence on historicity is reflected in the commitment to remember history, the criticism of the public disinterest, the objection to the repression of the traumatic memory which results in the denial of history, and the caution against misappropriation which threatens historicity. Appropriate figuration is advocated against idolatrous fantasies, which points to Jewish inauthenticity. In the meanwhile, redemptive healing is brought under way as a result of the insistence on Jewish authenticity and appropriate transmission of the Holocaust history.

In history representation including the fictional construction and deconstruction of Jewish memories and the Midrashic representation of the Holocaust, Ozick highlights her moral ethos in weighing the Jewish value attached to history and historicity, the "minority," and the American orientation toward the future and the prevailing trend in the excessive figuration of the Holocaust, the "majority," and foregrounds the "minority" in her literary practice wherein the diasporic space is established.

Chapter Four

Jewishness and Feminine Representation

In the diasporic space Ozick establishes in her fiction, Judaism engagement is enriched with the moral judgment she makes of the prohibiting Orthodox Judaic gender law that results in her representation of Jewish femininity, highlighting "Eros of ideas." Ozick's feminine representation is related to the tension she encounters as a Jewish woman writer.

Just as there is tension between Ozick's identities as a Jew and a writer, there is tension between her identities as a Jew and a woman, and as a woman and a writer in Diaspora. Dual marginality of Jewishness and femininity, together with the fissure between Jewishness and feminism, constitute the primary source of Ozick's tension as a Jewish woman writer in Diaspora. Since a Jewish woman suffers dual marginality and dual exile, the two minorities, Jewishness and femininity, are likewise in need of power in the diasporic space so as to turn into the majority and hence the possibility of the identity construction. Therefore, the construction of Jewish feminine identity and Jewish feminine literary identity chiefly stems from the fusion between Jewishness and feminism, for feminism has been argued by some as "the most important force in American Jewry" (Fishman 37). The discussion also takes into account the social impact of the Holocaust, which epitomizes the dual marginality of Jewish women and serves as an inevitable shaping force in the Jewish feminist imagination and the corresponding identity construction.

I. Cynthia Ozick's Tension as a Jewish Woman Writer in Diaspora

From Ozick's childhood through her professional career, she has encountered racial and gender biases. She suffered segregation in both religious and public schools because of her gender and her Jewish identity. The prejudice persisted when she attended college, and went on even after she became a university professor. The prejudice Ozick has experienced serves as the basis for her literary attempts in constructing Jewishness and femininity as the majority in her literary practice.

A. Prejudice in Ozick's Educational and Professional Life

Ozick is the daughter of Russian Orthodox Jewish immigrants William and Celia Regelson Ozick (Kremer 1994 265). In her childhood, she was rejected from Jewish seminary due to the rabbi's insistence that she was only a girl and therefore did not have a reason to learn Jewish law or history (Kauvar interview 384). Ozick's grandmother, however, insisted that Ozick receive a "standard [male] Jewish education" (Klingenstein 252), and Ozick reflects that when her grandmother came to pick her up at the end of the year,

> the rabbi said to my *bobe* (Yiddish term for Grandmother), *Zi hot a goldene kepele* ("She has a golden little head"). That was the last time anybody ever told me I was intelligent for my whole school time until I got to high school, and since the praise came from somebody who was an opponent of girls' education, it was something I held onto. (Kauvar interview 385)

Even as a child, Ozick challenged her rabbi's perceptions with her intellectual capability.

In public school, Ozick's sense of inferiority resulted from being a girl and a Jew. According to Daniel Walden, between the ages of five and fourteen, Ozick was the only Jewish child in P. S. 71, a fact that

116

led to "demeaning" and "baiting" reaction by her teachers and classmates (1995 886). In elementary school at P. S. 71, Ozick felt "friendless and forlorn. [She was] publicly shamed in Assembly because [she was] caught not singing Christmas carols and repeatedly accused of deicide" (Klingenstein 252)—of being a "Christ killer" (Kremer 1994 265). In second grade, a white Anglo-Saxon Protestant girl inquired into Ozick's faith-was she Catholic or Protestant? Ozick replied, "I'm Jewish," the girl repeated the same question, for the WASP girl could not fathom that another faith could exist (Strandberg 6). Ozick claims that she felt "stupid," that she was "never made aware of being good at anything. I had no sense of being intelligent" (Kauvar interview 385). "'I'm still hurt by P. S. 71,' Ozick said in 1989; 'I had teachers who hurt me, who made me believe I was stupid and inferior'" (Strandberg 6); and it "was very strange [for Ozick] to have two lives like this: on the school side, where I was almost always the only Jew, and in *cheder* where I was almost always the only girl" (Kauvar interview 385).

Due to her gender, Ozick suffered biased assumptions from her colleagues both in graduate school and as a writer. In graduate school at Columbia, Ozick encountered misogyny in a seminar consisting of all men except for one other woman, who was nicknamed "Crazy Lady" due to her loud voice and insistence on expressing her opinion (Strandberg 12). Her professor, a man of course, "couldn't tell [Ozick and the Crazy Lady] apart" (13). To the professor, one woman was like any other woman. In *Art and Ardor*, Ozick recounts that her male colleagues distrusted her opinions, since she was a "woman writer" and "woman teacher":

I learned that I had no genuinely valid opinions, since every view I might hold was colored by my sex. If I said I didn't like Hemingway, I could have no critical justification, no literary reason; it was only because, being a woman, I obviously could not be sympathetic toward Hemingway's "masculine" subject matter, the hunting, the fishing, the bullfighting, which no woman could adequately digest. (266)

Ozick "discovered two essential points: (1) that it was a 'woman' who had done the writing—not a mind—and that I was a 'woman writer'; and (2) that I was now not a teacher, but a 'woman teacher'" (226). Her experience pertains to her representation of women in fiction. The gender inequality she has personally experienced throughout her educational and professional life contributes to the germ of her construction of Jewish literary femininity while the basis for her experiences with patriarchy was often Orthodox Judaic gender law.

B. Orthodox Judaic Gender Law Prohibiting Women

The traditional prayer said by an Orthodox Jewish man upon awaking in the morning is "Blessed are You, God, ... who has not made me a woman" (Trepp 270). Self-evidently, "from its very beginning, Judaism has been outspokenly patriarchal" (268). While acknowledging that women have authority over all aspects of domestic decisions including children's upbringing and education, Orthodox Judaic law imposes an inferior status upon women outside the home and expects women, regardless of their intellectual achievements or contributions, to submit to their marital obligations. Rabbi Sholom Estrin, of the Congregation Sha'arei Israel-Lubavitch in Raleigh, North Carolina, describes women's maternal role as a means of ensuring and protecting their modesty. Rabbi Estrin states that Orthodox Judaism highly esteems women, and therefore avoids putting them in vulnerable situations: "by placing a woman in public, you in a sense are tainting her pureness."

Orthodox Judaic law requires segregation of men and women in study and synagogue attendance. During synagogue services, women must sit separate from men, behind a "mehitzah," or wall or screen, which divides the two genders (Trepp 271). The message Jewish schools convey to boys and girls early in life is that "sons are valued more than daughters [and] that the education of sons is more important than that of daughters" (Schneider 284).

According to Leonard Swidler, the Orthodox do not expect women to study the Torah or Jewish law: "the only connection with the study of the Torah that women could be expected to have was to send their sons and husbands off to study and to wait for them" (95), and "if any man teaches his daughter Torah it is as though he taught her lechery" (93). Women have been "kept ignorant of the processes of Jewish law" (Greenburg 10). Intellectual merit is among the prerequisites for Orthodox Jewish masculinity. Aviva Cantor asserts that Orthodox Jews define manhood "in terms of commitment to and achievement in learning Torah," as well as in scholarly achievement (92). On the contrary, women's "intellectual endeavors don't count. [Jewish women] want their *men* to read books, be 'intellectual,' because only what the men do and learn will change the status of the family as a whole" (Schneider 150). The Orthodox exclude women from the rabbinate, a symbol of wisdom and authority. According to Helene Rebecca Bogdanoff, the Orthodox refuse to accept women as rabbis (12). This accounts for the Orthodox conception that women are incapable of literate, intellectual endeavors.

Orthodox Judaism does not approve of women seeking or obtaining any other positions of authority, but instead advocates women's supportive role. Rabbi Estrin states that women's connection with rabbinical authority "is based on their husband's position as the rabbi [... she] traditionally has always played a major role in the community [by] helping her husband lead." The Orthodox put limitation on women and contend that "feminism [is] a capital crime" (Swidler 103). According to the Midrash, there are two versions of Genesis, the first of which tells the story of Lilith: "the first woman was Lilith. She stood before God, insisting on absolute equality with her husband, as both had been created in the same fashion and at the same time. This demand irritated God. Lilith then uttered the Name of God and became a demon to haunt mankind" (Trepp 268). God's irritation and Lilith's transformation into a demon to haunt humanity conveys an Orthodox deviance for women who demand equal rights.

However, Ozick demands equal rights in rejecting the label of "woman writer," which is related not only to her life experience but also to the negative reception of women's writing while her disruption of the oppositions between feminism and Judaism results from her efforts in constructing Jewish literary femininity.

C. The Negative Reception of Women's Writing

Before 1990, women's writing was negatively received by the Jewish intellectual community. Elaine M. Kauvar asserts in 1993 that "to write a novel twenty-five years ago with a woman as the narrator was to risk exclusion from the ranks of serious writing. More precisely, it often meant being regarded as the author of a woman's novel; which is to say, a romantic, pulp, trivia" (1993 2). According to Judith Baskin, "to become a Jewish woman writer was to become a cultural anomaly; often the price of such an achievement was equivocal exile from a male society profoundly uncomfortable with female intellectual assertiveness" (18).

It is a common practice that literary judgment is made on the basis of the writers' gender. "No book of poetry by a woman was ever reviewed without references to the poet's sex" (Strandberg 13). Ozick recalls in writing *Trust*, when she read book reviews that discussed writers' genders, she "was afraid to be pegged as having written a 'woman's novel'... no one takes a woman's novel seriously" (13).

Critics tend to treat men's writing more favorably. Tillie Olsen points out that "women writers, women's experiences, and literature by women, are by definition minor" (9). According to Kristie S. Fleckenstein, women who intend to be producers of knowledge must "be like men, think like men, speak like men" (115). Furthermore, even under such conditions, the knowledge of the gender of the author prevents the work from a fair critical reception.

Norma Rosen states that "any writer worth her salt struggled to write herself free of the epithet ' woman writer'" (146) and she presents her critical reception. Her first book is praised for "charm, for playfulness. " Her second book is confronted with a critical response which opens with an "Anthony Burgess quote: He prefers books with ' a strong male thrust', an almost pedantic allusiveness and a brutal intellectual content. " Her third book is assigned to a female reviewer, who claims that "one cannot read this novel without stumbling over queries about the female condition" (146-47). Female reviewers present no less alienating attention to gender than men to women's writings. The same is true of Joyce Antler's review of Anza Yezierska's writing: " feminist scholars have elaborated several interpretive strategies for elucidating the gendered meanings" in her writing (198).

Ozick herself is incapable of escaping criticism that focuses on women's assumed domestic roles. *Time* magazine calls her " a housewife. " Furthermore, the critical reception of her works is loaded with gender-biased conclusions. For example, the reviewer of *Trust* in the *New York Times Book Review* writes of the narrator's longing for "some easy feminine role, " allowing a "coming to terms with the recalcitrant sexual elements in her life" (Strandberg 14).

Ozick considers the practice of basing literary judgment on gender as a "Great Multiple Lie, " which takes for granted that women's imagination is sexually determined and that their gender "inherently circumscribed and defined and directed the writer's subject matter, perspective, and aspiration" (Ozick "Literature and the Politics of Sex: A Dissent" *Art & Ardor* 288-89). The "Lie" assumes the existence of a "female nature" in women's artistic creation on the basis of women's inferior psychological and emotional temperament. In addition, the practice believes in the influence of women's reproductive abilities on their writing sensibilities. Ozick declares that the conception of "woman writer" originates from the assumption that women require constant renewal of internal stimuli in order to write. In her judgment, women are no different from men.

To Ozick, "a writer is a writer" and the term "'woman writer' has no meaning" (Ozick "Literature and the Politics of Sex: A Dissent" *Art & Ardor* 285). In observing the difference in male and female Jewish writers' depiction of selfhood, Joyce Antler argues that

> for Roth, Bellow, and Mailer, the quest was for a self-sufficient manhood. For Yezierska, Olsen, Paley and other female writers, the goal was female independence, and independence expressed in relation to family and communal responsibilities. ... in creating themselves as authors, Jewish women have first had to defy tradition, religious and secular, in different ways than men. The struggles they experienced in becoming artists parallel many of their characters' conflicts as they express desires for independence that run counter to traditional responsibilities. (194-96)

Ozick's fiction affirms Antler's contention that Jewish women writers are expected to transcend Jewish perceptions of female capacities to convince the literary community of the value of women's writing.

Ozick advocates equal opportunities for men and women and asserts the timeless, genderless freedom of imagination:

> when we write, we are not women or men but blessed beings in possession of a Promethean art, an art encumbered by peril and hope and fire, and, above all, freedom. What we ought to do, as writers, is not wait for freedom, meanwhile idling in self-analysis; the freedom one waits for, or builds strategies toward, will never come. What we ought to do, as writers, is seize freedom now, immediately, by recognizing that we already have it. (Ozick "Literature and the Politics of Sex: A Dissent" *Art & Ardor* 290)

Imagination—with all its freedom—is very much intertwined with Ozick's Jewish and feminine literary identities.

The following analysis is to center around Ozick's literary representation of Jewish femininity, which is embodied in both the female protagonists and Orthodox Judaic gender law and the Jewish mother in the Holocaust, and her feminist mending of the Orthodox Judaic gender law in order to answer for her allegiance to Judaism and to carve a place in the male-dominated Jewish literary tradition.

Ozick's Jewish feminist imagination is informed by the fissure and fusion of Judaism and feminism. While feminist views emerge as the prevailing trend and the "majority," Ozick's allegiance to Judaism, the "minority," is challenged by her judgment of the obviously prohibiting Judaic gender law.

Ozick seeks to construct both femininity and Jewishness as the majority in transforming and synthesizing Jewish visions and feminist visions. On the basis of her adherence to Jewishness, she integrates feminist ideas into Judaism in order to claim a place for women as intellectual equals with men, hence the merging of the "minority" with the "majority" based on her moral ethos.

In her works, there are female protagonists on whom there has projected a reaction against the effects of gender bias. They are characters transcending the Orthodox Judaic gender law, which generally treats women as intellectually and socially inferior to men. In addition, there are mothers under duress, whose mothering is featured by their "mothers' thought," the feminist tribute paid to the female intellectual capacities, which has been an Orthodox Judaic ignorance.

II. Female Protagonists and Orthodox Judaic Gender Law

While feminism contends equal rights between men and women, the Orthodox Judaic law confines women and condemns feminism as "a capital crime." Integrating feminist ideas of equality between men and women into Judaism which is outspokenly patriarchal, Ozick disrupts the opposition between feminism and Judaism, challenges male sexism in both marital and professional oppression in a patriarchal society, and calls for the establishment of an unbiased society that values intellectual merit over gender.

My analysis focuses on two of Ozick's stories: "Levitation," which depicts marital oppression, and "Puttermesser and Xanthippe," which evaluates professional oppression.

What is in common between the female protagonists in the two stories is that both of them initially acquiesce to the conventional roles Judaism endorses on them, however, there emerges a reaction against the effects of gender bias when it comes to either the protagonist's realization of others' judgment of her as inferior or her own surrender to an inferior status.

Their initial deeds reveal that the narrators concur with patriarchal domination which characterizes Judaism, and the subsequent reaction against the gender bias pays tribute to the necessity in transcending the conventional limitations on women in Judaism.

A. "Levitation": Marital Oppression

"Levitation" rejects Judaism's assumptions about women. Lucy Feingold, the female protagonist, a Catholic who converted to Judaism in order to marry Jimmy, initially believes that she must acquiesce to the expectations of Orthodox Judaism for the behavior of a proper housewife, however, when she comes to the realization of her second-class status, she rebels.

"Levitation" is centered around a writing couple, Lucy and Jimmy, who give a party for elite literary intellectuals, only to have the attendance of second-class guests. Both of them feel it is a failure without their intended guests. In the living room Jimmy draws the conversation to the Holocaust. Listening from the hall, Lucy fails to empathize with the feelings Jimmy and other Jews share about their history. She envisions the Jews levitating toward the ceiling before she walks to the dining room to converse with the atheists gathering there. In the story, Lucy feels her inferiority as a writer and as a housewife.

Lucy is characterized as a dependant writer. The opening paragraph of the story suggests that Lucy is, in her writing, equal to her husband:

> A pair of novelists, husband and wife, gave a party. The husband was also an editor; he made a living at it. But really he was a novelist. His manner was powerless; he did not seem like an editor at all. He had a nice plain pale face, likeable. His name was Feingold. (3)

However, in addition to being a novelist, Jimmy is also an editor. What's more, it is as an editor that Jimmy makes a living, though he doesn't boast being an editor. His nonchalant attitude towards his editing undermines Lucy's passion for her fiction because she herself is but an unsuccessful novelist. Her lack of authorial confidence stems from her experience with her first novel which has been unsuccessful and critically ignored, and her self-evaluation of her second novel that it is utterly lacking in story and character. Afraid of failing again, Lucy is determined to abandon her fiction temporarily to work with Jimmy on his novel about Menachem ben Zerach, who survived "a massacre of Jews in the town of Estella in Spain in 1382" (5). Lucy, a novelist who writes about "domestic life," hopes that helping Jimmy with his writing may resolve the difficulty she confronts in "seizing on a concrete subject" (4). Lacking sufficient self-confidence, she has to cling to the writing of a male writer, Jimmy, a minor writer as he is, to gain credibility, since critics will at least take his writings seriously.

As a wife, Lucy's marriage to Jimmy depends upon her conversion to Judaism. In light of the Judaic insistence that women submit to their marital obligations, Lucy is characterized as a proper Jewish woman whose career is secondary to family. In this sense, despite the fact that she is the protagonist of the story, she is more defined as Jimmy's spouse than his intellectual equal, and hence an inferior status. According to Leonard Swidler, "Jewish women were not only to be seen as little as possible; they were also to be heard and spoken to as little as possible" (123). Jewish wives are not expected to converse with the guests, but to make sure that there is enough food and the house is clean.

Lucy initially submits to the Orthodox perception of a quiet and invisible housewife. Lingering in the center hall, which has been "swept clean" (10), she is all alone while the men have fun, eat and talk about art. When Jimmy snatches her arm and complains that the party is a "waste... no one's here" (10), he is not at all concerned with Lucy's alienation but instead the absence of the elite guests. In her reaction of "gazing back" silently and rocking "a stump of cheese," there couches her submission to the Orthodox convention of a housewife. Furthermore, her hostess duties confine her to the outskirts of the party since she is merely expected to serve food and clean after the guests and therefore she is refrained from participating in the conversations. During the party, she doesn't speak to anybody but Jimmy until the concluding paragraphs in the story.

However, Lucy is unable to feed her guests properly, the significance of which is intensified by the fact that she is a Catholic converted to Judaism. In the living room, Lucy locates the rabbi who has performed her conversion, and she notices that there are only scraps of food left for him: the potato chips are devoured, carrot sticks gone, and "of the celery sticks nothing left but threads" (11). Lucy feels uneasy in the presence of the rabbi, "as if every encounter was like a new stage in a perpetual examination" (12), and her unease stems likewise from her awareness of her failure to maintain what Jewish laws define as a proper entertainment, the shortage of food left for the rabbi and the other male guests in the living room.

At last Lucy comes to rebel against her role as a Jewish wife. Retreating to the dining room and cubing the remaining slice of cake for the male guests in the living room, she sticks "a square of chocolate cake in [Jimmy's] mouth" (13) to put an end to his retelling of the atrocities of the Jewish people. The food, which used to represent her performance of the obligations of a Jewish housewife, has now turned into her means to reduce Jimmy to silence under her will. What she used to serve has now served her needs.

It is in the dining room that she notices the failure of the party. The Jewish guests there—"the unruffled, devil-may-care kind: the humorists, the painters, film-reviewers who went off to studio showings of *Screw on Screen* on the eve of the Day of Atonement" (12)—are simply "playing with the cake crumbs on the tablecloth" (19). Nevertheless, she no longer feels responsible for the failure of the party. She comes to the realization that she has "abandoned nature [for] the God of the Jews" (18) and her conversion, specifically her gender, impedes her intellectual independence when she leaves the living room and the levitating Jews.

With Jimmy among other levitating Jews and their words reduced to "specks" (20), Lucy no longer feels bound to Jewish law and she can choose to behave in her manners at the party. Seeing a saucer has tipped over, she goes to clean it up. Now the cleaning up, though a womanly duty as it is, has become more a choice than an obligation. Furthermore, witnessing the Jews levitating in the air, Lucy is overwhelmed by a vision in which she stands in a small park and watches a musical performance. On the stage stands a female anthropologist from the Smithsonian Institute in Washington, D. C. , introducing a group of male musicians, whose accessories are rather sexually connotative: " long strap, which rub. " Besides, the anthropologist suggests that the songs are "mainly erotic, the dances are suggestive," and the "up-and-down dancing can also be found in parts of Africa" (17). The audience, "Italians—greenhorns from Sicily, steeled New Yorkers from Naples" (17), are mostly male. All of a sudden, the female anthropologist vanishes " out of Lucy's illumination" (18). What is implied in Lucy's vision is that the females are displaced in male performance regardless of their intellect.

Lucy's vision reminds of the debate Ozick witnessed, in which a female anthropologist attempted to argue for the necessity of female education only to be ridiculed for her intelligence. Like the Italians in Lucy's vision, the audience in the debate laughed and mocked the female intellectual's idea that women deserve the same educational opportunities as men. What both Lucy and Ozick are exposed to is the gender bias with no concern of female intellect.

When Lucy's vision comes to its end, she turns back to the living room and sees how "small" (19) the Jews have become. To her, all that counts to the levitating Jewish men is "death and death and death" (19) and "she is bored by the shootings and the gas and the camps, she is not ashamed to admit this" (19).

If "Levitation" points to the unfair bias that women suffer as an immediate project of marital oppression, "Puttermesser and Xanthippe" confronts professional oppression.

B. "Puttermesser and Xanthippe": Professional Oppression

While "Levitation" rejects Judaism's assumptions about women, "Puttermesser and Xanthippe" satirizes male domination over female. In "Puttermesser and Xanthippe," Ruth Puttermesser, the female protagonist, is characterized as a woman who is professionally inhibited by gender-based insecurities despite her intellectual potentials to change her life. A victim of patriarchy, Puttermesser is both feministic and Jewish.

Violating Orthodox Judaic law that devalues the education and career of the female, Puttermesser is feministic, having a remarkable educational and professional record including the "highest score in the entire city on the First-Level Management Examination," "editor-in-chief of *Law Review* at Yale Law School," and a *summa cum laude* degree in history from Barnard. However, her job is usurped by Adam Marmel majoring in Film Arts (Ozick "Puttermesser and Xanthippe" 87), for he is a New York University buddy of Alvin Turtleman's, her boss in the New York City Department of Receipts and Disbursements. Despite Puttermesser's richer experience and educational background, she is replaced by men only because of her gender.

Puttermesser creates a female golem Xanthippe after her frequent demotions for the availability of her positions for less qualified men. (Note: In the Jewish folklore, golems are mute humanoids that come to life who solve their creators' dilemmas. The creators of golems are usually wise men who could bring clay effigies to life through the combination of clay and breath, and by means of magic charms or sacred words.) Her creation of Xanthippe contributes to her professional ascending. With all of Puttermesser's intelligence, desires and the knowledge to fulfill the desires, Xanthippe, as Puttermesser's golem, actualizes Puttermesser's hopes as a result of her "PLAN" to reinvigorate New York by helping Puttermesser become the mayor after acquiring "fourteen thousand five hundred and sixty-two more signatures than the law calls for" to petition for the mayoral election (128).

Puttermesser's unconscious creation of her golem is in contrast to the tribulations men generally endured in creating their golems. Without realizing what she is doing, she molds the dirt from her houseplants into the shape of a young girl, finds her creation the following day, effortlessly performs the basic ritual for golem creation, and gives birth to Xanthippe. In contrast, it supposedly took Rabbis and their students entire nights in the wilderness to fashion clay bodies and pray for their golem's creation, while others simply failed to create true golems and instead produced only small calves or homunculi (100-04).

The contrast between Puttermesser's experience and that of men in golem creation indicates that she has easily accomplished what takes men countless hours of labor to perform. It is safe to say Puttermesser is feministic in enjoying at least potentials of intellectual equality with men, if not superiority to men.

Furthermore, Puttermesser's rise has resulted from Xanthippe's contribution. However, since Xanthippe's "PLAN" stems from Puttermesser's knowledge, which she transfers to Xanthippe through her breath, it is suggested that Puttermesser boasts potentials to change her life, except that the insecurities engendered in her by patriarchy have inhibited her.

Puttermesser's potential to change her life is manifested as well in the realization of her maternal wish, an eventful change in a woman's life. Apart from the professional success, Puttermesser longs for a daughter. The creation of Xanthippe has accomplished the aspiration and she obtains the daughter to whom she "sometimes thought that she would never give birth" (91).

However, Puttermesser is Jewish as well as feministic. While the reaction against the effects of gender bias occurs when Lucy Feingold in "Levitation" comes to the realization of others' judgment of her as inferior, the reaction in "Puttermesser and Xanthippe" is more related to Puttermesser's own surrender to an inferior status.

Puttermesser is characterized as dependent. Rather than transcending gender constraints, she has achieved her goals via others' assistance. Her mayoral status is achieved through Xanthippe, whose feverish sexual desire overcomes her reason and eventually destroys Puttermesser's administration.

Xanthippe has an affair with Puttermesser's ex-lover, Morris Rappoport, and when Puttermesser attempts to stop it, Xanthippe comes to have sex with the men in every high-level administrative position in the mayoral cabinet. The harmony that Puttermesser and her administration have so far established is disrupted. In order to prevent the golem's growing sexual urges from triggering further disasters, Puttermesser solicits the assistance of Morris Rappoport to de-create Xanthippe, for she deems it too difficult an act to conduct alone.

Puttermesser's idea that de-creating Xanthippe is too tough a task to accomplish on her own, and the fact that she relies on Rappoport to perform the destruction ceremony signify female subordination and dependency on men.

In order to carry out the de-creation, the executioner is required first to walk seven times around the golem in the opposite direction from that in which the creator walked when breathing life into it, and then to remove from the golem's forehead *aleph* among the three Hebrew letters—*aleph, mem, tav*—which mean "truth" when put together. Without *aleph*, "the remaining letters, *mem and tav*, spell *met*—dead" (101). Rappoport follows the ritual and scrapes from Xanthippe's forehead the *aleph* with a small knife. It is Rappoport who performs the crucial work, therefore, though Puttermesser collaborates in the de-creation, she, as in her creation of Xanthippe and in her subsequent professional success, remains disengaged from taking positive steps to further her aspirations.

While Puttermesser's dependency is insulting to feminist pursuits, her dependence upon either the golem in her mayoral rise or Morris Rappoport in the golem de-creation reveals the Jewish tint. It is as a result of drawing on Jewish folklore that she creates a female golem, and it is in light of Jewish women's supportive role that she depends on the golem, her creation, and Rappoport, her ex-lover.

Puttermesser's Jewish tint, contradictory to her aspiration for gender equality, is also reflected in her treatment of Xanthippe. It seems that Puttermesser is feministic in being the first female creator of a female golem. However, despite the belief she expresses in her letters to Mayor Mavett that men and women should be judged on merit rather than on gender, she herself fails to treat Xanthippe as an intellectual equal. Instead, Xanthippe is treated as a Jewish wife and a domestic servant who is expected to clean and stay quiet. Even when Puttermesser praises Xanthippe as "cheerful and efficient, an industrious worker" for the contribution to her Mayoral rise, the praise is but analogous to Xanthippe's "zealous" cooking ability (127). There is tension between Puttermesser's attempt for gender equality in her golem creation and her actual treatment of Xanthippe.

It is common that golems are mute with no language capacity, however, Xanthippe, though mute, is capable of scribbling. Furthermore, Xanthippe even utters two words "my mother" (155) when Puttermesser sentimentally stares down on her during the de-creation ceremony. According to Gershom Sholem, "sinless beings would be able to transmit the soul of life, which includes the power of speech, even to a golem. Thus the golem is not mute by nature, but only because the souls of the righteous are no longer pure" (193). Golems can speak only if their creators possess pure souls.

Through Xanthippe's last words, the legitimacy of Puttermesser is established. Now that Xanthippe is capable of speech, if Ozick is following Scholem's principle, Puttermesser must be sinless and possess a pure soul. With a pure soul and with no sin, Puttermesser, who is both feministic and Jewish, is represented as a figure in the diasporic space, with the fissure and fusion of Jewishness and feminism.

In a sense, both Lucy Feingold in "Levitation" and Ruth Puttermesser in "Puttermesser and Xanthippe," with both their Jewish and feminist traces, represent Ozick's endeavor: she disrupts the fissure between feminism and Judaism and attempts to bring them into a fusion. As Jewish women, Lucy and Puttermesser are dually marginalized in Diaspora. Ozick's endeavor is constructing the minority in the dual marginality as the majority and presents it in her literary creation so as to give a voice of their own benefiting from the literary power of a Jewish woman writer.

In addition to Lucy and Puttermesser who are bearers of both feminist and Jewish traces in the diasporic space as a result of marital and professional oppression, in Ozick's works there are dichotomous mothers whose mothering, as a result of the oppression and racism in the Holocaust and its aftermath, shows characteristics that are seemingly unmotherly in light of the stereotyped motherhood, such as, Rosa in "The Shawl" and Hester Lilt in *The Cannibal Galaxy*. Their mothering demonstrates the de-stereotyped nature of the Jewish mothering under an extreme circumstance.

Ⅲ. Jewish Mothering in the Holocaust

The following analysis is to take as a sample the Jewish mothering of Rosa in the Holocaust in "The Shawl. " The focus is on the social construction of mothering, the dismantling of mothering stereotypes, and the way in which the racial tragedy and survival define a Jewish mother's role, and by extension, Jewish feminine identity in Ozick's diasporic space.

A. Mothering Stereotypes

The term "mother" is defined as "source, origin; a woman in authority" while "to mother" is "to care for or protect" (*Merriam-Webster's Dictionary*).

Chodorow emphasizes what she terms the "sense of oneness" between a child and the mother (78). She furthers attests that a child "develops a self only by convincing itself that it is in fact a separate being from [the mother]. . . . The infant comes to define itself as a person through its relationship to her, by internalizing the most important aspects of their relationship" (Chodorow 78).

Diane Eyer contends that "One of the most popular ideas in psychology is the notion of attachment, . . . which claimed mothers are biologically programmed to care for their children. . . this idea acts as the bedrock foundation for our contemporary standards of the Good Mother" (69).

Laying emphasis on protection, attachment, and oneness, however, these viewpoints fail to confront two basic issues: First, is it legitimate to apply contemporary standards to mothers from other eras under particular social impact? Second, what determines a mother's way to mother? Both nature and nurture should be taken into account, hence essentialism and social constructionism (Fishbone 6).

B. Essentialism and Social Constructionism

Diana Fuss presents useful definitions of essentialism and social constructionism for women. She defines essentialism as

> a belief in true essence—that which is most irreducible, unchanging, and therefore constitutive of a given person or thing. ... In feminist theory... essentialism can be located in appeals to a pure or original femininity, a female essence, outside the boundaries of the social and thereby untainted (though perhaps repressed) by a patriarchal order. (2)

According to essentialism, there are innate qualities in a mother that are genetically determined. It is these qualities that determine her thinking process and manipulate her decision-making process. However, co-existing with these innate qualities are environmental determinants.

Fuss also defines constructionism, suggesting that

> Constructionism, articulated in opposition to essentialism and concerned with its philosophical refutation, insists that essence is itself a historical construction... constructionists are concerned above all with the *production* and *organization* of differences, and they therefore reject the idea that any essential or natural givens precede the process of social determination. (2-3)

Fuss further draws upon Ernest Jones's question: "Is woman born or made?" to sum up the difference in philosophical positions. In his opinion, for an essentialist like Jones, woman is born, not made; for an anti-essentialist like Simone de Beauvoir, woman is made, not born (3). Then is a mother born or made?

A mother is chiefly bound to child rearing. No woman is born a mother capable of mothering, which necessitates advice-seeking. As Sharon Hays stresses in *The Cultural Contradictions of Motherhood*, mothers take advice from a variety of sources, including "their past and present social positions and their past and present cultural milieux... [and thus] in ... deciding what is worthy, individual mothers therefore actively engage in reshaping the social ideology of appropriate child rearing" (72). While reshaping the social ideology, the mothers, in the process of advice-seeking, are reshaped inevitably.

Hays reiterates that

> Every mother's ideas about mothering are shaped by a complex map of her class position, race, ethnic heritage, religious background, political beliefs, sexual preferences, physical abilities or disabilities, citizenship status, participation in various subcultures, place of residence, workplace environment, formal education, the techniques her own parents used to raise her—and more. (76)

Therefore, inadequacies with essentialism in isolation are self-evident in that the way a mother mothers and her process of decision-making are subjected to external events, as a result, her decisions are liable to be adjusted and affected.

The Holocaust, directly related to race, culture, and above all, to survival, presents such extenuating circumstances. Mothering during the Holocaust is doomed to differences from the stereotyped mothering, and the deviations are linked to the mother's ability to survive, as well as her ability to keep the offspring alive.

On the basis of distinct mothering in different circumstances, I would argue that a mother, although influenced by essential facets of her separate self, is made. Social constructionism, then, is at the crux of the discussion due to the Jewish-American mothers addressed within their specific environments. The mothers are "made."

Evelyn Nakano Glenn supports social constructionism, especially in discussing women and mothers who tend to be marginalized in society for secondary differences beyond gender. She notes that

> Third World women, women of color, lesbians, and working-class women began to challenge dominant European and American conceptions of womanhood, and [began] to insist that differences among women were as important as commonalities, [and thus] have brought alternative constructions of

motherhood into the spotlight. (3)

This argument "confirms that mothering... is socially constructed, not biologically inscribed" (3).

My discussion is to focus upon Jewish mothering under racial and cultural oppression in one of the most extreme circumstances, namely, in the Holocaust, as reflected in the crucial mothering character in "The Shawl." Ozick presents a dichotomous mother who is at once soft and hard, loving and cruel for the sake of her offspring. In the end, the mother makes choices regarding her child based upon the specific reality. Her choice demonstrates the de-stereotyped nature regarding how Jewish motherhood, and Jewish feminine identity by extension, should be defined and conducted.

C. Rosa in "The Shawl"

Despite the general understanding of mothering as caretaking, nurturing, and instructing, its primary function is protection that stems from the need of the survival of self and offspring, which will ensure the existence and continuity of the future generations of the family.

Survival is what Rosa has to deal with in "The Shawl"—the survival of herself, her daughter, and her niece in a concentration camp during the Nazi regime. Moreover, she is faced with a conflict, survival of body versus survival of voice, because in the Nazi regime, life and voice are not compatible. She has to decide whether to silence her daughter, whom she believes to be mute for months, to save the child's life, or to allow her to exhibit her recently acquired voice and die. Appreciating both and incapable of ensuring neither, Rosa hesitates and her daughter dies.

Vera Kielsky states that Ozick "regards the Holocaust as the central event in Jewish history" (28). Furthermore, for Jews the Holocaust is a "fundamental threat to continuity and integrity" (Powers 2001 23). Not surprisingly, the Holocaust, with racial and gender bias and persecution, has left its shaping mark on Rosa's mothering in "The Shawl."

Rosa, as a mother, is socially made, and her mothering is historically and culturally influenced, for her way of mothering and her process of decision-making are subject to the specific external environment.

As a mother, Rosa's first and foremost instinct is to protect her daughter, Magda, at all costs. As is expected in the Jewish community, "Woman [was] the bearer, the guardian, and preserver..., and only in so far as she carried out this, her primary function... [did] she come into her own domain" (Pappenheim 149). From the onset of the novella, Rosa serves as the all-encompassing mother to Magda. She was a "walking cradle" to Magda who was "curled up between sore breasts" (Ozick "The Shawl" 3-4). In the diasporic exile under the Nazi regime, she has to bury her baby "away deep inside the magic shawl, mistaken there for the shivering mound of Rosa's breasts," pretending to the world that she does not exist (5-6). She has to decide whether to keep Magda in "the little house of the shawl's windings" or to "leave the line for a minute and push Magda into the hands of any woman on the side of the road," denying and deserting her while at the same time preserving her (4). Since Magda is Aryan-looking as a result of a Nazi rape, it is likely that she would be raised.

Rosa's seemingly unmotherly and aberrant ideas and actions in her mothering are socially constructed by the environmental determinants in the concentration camp, where life and voice are incompatible. She has to deny her daughter's existence and silence her voice in order to preserve her life. Additionally, due to the Nazi policy that no infant should be spared, she has to decide whether to desert her in order to preserve her.

What results from her mothering is fear. She fears being shot. She also fears that the woman to whom she might hand Magda would not take her, or in surprise or fear, the woman might drop Magda and

Magda would die (4).

Rosa's decision comes from the environmental determinants in which her mothering is constructed. Fears of various kinds force Rosa to come to the conclusion that concealing her daughter in "the shawl as if it covered only herself" is the best way to protect her (Ozick "The Shawl" 6). Rosa stifles the voice and denies the existence of her child in order to ensure her survival.

The stifling of the child's voice and the denial of her existence have to occur every day in the marching and in the roll-call.

> Rosa had to conceal Magda under the shawl against a wall of the barracks and go out and stand in the arena with Stella and hundreds of others, sometimes for hours, and Magda, deserted, was quiet under the shawl, sucking on her corner. Every day Magda was silent, and so she did not die. (7)

Rosa abandons her fifteen-month-old baby every day in order to protect her. Both the child's existence and her voice have to be denied for survival. The child has to be deserted in silence and darkness in order to survive.

On account of the extreme circumstances, Rosa alters her mothering and takes seemingly aberrant steps for a loving mother in order to protect her child. Rosa "was afraid to fall asleep; she slept with the weight of her thigh on Magda's body; she was afraid she would smother Magda under her thigh" (6). But she has no other choice, for she fears both the Nazis and other victims in the barracks, including Stella, who might want to eat Magda to survive a bit longer. She has to risk smothering Magda with her thigh in order to save her from being killed by others. To her, potential killing in protecting is better than having the child maliciously killed.

Rosa's socially constructed mothering, apart from its altered mothering from the stereotype, is reflected as well in her self-adaptation. Rosa's own body must adapt so that she can give all of her food to her daughter. As Dalia Ofer and Lenore J. Weitzman note in the introduction to their collection of Holocaust commentaries, "Seeing their children and husbands endangered filled [women] with a sense of mission and superhuman strength—... [they spent] long days at exhausting work ... tried to ignore their own hunger while sharing their meager rations, and ... coped with rampant sickness" (10). This is exactly what Rosa does as a mother. In addition, she learns to "drink the taste of a finger in one's mouth" (Ozick "The Shawl" 5). She learns this from Magda, her child, who sucks on the shawl when there is literally nothing else.

Both Rosa's altered mothering and her self-adaptation suggest her readiness to succumb to the Nazi order and regime. In fact, what she has done is to learn to modify her mothering techniques within the changing environmental confines in order to offer stability in an unstable world and protect her offspring. Even if the instinct of protecting the offspring is innate to a loving mother, the process of mothering is socially constructed. Consequently, when the environment changes, a mother must adapt correspondingly. Rosa has to face her greatest challenge in the adaptation of her mothering.

Rosa's mothering, unmotherly and aberrant, has been altered at the mercy of the unimaginable horrors in the Nazi regime. Elaine Kauvar delineates that "It is silence that saves... it is silence and darkness which offer a chance for survival" (1993, 182).

However, Magda broke the silence and ran into the light one day when Rosa realizes "that today Magda was going to die," but as a mother, she tries everything she can to put off what is inevitable (7).

> Magda flopped onward with her little pencil legs scribbling this way and that, in search of the shawl; the pencils faltered at the barracks opening, where the light began. [...] But [...] Magda was in the square outside the barracks, in the jolly light. It was the roll-call arena. (7)

Stepping into the light, Magda utters a voice that reaffirms her existence that her mother has denied her. Watching Magda, "a fearful joy ran in Rosa's two palms, her fingers were on fire, she was astonished, febrile.... [for] Magda was howling" (7). For months, Rosa believed Magda was mute due to malnutrition and environmental issues.

> Rosa believed that something had gone wrong with [Magda's] vocal cords, with her windpipe, with the cave of her larynx; Magda was defective, without a voice; perhaps she was deaf; there might be something amiss with her intelligence; Magda was dumb. Even the laugh that came when the ash-stippled wind made a clown out of Magda's shawl was only the air-blown showing of her teeth. Even when the lice, head lice and body lice, crazed her so that she became as wild as one of the big rats that plundered the barracks at daybreak looking for carrion, she rubbed and scratched and kicked and bit and rolled without a whimper. But now Magda's mouth was spilling a long viscous rope of clamor. "Maaaa—". (7-8)

Magda's voice, for Rosa, serves as a hope whose absence has been accepted as common. However, the ephemeral feeling of hope is mixed with impending death, because of the incompatibility of voice and life. "A tide of commands hammered in Rosa's nipples: Fetch, get, bring! But she did not know which to go after first, Magda or the shawl" (8).

The conflict Rosa has to address is not simply "whether to get Magda or the shawl first, but rather, whether to save her child for a life of silence and horror in the camps with no sure outcome, or instead, to allow her to die with a voice that expresses not only her needs, her anger, her frustration, her indignation, but also her love" (Fishbone 100). Rosa is in a plight:

> If she jumped into the arena to snatch Magda up, the howling would not stop, because Magda would still not have the shawl; but if she ran back into the barracks to find the shawl, and if she found it, and if she came after Magda holding it and shaking it, then she would get Magda back, Magda would put the shawl in her mouth and turn dumb again. (8)

In such an abnormal and horrific situation, Rosa has to make decisions which are likewise horrific. She chooses to get the shawl first, for the sake of the life of her daughter, believing she will save her daughter's life with the sacrifice of her voice. The "voices" in the hum of the electric fence tell "her to hold up the shawl, high [...] to shake it, to whip with it, to unfurl it like a flat" and she "lifted, shook, whipped, unfurled" (9). However, Magda, who "leaned across her air-fed belly, reaching out with the rods of her arms," was already being carried off to be hurled at the electric fence by a Nazi soldier (9).

In this moment, asserts Lowin, "The maternal instinct and the instinct for self-preservation wage a silent battle within Rosa as, helpless, she observes the Nazi electrocute her daughter by hurling her against the fence" (1988, 107). At last, when "the steel voices went mad in their growling, urging Rosa to run and run to the spot where Magda had fallen from her flight against the electrified fence," unstereotypically, Rosa does "not obey them" (Ozick "The Shawl" 10). Ozick explains:

> [Rosa] only stood, because if she ran they would shoot, and if she tried to pick up the sticks of Magda's body they would shoot, and if she let the wolf's screech ascending now through the ladder of her skeleton break out, they would shoot; so she took Magda's shawl and filled her own mouth with it, stuffed it in and stuffed it in, until she was swallowing up the wolf's screech and tasting the cinnamon and almond depth of Magda's saliva; and Rosa drank Magda's shawl until it dried. (10)

Sarah Cohen contends that "near-dead Rosa must disown her baby" for her own survival. Now that Rosa cannot "publicly mourn for her," she has to "mother herself" with the shawl (148, 153, 152). As in Magda's case, Rosa's body has to be denied for its saving, and Rosa's voice has to be repressed for survival. As S. Lillian Kremer notes,

> Rosa must resist the instinctive maternal response. [...] She must deny her

> body in order to save it; she must still her despairing voice and mute her grief, stop her legs from running to the electrocuted child, and suppress her maternal impulse to honor the survival instinct, for to retrieve her baby's charred corpse will invite the guard's bullet for herself. Even her scream will be a prologue to death. Rosa muffles her cries in the shawl, now her life preserver. (152)

Torn between the grief of her lost daughter, the inability to mourn her publicly, and the last bit of innate desire for self-preservation, Rosa is rendered immobile and mute, as she once believed her daughter to be. The fact that the denial of the body for its saving and the repression of the voice for the survival occur in both Magda's and Rosa's cases points to the environmental determinants in the Holocaust, the marginality that Jewish women suffered.

Rosa's decision and choice have resulted from the judgment she makes as a critical thinker on the basis of the assessment of the actual conditions she is forced to face. Despite the superficial de-stereotyped nature, Rosa's mothering is meant to protect and save. Hiding the baby in the shawl and denying its existence is considered the best way for protection while potential killing in protecting is deemed better than having the child maliciously killed.

While mothers are stereotypically viewed as soft, selfless, and abounding with patience, in fact, they have the capacity to be selfish, angry, and cruel in the process of being protective of their charges.

Mothers, by extension women, work to maintain what they regard as right in terms of their definitions of life resultant from their critical thinking. Adrienne Rich contends that a woman's, a mother's, "choices—when she has any—are made, or outlawed, within the context of laws and professional codes, religious sanctions and ethnic traditions, from whose creation women have been historically excluded" (128). While mothers are expected to be charged with the protection, at all costs, of the children of whom they are the source or guardian, they are deprived of the necessary rights or power to make the rules in the materialization of the protection.

Motherhood, by extension femininity, then, must come into its own. Sarah Ruddick re-establishes motherhood in asserting the "mother's *thought* — the intellectual capacities she develops, the judgments she makes, the metaphysical attitudes she assumes, the values she affirms" (214). Ruddick gives motherhood power and essence in suggesting that a mother "establishes criteria for the truth, adequacy, and relevance of proposed answers; and she cares about the findings she makes and can act on" (214). She also discerns that "The discipline of maternal thought consists in establishing criteria for determining failure and success, in setting the priorities, and in identifying the virtues and liabilities the criteria assume" (214). Her reestablishment of motherhood with such power and essence allows one to truly examine the Jewish mothering under duress. For example, Rosa chooses to conceal her daughter in the shawl, stifling the voice and denying the existence of her child in order to ensure her survival; she considers giving away her Aryan-looking daughter, knowing she would be likely raised by the enemy, in order to save her; she sleeps with a potentially crushing leg on Magda to make sure she does not lose her; she resists the instinctive maternal response to mute her grief over the loss of her daughter. In short, Rosa's mothering is featured by the judgments she makes on specific occasions as a result of her intellectual capacities that allow her to keep herself, and those in her charge, alive or in the best place possible.

Rosa, as a mother, has the obligation to determine what the appropriate mothering is in her situation. The source of her decision and choice stems from what Sarah Ruddick terms "mother's thought." In Rosa's "mother's thought," the corresponding virtues are nonexistence resulting from immobility and silence, superficial denial and deserting, and potential killing in protecting outweighing having the child maliciously killed.

What primarily features her "mother's thought" is the social reality that a female, in both Magda's case and hers, when denied as non-

existent, deserted and mute, can temporally survive, however, once
she is ready to give an expression, she has to be silenced at the cost of
her life. Rosa's motherhood is forced as a result of Nazi raping while
her mothering has been constructed in a society which has not always
been friendly to a Jewish woman, who is dually marginalized in the
Holocaust. It's not her fault for all the altered mothering. It's not her
fault to choose life over voice. It's not her fault to sacrifice Magda's
voice for her life. It's not her fault to sacrifice her voice for her own
life. If Rosa's mothering seems unmotherly, it is because "the culture
blames mothers for what's wrong with society" (Eyer title).

As is reflected in Rosa's mothering in the Holocaust, Jewish
femininity in Ozick's vision is not only featured by the stereotyped
protective role but also by altered protection dependent upon subjective
judgment in accordance with given environmental determinants. What
is highlighted is the subjective judgment of the females as resultant
from *thought*, the intellectual capacities, which has been ignored by
Orthodox Judaism.

To sum up, the construction of Jewish femininity under
oppression, including the marital oppression as is shown in Lucy,
professional oppression as is shown in Puttermesser, and the oppression
and persecution from the Holocaust as is shown in Rosa, reveals
Ozick's efforts in casting feminist visions into Judaism so as to disrupt
the fissure and establish the fusion, and in turning both Jewishness and
femininity from minority into majority.

With the marginalization of Jewishness, the allegiance to Judaism
and Jewish values consequently ends up as the "minority." Ozick's
practice in imbuing Judaism with feminist visions is evidence of her
steadfast allegiance to Judaism, which finds its expression in Ozick's
feminist mending of the Orthodox Judaic gender law.

IV. "Eros of Ideas": Feminist Mending of Orthodox Judaic Gender Law

In *Honey Mad Women: Emancipatory Strategies in Women's Writing*, Patricia Yaeger describes the ways women seek freedom through writing as "emancipatory strategies" including "use of fragmented texts" and "play with language," and she argues that women writers take pleasure in strategically writing their way out of the patriarchal bondage (18).

Due to Ozick's own strategy of "cannibalizing" and "usurping" other writers' works and transforming them within the body of her own writing, it is particularly apt for reading Ozick to draw on Patricia Yaeger's use of the metaphor of the "honey-mad woman" in her examination of the works of the 19th-century women writers to represent how women writers pleasurably devour language in order to transform it. For instance, in her "Preface" in *Bloodshed and Three Novellas*, Ozick acknowledges her "prey" for her novella "Usurpation":

> The tale called 'The Magic Crown' in my story is a paraphrase, except for a twist to its ending of Malamud's 'The Silver Crown'; the account of the disappointed messiah is Agnon's; and David Stern's 'Agnon, A Story' is the mischievous seed of my metamorphosis of the Nobel Prize winner. (7-8)

Similar themes are apparent in *The Cannibal Galaxy*, "Virility," and the Puttermesser stories.

Yaeger further points out that women writers "devour and transform patriarchal language inimical to their identities as women" (134). Ozick is confronted with a dual challenge of transforming myths antagonistic both to her identity as a woman and as a Jew.

Though Ozick resists the label of "woman writer," she has actually employed some of the so-called feminist literary strategies, in particular, play with language. It is not as important whether these literary strategies are feminist as whether Ozick's employment of these strategies is feminist in effect.

Before coming to the illustration of her strategy employment, I'll first present its guideline.

A. "Eros of Ideas"

Intending not to write like a woman, Ozick distances herself from other Jewish women writers, such as E. M. Broner, Erica Jong, and Grace Paley who reclaim the female body. Ozick repudiates the notion of writing from the body and attempts instead to create what Moelis calls an "Eros of ideas" (105).

Ozick has been criticized as an "overly cerebral writer," which, ironically, is what she parodies herself in Puttermesser, who has been argued by critics as her alter-ego. In addition, in "Defenders of the Faith," a review of both Ozick's *The Messiah of Stockholm* and Philip Roth's *The Counterlife*, Robert Alter, the author of *Defenses of the Imagination* (1977), points out Ozick's lack of imagination and comments that she attempts to compensate for the lack with "razzle dazzle" of language. The "violent extravagance of [her] metaphors," he argues, "betrays an attempt to substitute rhetorical intensity for experiential depth" (Alter 53-54).

Ozick's style, however, reflects not only her role as a "defender" of Jewish identity, but also as a somewhat defensive woman who has been excluded from the Jewish literary circle. Rendering her language "cerebral" and "genderless," she is determined not to be mistaken for a "woman writer."

For Ozick, writing and ideas themselves are a passion, like Puttermesser, who has the "habit of flushing with ideas as if they were passions" (Ozick "Puttermesser and Xanthippe" 99), and who "caresses [the] meticulousness" of the "law and its language" (82). There's little difference between what Alter terms Ozick's "wild hyperbole [that] knows no limits" (53) and Portnoy's imaginings of "going wild in public" (Roth 1985 278). As Moelis argues, "If Roth's

Portnoy takes pleasure and finds liberation from sexual repression in talk of masturbation, Ozick's characters find erotic and emancipatory pleasure in talking about language and in the self-reflexivity of word play" (113). Therefore, Ozick's writing and ideas constitute her own kind of eroticism, which does not so much *represent* the "human" and the "sexual," but itself embodies passion.

What Ozick is after is neither Helénè Cixous's idea of *jouissance*, with wild abandon in pleasure and freedom of imagination, nor Roland Barthes's sheer indulgence in language, for her imagination, however feminist it is, has Jewish imagination as the premise while her indulgence in language is confined against the risk of idolatry. Her eroticism, instead, more closely resembles the kind of passion Audre Lorde, a feminist writer, describes in her essay "Uses of the Erotic: The Erotic as Power." In Lorde's explanation, the erotic is not confined to sexual passion, but deeply connected to any pursuit-physical, emotional, or intellectual (53-59).

Drawing upon Lorde's theory, Judith Plaskow, a Jewish feminist, illustrates the role of the erotic in feminist spiritual pursuits in *Standing Again at Sinai: Judaism from a Feminist Perspective* (196-206). In response to Julia Kristeva's theory that to speak and write as a woman is to suffer, Patricia Yaeger argues that women writers take pleasure in their emancipatory writing out of the patriarchal bondage, which sheds additional light on the connection between eroticism and Ozick's intellectual pursuit.

However, what differentiates Ozick from Yaeger's subjects is while they rebel in order to break away from the patriarchal institutions, Ozick intends to integrate herself within Jewish literary and religious traditions.

Powered by an "Eros of ideas," Ozick employs literary strategy considered by some critics as feminist to claim her place as a Jewish writer. The following analysis focuses on Ozick's employment of one of the emancipatory strategies, namely, flights of imagination as a specific embodiment of "play with language."

B. Imagination for the Female Protagonists: "Conjuring" and "Purifying"

Insisting that her writings are informed by Judaism, not by femininity, Ozick advises the critics on reading her work, hinting and often warning them that she is a Jewish writer, not a woman writer. One of the most explicit statements in this regard is made in "Literature and the Politics of Sex: A Dissent," where she calls *woman writer* a "new political term" (Ozick *Art &Ardor* 284) and claims that "Outside its political uses, 'woman writer' has no meaning—not intellectually, not morally, not historically" (285). What she rejects in "woman writer" is the identity as a writer who writes as a woman.

I suggest, however, what distinguishes Ozick from other Jewish women writers is more her identity as a writer who writes for women and further for Judaism than her identity as a writer who writes as a woman. Via feminist mending of the prohibiting Orthodox Judaic gender law, which stems from Ozick's moral weighing of the prohibition and the necessity to bring it to a feminist mending in her literary practice, Ozick eventually achieves the allegiance she pays to Judaism.

Therefore, Ozick, emphasizing feminist visions rather than stressing femininity, imbues feminine representation with "Eros of ideas." Conjuring fantasized flights of imagination itself is likely to be mared in idolatry for Ozick, and the "Jewish writer" must dialectically shift between "conjuring" and "purifying" (Ozick *Art &Ardor* 198). What distinguishes Ozick's construction of imagination flights for the female protagonists is that they are not only conjured but also purified. While the process of "conjuring" flights of imagination is passion-driven and suggestive of Eros, the process of their "purifying" is idea-oriented in essence.

I'll illustrate Ozick's conjuring and purifying fantasized flights of imagination in "Levitation," "Rosa" (the sequel of "The Shawl" in *The Shawl*), and "Puttermesser and Xanthippe."

a. Lucy's Flight of Imagination

As is argued in the previous chapter about "Levitation", Ozick's description of Lucy's writing in relation to her role as Jimmy's wife conforms to the traditional status of women in Orthodox Judaic law: domestic and supportive. However, as a writer, Lucy's abandonment of her hostess responsibilities at her party and her rebellion against Orthodox Judaic laws represent Ozick's wish that women writers carve their way into the male-dominated Jewish literary tradition.

Fantasized imagination is conjured for Lucy in her vision when she witnesses her husband and the other Jews levitating higher and higher into the air. The dancing men's performances in her imaginary vision suggest male homosexuality.

In the vision, she stands in a small park and witnesses a musical performance, in which a dozen men fill the platform, mostly middle-aged, some young, and one old. One young man begins the ritual by churning butter, while others follow by blowing into pipes (16-17). Figuratively, this performance implies sodomy in the butter churning and fellatio in the pipe blowing. The songs produced by the "instruments" are suggestive. In Lucy's fantasized imagination, there are only men performing the "instruments," and the female anthropologist, the only woman on stage, disappears out of the vision. It is suggestive that the dancing men are indulging themselves in homosexual desires: "a pair of [male] dancers seize each other. Leg winds over leg, belly into belly, each man hopping on a single free leg. Intertwined, they squat and rise, squat and rise. They send out elastic cries" (18).

Watching the dancing performances in her fantasized imagination, Lucy feels "glorified [....] exalted. She comprehends" (18).

Homosexuality conflicts with Judaism's tenet, for the Orthodox

Jews believe God intended sex only for procreation. Homosexuality represents an affront against God in its failure to bring about covenanted offspring. Jewish law considers homosexuality sinful, and witnessing non-Jewish men publicly engage in acts suggestive of homosexuality reveals to Lucy the limitations of Orthodox Judaism. Characterized as a converted Jew, Lucy's idea is not necessarily that of Ozick's, however, together with Lucy's comprehension is Ozick's passion for ideas in her writing. The fantasized flight of imagination that Ozick allows for Lucy reflects her critique of the Jewish laws pertaining to women for limiting women's intellectual freedom, the marginalization of women in their passionate literary expression.

When Lucy realizes that she forfeited her intellectual independence by marrying Jimmy, she rebels. She rejects the Jewish laws that have impeded her artistic progress. No longer will she have to rely on her husband's creativity. Ozick's idea is her advocacy for gender equality in American society, in fiction, and in Judaism.

With the fantasized flight of imagination, Ozick enables Lucy to emancipate herself from the oppression in her marriage, which Ozick compares with the gender biases that affect critical receptions of women writers. In *Art and Ardor*, Ozick discusses critics' presumptions concerning men's and women's fiction:

> The political term *woman writer* signals in advance a whole set of premises: that, for instance, there are 'male' and 'female' states of intellect and feeling, hence of prose; that individuality of condition and temperament do not apply, or at least not much, and that all writing women possess—not by virtue of being writers but by virtue of being women-an instantly perceived common ground. (284)

It is Ozick's idea that marginalizing women's intellectual capabilities perpetuates a separation of sexes, which she believes undermines the creative capacities women could contribute to the literary community.

While Ozick enables Lucy to witness what men are free to enjoy in their self-expression in her conjured flights of imagination, she conjures flights of imagination for Rosa in the post-Holocaust to heal from the traumatic memories of mothering and the grief of losing her daughter for rebirth of her own.

b. Rosa as a Woman Writer

"The loss of the daughter to the mother . . . is the essential female tragedy" (Rich 237). After witnessing her daughter's death, Rosa is torn between grief and the inability to mourn in public, rendered immobile and mute. In the post-Holocaust, after tearing down her antique shop in New York for the customers' indifference to her Holocaust testimony, she lives in a hotel in Miami, scavenging paper so that she can write letters to her deceased daughter.

Letter writing constitutes her life, and Rosa, with the flights of imagination conjured by Ozick, becomes a woman writer, distinguished by an imaginative sensibility, the ability to creatively use domestic, ordinary materials, and the desire to create meaning and order out of her experience of writing.

While writing for Ozick is an intellectual passion in presenting ideas, the flights of imagination for Rosa are somewhat a healing of the trauma when there are no other alternatives to rely upon. While Rosa, in writing, emancipates herself from grief, Ozick, in employing the emancipatory strategy, namely, in conjuring fantasized flights of imagination, gives voice to a woman writer, an oppressed and victimized being who is characterized as an imaginative creator.

First of all, Rosa's imaginative sensibility is reflected in the fact that both the past and the future witness their presence in the letters. It is likewise reflected in the establishment of the connection between grandmother and granddaughter, and the gendering of the child as female in the "motherline." The imaginative sensibility highlights the continuity, which is actually in absence. Rosa's writing, then, is historically meaningful.

In the letters Rosa not only recounts her past but also reinvents time in creating an imaginary future for her deceased daughter, an unmarked territory which she hopes will offer more possibilities than she herself experienced. Non-linearity is established as a result of the disruption of the chronological time. Three reveries reveal the mother's invention of the life that she expects Magda to have. Rosa visualizes Magda as a lovely young girl of sixteen at the threshold of adulthood; at thirty-one, a physician married to a physician living in a large house in a New York suburb; or a professor of Greek philosophy at a prestigious university.

In addition, the mother-child connection skips a generation and forms between grandmother and granddaughter. Rosa recalls with great fondness the Yiddish lullabies her grandmother once sang to her. Her own mother forbade the speaking of Yiddish, which was distained as a hybrid language. What's more, Ozick's gendering of the grandchild as female establishes a "motherline" and locates Rosa as both an inheritor and a transmitter of culture and rescues her from silence, in particular with Rosa's imagination of Magda as a painter or musician.

Second, Rosa transforms domesticity from the ordinary and everyday into the beautiful and transcendent. A shawl, the central symbol of the text, resonates as both a domestic and sacred object when it is transformed from the garment that once cradled the infant Magda to the vehicle which carries a mother's prayers. By transforming domesticity, the female is at the same time transformed from a domestic being into an imaginative creator. Therefore, Rosa's writing is intellectually meaningful.

Third, Rosa is a witness and survivor who is situated inside, rather than marginal to, history. Her experience becomes the vehicle for a critique of racial oppression and persecution. Rosa is represented as an angry prophet who warns that the apocalypse, in the form of the Holocaust, has already come.

Rosa's search for meaning and order and her desire to tell the story of her experience have enabled her to channel her creative passion into her writing so as to divert herself from the traumatic memories and consequently give birth to herself. As a mother incapable of normal mothering, Rosa witnesses the death of her daughter. She has experienced guilt, despair and melancholia. Her letters to Magda represent an attempt to heal her grief. The pursuit of creativity and self-expression provides her with an opportunity for regeneration and rebirth. Consequently, Rosa's writing is morally meaningful.

In short, Rosa's writing, as resultant from Ozick's conjuring flights of imagination, is historically, intellectually and morally meaningful. This recalls what Ozick claims of the label of a "woman writer" in *Art &Ardor*, "Outside its political uses, 'woman writer' has no meaning—not intellectually, not morally, not historically" (285). The fact that Rosa, characterized as a woman writer in the flights of imagination conjured by Ozick, writes in an intellectually, morally, and historically meaningful way reveals Ozick's idea that Rosa, a woman, is writing as an intellectual equal to men writers. Therefore, the conjured flights of imagination are purified.

Like Lucy and Rosa, Puttermesser is characterized as a marginalized female protagonist under oppression. While fantasized flights of imagination are conjured to Lucy and Rosa respectively, Puttermesser conjures hers.

c. Puttermesser's Flights of Imagination

Puttermesser confronts great difficulty, if not futility, in attempting to gain equal status in the Department of Receipts and Disbursements with her male colleagues. Despite her diligent efforts, she is rendered invisible and becomes an outcast. Ozick conjures for Puttermesser two flights of imagination, the imagined Uncle Zindel, and Puttermesser's creation of a female golem.

1. The Imagined Uncle Zindel

The flight of imagination is first conjured in Uncle Zindel, a *melamed* （teacher） from the "old country," who helps with Puttermesser's nightly studies of Hebrew. With the imaginary uncle, Puttermesser establishes a temporary connection to her Jewish past. Each night, she takes Hebrew lessons and engages in the banter with this lively imagined uncle. Chewing a hard-boiled egg, Zindel himself presents the Hebrew characters in a vivid manner. "First see how a *gimmel* and which way a *zayen*. Twins, but one kicks a leg left, one right. You got practice the difference. If legs don't work, think pregnant bellies. Mrs. *Zayen* pregnant in one direction, Mrs *Gimmel* in the other" (35). Puttermesser indulges herself in the imaginary world, and Uncle Zindel begins to arrange for Puttermesser's move to Israel where she will find a husband.

However, the narrator breaks into the imagined scene and interrupts: "Stop. Stop, stop! Puttermesser's biographer, stop! Disengage, please. Though it is true that biographies are invented, not recorded, here you invent too much. A symbol is allowed, but not a whole scene" (35). Commanding Puttermesser's biographer to return Zindel to the dust of his long-ago crumbled *shul* (synagogue), the narrator shatters Puttermesser's imagined world in emphasizing that Zindel's shul was not torn down or even abandoned, but that over time it disintegrated. "The congregation too began to flake off—the women first, wife after wife after wife, each one a pearl and a consolation, until there they stand, the widowers, frail, gazing, palsy-struck [until] they too flake away" (36). While Puttermesser "demands connection—surely a Jew must own a past" (36), this connection to an immigrant past is worn out.

It is Ozick who conjures the imagined world and then shatters it. The reason for its conjuring lies in the necessity to establish a connection to the Jewish past while the reason for its shattering is that Uncle Zindel in a sense represents Jewish tradition that does not recognize women as intellectual equals, for his attempted arrangement of moving Puttermesser to Israel to find a husband. Therefore, the purifying of this conjured flight of imagination lies in its voluntary deconstruction.

Ozick's rejection of Zindel, the immigrant ancestor, somewhat gestures her intention in separating herself from the other contemporary Jewish writers who write about the immigrant experience and have thus defined themselves. In contrast, Ozick seeks entrance to Jewish religious and mythic traditions. Putting Uncle Zindel to rest, Ozick conjures a wilder imaginative flight for Puttermesser in manipulating Puttermesser to take the role of a creator, not a biological producer of children, but a creator of a female golem, who will satisfy Puttermesser's craving for imagination, and who will help Ozick to assert herself in the male-dominated literary world. Above all, through this wilder imaginative flight, a connection to the Jewish past is established.

Uttering aloud the holy letters of the Name of Names, *heh, shin, mem* (in Hebrew, *hashem*, literally "the name," referring to God), inscribing on the slip of paper on the golem's tongue, Puttermesser brings to life a female golem.

Puttermesser's creation of a female golem, resultant from Ozick's flights of imagination, reflects Ozick's attempts to disrupt the fissure between feminism and Judaism and to bring them into a fusion.

2. The Rewriting of the Golem Legend

In "The Idea of the Golem," Gershom Sholem, the historian of Jewish mysticism, presents a history of a variety of myths relating to the golem. Generally, the golem is a creature made from clay and water, which when breathed upon, and with the utterance of the holy Name, is given life. According to the legends, the purpose of the golem, such as the famous golem of Prague, is to save the Jewish community. After the golem has accomplished its mission, it must be destroyed. Among the most distinguishing characteristics of the golem are its inability to speak or love, and its lack of sexual urge, lest it be dangerous to women. Gershom Scholem notes what he deems "the utterances. . . of a modern author inclining toward Kabbalism, which he puts into the mouth of the 'Great Rabbi Loew' of Prague. . . 'The golem had to be made without generative power or sexual urge, for if he had this urge, even after the manner of animals in which it is far weaker than in man, we would have had a great deal of trouble with him, because no woman would have been able to defend herself against him' " (Sholem 1965 194). Though most golems are male, Scholem mentions several female golems, created by men, whose functions are domestic and sexual. The most famous of these is Ibn Gabirol's creation of a female golem. Scholem, quoting a seventeenth-century Jewish author, points out that "he created a woman who waited on him. When he was denounced to the government [evidently for magic], he proved that she was not a real, whole creature, but consisted only of pieces of wood and hinges, and reduced her to her original components. And there are many such legends that are told by all, especially in Germany" (199).

Puttermesser created the golem after her frequent demotions. It is out of her feminist pursuit for equality that she turns to the Jewish legend, the golem creation. While Puttermesser is among the first female creators of a golem, Ozick as author innovates with the golem legend in terms of both women's voices and women's sexuality (Moelis 124).

Noticing the creature's imperfections, Puttermesser begins to reshape them and her special attention is paid to the mouth, which signifies eroticism and expression: it "above all required finishing" (94). Just as Puttermesser remolds the golem's body, Ozick reshapes the legend of the golem, thereby altering and recasting Jewish literary and religious traditions.

Like other conventional golems, Xanthippe cannot speak. Ozick, however, makes a crucial alteration in this aspect of the legend by endowing Xanthippe the capacity to write. In addition, her self-assertion, as the projection of her voice, is apparent in her self-naming. Rejecting the name "Leah" after Puttermesser's imagined daughter, the golem insists on "Xanthippe," the shrewish wife of Socrates (97-98), the only person who "had the courage to gainsay him" (105).

Ozick not only gives a voice to the female golem but also frees her from the traditional role for men's sexual pleasure and domestic service. As a result, the patriarchal Jewish myth is feministically rewritten.

In contrast to Ibn Gabirol's female golem, created to serve and wait on him, Xanthippe is self-gratifying and ambitious. Soon tired of cleaning, cooking and shopping, Xanthippe steps beyond the domestic bounds and helps Puttermesser with her professional rise to the mayor of New York. Ozick has transformed the meaning of "golem" from its Talmudic connotation of a physically barren woman (Goldsmith 16) to one of intellectual power.

However, with rampant sexuality running out of control, Xanthippe's self-gratification turns out to be destructive. Devouring man after man, the golem destroys the New York she has helped to rebuild and jeopardizes Puttermesser's "well-earned" position as mayor. Xanthippe's rampant sexuality is somewhat a parody of feminism and imagination taken too far.

With her self-gratifying and ambitious female golem, Ozick parodies and thus transforms what is generally a sexist legend. Through her creation, Ozick shifts the role of women from sexual objects and domestic servants to active intellectual equals, and at the same time finds a way to establish a connection to the Jewish tradition.

While conjuring flights of imagination, Ozick always bears in mind the "purifying" aspect of Abraham as combating the "conjuring" aspect of Terach (Ozick *Art & Ardor* 198), hence Ozickian ideas in each conjured flight of imagination.

In Lucy's case, the idea is that marginalization of women's intellectual capabilities perpetuates a separation of sexes, which undermines the creative capacities women could contribute to the literary community. In Rosa's case, the idea is that a woman writer can by all means write, as a man, in an intellectually, morally, and historically meaningful way. In Puttermesser's case, the idea is that women as active intellectual equals are capable of establishing a connection to the Jewish tradition and carving a place into man-dominance.

Ozick's Jewish feminist imagination is, in nature, Jewish imagination due to the co-existence of the "purifying" Abraham and the "conjuring" Terach. With all the ideas resulting from the "purifying" aspect, Ozick not merely presents a feminist world view that confronts the patriarchal nature of Judaism, she intends to mend Judaism, as she advocates, in concluding her essay "Notes Toward Finding the Right Question," to "mend" Torah by working into it the missing Commandment: "Thou shalt not lessen the humanity of women" (150).

The Jewish nature of Ozick's feminist imagination is further attested in her denial of the feminist motives in repairing Torah as she emphasizes that the purpose of such mending is not for the sake of women, nor for the broader good of the Jewish people, but to "preserve and strengthen Torah itself" (151). Therefore, Ozick, likewise, intends to preserve and strengthen Judaism itself when she integrates feminist ideas into Judaism, which attests to the authentically Jewish nature of her creation.

In short, with literary representation of female protagonists who are at once acquiescent to and rebellious against Orthodox Judaic gender law, Ozick is aiming to foreground both Jewishness and femininity. With representation of Jewish mothering in the Holocaust, Ozick highlights "mothers' thoughts," integrating feminist insight into Jewish femininity. With flights of imagination both conjured and purified, "Eros of ideas" is fulfilled, and the Jewish nature of Ozick's feminist imagination is revealed. With the insistence on mending

Judaism for its own sake, Ozick's authentic Jewishness bespeaks itself. Therefore, the dual minorities, Jewishness and femininity, are represented as the majority in Ozick's characterization of female protagonists and the Jewish mother in the Holocaust whereas Ozick's allegiance to Judaism is eventually materialized via her moral ethos in mending Orthodox Judaic gender law prohibiting women from acting as men's intellectual equals and in creating "Eros of ideas."

Chapter Five

Jewishness and Literary Narrative

As is foregrounded in the conflicts between Jewishness and "literature as idol," Jewishness and history representation, and Jewishness and feminine representation, moral ethos is manifest in Ozick's application of postmodernist literary narrative for her realistic needs, to stay Jewish. As a matter of fact, Ozick expands the scope of moral ethos to her employment of literary narrative.

In the postmodernist context, postmodernism dominates and acts as the prevailing trend, hence the "majority." With the marginalization of Jewishness, Ozick's wish to foreground Jewish visions through literary practice based on her allegiance to Judaic belief leading to her realistic needs to stay Jewish consequently turns out to be the "minority." However, the "minority" is foregrounded as a result of Ozick's highlighting of the moral ethos in weighing the postmodernist literary narrative and her realistic needs, which eventually gives birth to the realistic function that these postmodernist literary narratives serve in her fiction.

In the influential essay "The Debate on Postmodernism," the American literary theorist Hans Bertens asserts that postmodernism is, from the start, "many things at once" (Bertens 4). During the long-term debate on postmodernism, theorists hold diversified viewpoints. Brian McHale suggests that the shift from modernist fiction to postmodernist fiction is "the shift from epistemological dominant to an ontological one" (McHale 10). Susan Sontag and Leslie Fiedler revolt against the pretentiousness and the privileging of timeless, transcendent "meaning" that are associated with modernism. Mike Featherstone and Scott Lash define postmodernism as a life style based on consumption and an aestheticization of experience. And Michel Foucault proposes the absence of representation and lays emphasis on power. With regard to the postmodernist writings, David Lodge lists five strategies, namely, contradiction, discontinuity, randomness, excess and short circuit while Ihab Hassan puts forward two distinctive features of indeterminacy and immanence.

Therefore, postmodernism, as a cultural phenomenon in the Western world, is complicated, plural and synthetic. While the theoretical basis is a mixture of all kinds of philosophies, sociologies and ideological trends, its literary practice reflects distinct aesthetic propositions and artistic pursuits. However, postmodernist fiction, as a whole, advocates thorough pluralism in thinking modes, writing techniques, artistic genres and language games. It subverts the internal formation and structure of traditional novels, and shows its doubt about form and narrative likewise. For postmodernists, there are no transcendent meanings at all in the world and the so-called meanings are only produced by artificial language signs.

In *The Postmodern Turn: Essays in Postmodern Theory and Culture*, American critic and scholar Ihab Hassan amply elaborates postmodernist features and defends the liberal values of pluralism. He contends that modernism and postmodernism coexist—except that new lines merge from the past—until the latter rises. Therefore, changes take place in concepts that used to constitute modernism like urbanism, technologism, dehumanization, experimentalism, etc., and they are redefined in the realm of postmodernism. The focus of these concepts shifts from doubtable nature, emphasis on style, new languages and new concepts of order, to the bold postmodernist conception of Global Village and Spaceship Earth, contention of antielitism, antiauthoritarianism, communal, optional and anarchic art as well as open, discontinuous, improvisional, indeterminate self-reflexive structures. These changes are embodied in art, especially in literature. Consequently, new postmodernist fictional formats emerge accordingly, including the French New Novel, the Black Humor Novel, the Latin American Magic Realist Novel, the Metafiction, and the Postmodernist Historical Novel, etc.

Writing in a postmodernist context, Ozick applies postmodernist literary narrative, as postmodernism acts as the "majority" in the diasporic space. However, there is inconformity to the postmodernist tenets in Ozick's employment of these postmodernist literary narratives. They are employed, instead, to serve her realistic needs to stay Jewish, the "minority" in the diasporic space. It is with the application of the postmodernist literary narrative featured by "indeterminacy" that Ozick's determinate realistic needs to stay authentically Jewish are satisfied.

While criticizing "The novel is now said to be 'about itself,' a ceremony of language" (Ozick "Towards a New Yiddish" *Art & Ardor* 164), Ozick highlights the Judaized novels in the inspiration of the Jewish covenant and the concern with "conduct" when she pointed out "The novel at its nineteenth-century pinnacle was a Judaized novel: George Eliot and Dickens and Tolstoy were all touched by the Jewish covenant: they wrote of conduct and of the consequences of conduct: they were concerned with a society of will and commandment" (164).

In her own literary practice, when it comes to the employment of literary narrative, Ozick's conduct and the consequences of her conduct merit critical attention. What governs the conduct and the consequences is but her moral ethos in highlighting the "minority" via its mergence with the "majority" in the diasporic space, which bespeaks the Jewishness in Ozick's fiction.

Cynthia Ozick has employed such postmodernist literary narrative as "heteroglossia" and "polyphonic narrative," "metafictional intrusion narrative," "writing degree zero," and "intertextuality" in her fiction to highlight the moral ethos in the diasporic space.

In highlighting the moral ethos concerning Jewishness and "literature as idol," especially when the relationship between idolatry and imagination is elaborated, as in "The Pagan Rabbi," Ozick presents "heteroglossia" and turns to "polyphonic narrative."

I. Heteroglossia and Polyphonic Narrative

"Heteroglossia" is featured by diversities of discourses in which none of the individual voices is privileged and each authorizes itself.

In "The Pagan Rabbi," as is analyzed in Chapter Two, the diversities of discourses are embodied in the voices of the three characters, and Ozick's voice is among the collision between the three voices relating to the attitude to and attribute of imagination as the primary means for literary representation, and to pity consequent on the capability or incapability of imagination which leads to success or failure to sympathize and empathize.

As an artistic orchestration of a diversity of the distinct discourses, the story, with its employment of hereroglossia and polyphonic narrative, represents the component oppositions in Ozick's meditations on the relationship between Jewishness and imagination.

The collision between the oppositions as represented in the distinct discourses is based on Ozick's self-positioned paradox pertinent to the relationship between idolatry and imagination, and by extension, to the relationship between Jewishness and representation of literature. Furthermore, the collision, and in particular the Jewish insistence on idolatry resistance, is presented via Ozick's literary practice as a result of her imagination.

It is Ozick's imaginative representation that has made manifest her resistance against idolatry in imagination as idol. Heteroglossia and polyphonic narrative is but to illustrate the opposing forces that struggle in the conflict whereas Ozick's Jewish vision of anti-idolatry is eventually highlighted as the subject matter in her imaginative representation. Her realistic intention to stay Jewish is satisfied via her application of postmodernist heteroglossia and polyphonic narrative.

Among others, the fundamental basis for heteroglossia and polyphonic narrative is but the distinctive features of the distinct discourses, which result from distinction and lead to judgments.

The capacity of distinction-making is valued as one of the two momentous standards in the Jewish Idea. In "Bialik's Hint," Ozick argues,

> The Jewish Idea, I believe, was characterized by two momentous standards. The first, the standard of anti-idolatry, led to the second, the standard of distinction-making—the understanding that the properties of one proposition are not the properties of another proposition. Together, these two ideals, in the form of urgencies, had created Jewish history. (Ozick *Metaphor & Memory* 224)

The two momentous standards for Jewish Ideas are both highlighted: anti-idolatry serves as the subject matter while distinction-making acts as the source of the awareness of the opposing claims of Jewishness and "literature as idol," and furthermore, the premise of their literary presentation. It is on the basis of the understanding that imagination, in its conventional sense, is not of the properties that define Jewishness, hence the necessity for "the fusion of secular aesthetic culture with Jewish sensibility" (Ozick *Metaphor & Memory* 229), which Ozick has attempted. It is distinction-making that initiates her tension as being a Jew and a writer whereas it is the practice of fusing imagination with Jewish sensibility that has established her status as an acclaimed American Jewish writer.

In addition, it is with the capacity to make judgments that Ozick comes to the decision to foreground idolatry-resistance in her literary creation. Her practice is a testimony to her view that "The Jewish writer, if he intends himself really to be a Jewish writer, is all alone, judging culture like mad, while the rest of culture just goes on being culture" (Ozick *Art & Ardor* 166).

In foregrounding the moral ethos relating to Jewishness and history representation, Ozick utilizes "metafiction" and "writing degree zero." In her fictional construction and deconstruction of Jewish memories, Ozick employs "metafiction," in particular "metafictional intrusion narrative."

II. Metafictional Intrusion Narrative

In "Intertextuality," Ulrich Broich comments on the term of metafiction and reckons it as "the very trademark of postmodernism" (Broich 249). Inger Christensen explores the origin of the term "metafiction" in his book *The Meaning of Metafiction,* claiming that it is first lodged by the American critic and self-conscious novelist William. H. Gass in 1970 when he refers to the works of Borges, Barth and O'Brien (Christensen 9). Later, many other critics also propose their understandings of the term.

Larry McCaffery holds that the explicit feature of metafiction is " its direct and immediate concern with fiction-making itself " (Christensen 10). Mark Currie considers the synonym of metafiction as "theoretical fiction" which combines criticism and narration together. And Patricia Waugh defines metafiction as a term "given to fictional writing which self-consciously and systematically draws attention to its status as an artifact in order to pose questions about the relationship between fiction and reality " (Waugh 2). In the eyes of postmodernists, there is no timeless and transcendental "meaning," instead, meaning only comes out of the difference of the artificial language signs. Hence the postmodern world is no longer a permanent reality and cannot be represented. Therefore, postmodernist metafiction is "both a response and a contribution to an even more thoroughgoing sense that reality or history is provisional: no longer a world of eternal verities but a series of constructions, artifices, impermanent structures" (Waugh 7).

In a word, metafiction emphasizes the fabrication of fiction and comments on the writing itself during the process of writing. It challenges the traditional novelists' efforts of trying to represent a realistic world, and blurs the boundaries between reality and fiction, writing and criticism.

As a postmodern writer, Cynthia Ozick makes use of postmodernist narrative in her fiction, and one of the most obvious is her utilization of metafiction in "Puttermesser: Her Work History, Her Ancestry, Her Afterlife."

As is touched upon in Chapter Three, the concrete feature of Ozick's application of metafiction in "Puttermesser: Her Work History, Her Ancestry, Her Afterlife" is the intrusion narrative, in which the narrator steps into the fictitious world and becomes part of it. Intentionally, the narrator intrudes into the narrative and criticizes in a detached and objective tone, intending to break the dividing line between writing and criticism as metafiction is featured. More specifically, the narrator interrupts the narrative in a voice that takes issue with "Puttermesser's biographer" to question Puttermesser's reliance on her invention of the connection with "Uncle Zindel" and accuse the biographer of excessive fabrication. In addition to the insistence that the biographer distinguish between Puttermesser's fantasy and her life, there is in the metafictional intrusion a moral imperative proposed to the reader, namely, to resist temptation to "posit ancestry."

The realistic significance of Ozick's employment of postmodernist metafictional intrusion narrative lies in the following two aspects:

First, as Robert Scholes remarks, "metafiction assimilates all the perspectives of criticism into the fictional process itself" (Scholes 23). That Ozick uses metafictional intrusion narrative to bring Puttermesser's invention of "Uncle Zindel" to a challenge indicates that fictional construction of Jewish memories is but figuration and its effects of fictionality are made explicit: figuration does suffice identity construction or establishment of a tie with the Jewish past.

Second, as is analyzed in Chapter Four, there is another realistic function in Ozick's rejection of Zindel, the immigrant ancestor. With the metafictional intrusion narrative which brings Puttermesser's invention of "Uncle Zindel" to an end and paves the way for Ozick's further conjuring imagination of the female golem Xanthippe, Ozick distinguishes herself from the common practice of the other contemporary Jewish writers who have defined themselves through writing about the immigrant experience. Ozick, however, intends to carve her way into Jewish American literature by means of mingling Judaism engagement with moral ethos.

While Ozick applies "metafictional intrusion narrative" in her fictional construction and deconstruction of the Jewish memories, she adopts "writing degree zero" in the Holocaust representation.

III. Writing Degree Zero

In *Writing Degree Zero*, which appeared in its original French version in 1953, Roland Barthes discloses that "the whole of Literature, from Flaubert to the present day, became the problematics of language" (Barthes 3) and inevitably writers in the postmodern era became enslaved and strove to write at the zero degree.

According to Barthes, "writing at the zero degree is basically in the indicative mood, or if you like, amodal; it would be accurate to say that it is a journalist's writing, if it were not precisely the case that journalism develops, in general, optative or imperative (that is, emotive) forms" (Barthes 76-77). In addition, "the zero degree of writing" is referred to as one of the "neutral modes of writing" (Barthes 5) and Barthes further explains

The new neutral writing takes its place in the midst of all those ejaculations and judgments, without becoming involved in any of them; it consists precisely in their absence. But this absence is complete, it implies no refuge, no secret; one cannot therefore say that it is an impassive mode of writing; rather, that it is innocent. (Barthes 76-77)

To sum up, "writing degree zero" is featured by the neutral journalist writing in the indicative mood.

In "The Shawl," where the Holocaust is represented in the Midrashic mode as is discussed in Chapter Three, Ozick gives full play to "writing degree zero."

First, the characters in "The Shawl" are presented "in the indicative mood" (Barthes 76). Rosa is "a walking cradle," "a floating angel" (Ozick "The Shawl" 3); "Magda wound up in the shawl," (3) "mistaken there for the shivering mound of Rosa's breasts" (6); Stella's "knees were tumors on sticks, her elbows chicken bones" (3).

Second, the death of the infant Magda is presented in a journalist's manner: "Then Stella took the shawl away and made Magda die" (6). Moreover, what epitomizes Ozick's writing at the zero degree is the "neutral mode" she adopts in her journalist's representation of Rosa's witnessing of Magda's death, revealing no emotion of the narrator. "The electric voices began to chatter wildly. 'Maamaa, maaamaaa,' they all hummed together" (9). "Maamaa" is the first and the last utterance of Magda.

> All at once Magda was swimming through the air. The whole of Magda traveled through loftiness. She looked like a butterfly touching a silver vine. And the moment Magda's feathered round head and her pencil legs and balloonish belly and zigzag arms splashed against the fence, the steel voices went mad in their growling, ... (10)

There is no revelation of the narrator's emotion from the beginning to the end of the story. The narrator is but telling of the death of an infant in a concentration camp in the Holocaust in a neutral journalist manner, leaving much emotional experience, value judgment, and meaning construction to the reader.

While writing at the zero degree, Ozick invites and maximizes the reader's judgment and interpretation. As she identifies Jewish writing as "literature which dared to introduce into the purely imaginative the elements of judgment and interpretation" (Ozick *Metaphor & Memory* 223), her invitation and maximization of the reader's judgment and interpretation is but evidence of her construction of Jewish writing.

In addition to "heteroglossia" and "polyphonic mode," "metafictional intrusion narrative," and "writing degree zero," Ozick makes use of "intertextuality" to foreground the moral ethos concerning Jewishness and feminine representation.

IV. Intertextuality

"Intertextuality" is a term coined by Julia Kristeva to designate the various relationships that a given text may have with other texts. These intertextual relationships include anagram, allusion, adaptation, translation, parody, pastiche, imitation, and other kinds of transformation. In the literary theories of structuralism and post-structuralism, texts are seen to refer to other texts (or to themselves as texts) rather than to an external reality. The term "intertext" has been used for a text drawing on other texts, for a text thus drawn upon, and for the relationship between both.

In "Levitation," a tale about two married novelists, Ozick makes use of intertextuality and represents artists' lives. The employment of intertextuality attests to Ozick's insistence on history, for drawing upon other texts and establishing a relationship with other writers is in a sense being in history in terms of other texts and writers whereas for distinct meaning.

Transformations in the intertextuality in "Levitation" chiefly fall into two categories, adaptation and allusion. Adaptation finds its expression chiefly in the intertexts with the experience of Menachem ben Zerach and the compassionate Christian knight as recorded in Heinrich Graetz's *History of the Jews*. There are the allusion of Lucy Feingold to Saint Lucy, the allusion to the flood and Noah's two birds in Genesis in the Feingolds' experience at the party, and the allusion of Lucy's mind-pictures and sensory memories to the fundamental divergence between the pagan and the Judaic conception of the divine in Heinrich Graetz's "The Structure of Jewish History."

Unknown and excluded from the ranks of famous writers in New York, the Feingolds take delight in their productivity. Despite his awareness that "he did not want a Jewish wife," Feingold married a "minister's daughter" who was converted to Judaism. Despite Lucy's belief that she and Feingold have "the same premises," from the very beginning of the story Ozick differentiates Lucy from Feingold.

Indifferent to history and inclined "to speculate and ruminate" and "tempted to write solipsistically, narcissistically, tediously, and without common appeal," Lucy reads only Jane Austen's *Emma* and has written a novel "about domestic life" (4-5) whereas Feingold is drawn to history and "event," owns volumes and volumes of Jewish history, and writes "about Jews" (4). He is attracted to the Middle Ages, one of the darkest eras of Christian Europe when Jews were persecuted, humiliated, and massacred.

The intertextual relationship between "Levitation" and *History of the Jews* is in nature adaptation. The intertextual relationship of adaptation is ironic, for "the nineteenth-century historian was nothing like the novelist" (Kauvar 112).

A. Adaptation

The story Feingold attempts to construct is based on the history presented in *History of the Jews* by Heinrich Graetz, a nineteenth-century historian. For Graetz, the Middle Ages were exemplary:

> Enslaved a thousand times, this people [the Jewish people] still knew how to preserve its intellectual freedom: humiliated and degraded, it still did not become a horde of gypsies nor lose its sense for the lofty and holy; expelled and homeless, it built for itself a spiritual fatherland. ... post-talmudic Jewish history... knows no Middle Ages, in the pejorative sense of the word, which is

afflicted with the symptoms of intellectual stupor, brutishness, and religious madness. (Graetz *Structure* 136-37)

Feingold has chosen as the subject for his novel Menachem ben Zerach, a survivor of a fourteenth-century massacre in Spain as recorded in Graetz's *History of the Jews* and Feingold writes:

> From morning to midnight he hid under a pile of corpses, until a
> "compassionate knight" plucked him out and took him home to tend his wounds. ...
> Six thousand Jews died in a single day in March. ... It was nevertheless a
> triumphant story: at the end Menachem ben Zerach becomes a renowned
> scholar. (4-5)

The massacre to which Feingold refers began on the Sabbath with mobs of people demanding either the death of Jews or their conversion to Christianity whereas what draws the attention of Graetz is the twenty-two-year-old Menachem ben Zerach who was rescued by a "compassionate knight" but lost his entire family in the massacre. On recovering, Menachem ben Zerach vowed to devote himself to Talmudic studies and later wrote a compendium of theoretic and practical Judaism, but he "did not rise above the mediocrity of his times" (Graetz 144-45), thoroughly different from the "triumphant story" Feingold constructs in his novel.

In addition, while drawing upon Graetz's history of the Jews, Feingold rejects Graetz's beliefs. Drawing on the historical figure in the massacre, Feingold chiefly turns to the compassionate knight for whom he plans to write a journal, thereby converting the knight into a writer who, as Lucy observes, is really Feingold himself. He identifies himself with a Christian knight and "is married to a gentile woman whose apathy toward history contravenes Graetz's idea of Judaism" (Kauvar 112). However, Judaism was significant to Graetz not only because it "negates paganism" but because it proved "the utter insignificance of paganism as far as truth is concerned as well as its damaging effect on society" (Graetz *Structure* 66).

The vitality that imbues Graetz's account stems from his "impassioned opinions, his focus on biography rather than on neutral historical forces, his talents as a writer" (Kauvar 113), which are precisely what both Feingold and Lucy lack.

Drawn to the powerful Christian knight, Feingold displays his fascination with power. Obsessed with the events of the Middle Ages— "blood libels, " host desecration myths, the Fourth Lateran Council, the Crusades—Feingold links himself to martyrdom and impotence (Kauvar 113).

Lucy, a minister's daughter, has refused her father's gift of transmission. What merits specific attention is the fact that the minister's reading of a psalm determined Lucy to convert to Judaism, yet to her "Jews and women... were both beside the point." Nonetheless, she married a Jew, took his faith as her own, and "supposed the inner life of a housebound woman—she cited *Emma*—to contain as much comedy as the cosmos" (9, 8). She perceives that cosmos with "huge, intent, sliding eyes, disconcertingly luminous" (4).

In addition to adaptation, intertextuality is also shown in Ozick's allusion.

B. Allusion

In the description of Lucy, Ozick alludes to Saint Lucy, "the virgin martyr of Syracuse who was killed when her betrothed denounced her to the authorities as a Christian" (Kauvar 113).

Lucy Feingold, named after Saint Lucy, is featured by "the beauty of her eyes, which Saint Lucy is thought to have torn from her head as protection for her suitor" (Kauvar 113), hence the significance of her name: with a meaning of "light, " Lucy, as a name, symbolizes "divine light and wisdom." However, alluding to Saint Lucy with the same name, Ozick implies that Lucy Feingold "has martyred herself not out of religious faith but for an allegiance to a man whose religion she finds irrelevant" (Kauvar 113). Lucy Feingold possesses none of the attributes of Saint Lucy, despite the sameness in their name.

As a result, Feingold and Lucy end up as "Anonymous mediocrities. They could not call themselves forgotten because they had never been noticed" (Ozick "Levitation" 8).

Unnoticed in New York and separated from their parents, the novelists arouse no curiosity in anyone: "no one said their names. . . no one ever asked if they were working on anything new" (7, 8). In Lucy's judgment, their predicament is the fate of those who "sunk in a ghetto, " however, Ozick suggests it is their detachment from their families and their traditions that has rendered them powerless to make themselves known, pointing to Ozick's insistence on continuity in history and inheritance.

Besides the allusion to Saint Lucy, Ozick alludes to the flood and Noah's two birds in Genesis in her presentation of the Feingolds' experience at the party. In addition, Lucy's mind-pictures and sensory memories are alluded to the fundamental divergence set forth by Heinrich Graetz between the pagan and the Judaic conception of the divine in "The Structure of Jewish History. "

Ozick alludes to the flood in Genesis at the beginning of the story, the "party washed and turned like a sluggish tub; it lapped at all the walls of all the rooms"; all of the guests seemed "afloat in a tub" (9, 10). Toward the end of the story, the living room "ascended. It rose like an ark on waters" (15). Lucy's "mind-picture" invokes the flood in Genesis when the "ark . . . rose above the earth, " saving only Noah and those who accompanied him. The biblical event is transformed into a levitation to the effect of a separation between Lucy and the Jews. What is implied in the allusion is that only those who have recovered the Covenant will be renewed, like Noah and the people in the ark.

Moreover, Noah's two birds in Genesis are referred to. Lucy's and Feingold's experiences at the party disclose their distinctions not only in religion but also in writing, which are "inextricable from the novelists' respective attitude toward tradition" (Kauvar 113).

Lucy's alienation from her father's faith indicates that her denial of tradition is voluntarily decisive. Voluntarily detaching herself from tradition, Lucy hinders her imagination as a result. Confining Lucy to the earth, Ozick suggests the limitations of Lucy's imagination as well. While "Feingold is impelled upwards beyond the boundaries of what he can visualize into a realm where he must imagine the unimaginable," Lucy is anchored on the ground, which revives Ozick's description of the couple early in the story: "They wrote not without puzzlements and travail; nevertheless as naturally as birds" (4). That Feingold is later imagined by Lucy aboard the ark with the Jews suggests Ozick's simile referring to Noah's two birds in Genesis, the white dove and the black raven, one a messenger bearing glad tidings of Jerusalem's survival, the other a devourer feeding on carrion (Genesis 8: 7). While journeying upward is to ascend to freedom and redemption, remaining on the earth is to be a fallen bird bereft of the capacity to fly.

Meanwhile, there is an intertext in Lucy's mind-pictures and sensory memories, alluding to the fundamental divergence between the pagan and the Judaic conception of the divine as is set forth in Graetz's "The Structure of Jewish History."

It is mind-pictures or sensory memories that enable Lucy to decode an event or to decipher her feelings about it. In "The Structure of Jewish History," Graetz presents the primary divergence between the pagan and the Judaic conception of the divine:

> To the pagan, the divine appears within nature as something observable to the eye. He becomes conscious of it as something seen. In contrast, to the Jew ... God reveals Himself through a demonstration of His will, through the medium of the ear. ... Paganism sees its god, Judaism hears Him; that is, it hears the commandments of His will. (68)

Lucy scrutinizes the surroundings and derives pleasure from looking, displaying her Jewish inauthenticity. Ultimately, the living room ascends, carrying the Jews while leaving Lucy on the ground with her "great, luminous eyes. "

Therefore, intertextuality in "Levitation" chiefly embraces such transformations as adaption and allusion. Thanks to the adaptation shown in the intertextuality between Feingold's Menachem ben Zerach and the Christian knight in "Levitation, " and those in Heinrich Graetz's *History of the Jews*, the differences between Feingold and Graetz are made explicit; thanks to the ironical allusion of Lucy Feingold to Saint Lucy, the virgin martyr of Syracuse, it is revealed that Lucy Feingold possesses none of the attributes of Saint Lucy; thanks to the allusion to the flood and Noah's two birds in Genesis in the Feingolds' experience at the party, together with the allusion of Lucy's mind-pictures and sensory memories to the divergence between the pagan and the Judaic conception of the divine in Graetz's "The Structure of Jewish History, " Lucy is distinguished from Feingold, and furthermore, Jewish authenticity is highlighted and Ozick's Jewish visions pertinent to history and heritage inheritance are foregrounded.

In short, thanks to heteroglossia and polyphonic mode narrative employed in Ozick's insistence upon anti-idolatry, distinction and judgment, the two distinguishing elements to Jewish Ideas and Jewish writing, are highlighted; due to metafictional intrusion narrative in Ozick's fictional construction and deconstruction of the Jewish memories, the insufficiency of figuration is disclosed for identity construction; writing at degree zero in the Holocaust representation, Ozick invites and maximizes the reader's judgment and interpretation, evidence of her construction of Jewish writing; on account of intertextuality embracing such transformations as adaption and allusion, Ozick's insistence upon history is made explicit, though in a sense of being in history to relate to other texts and writers whereas for distinct meaning. Therefore, despite Ozick's employment of these postmodernist literary narratives, there is inconformity to the postmodernist tenets. Contrasted with Hassan's contention that postmodernism is featured by "indeterminacy" and "immanence," Ozick satisfies her determinate realistic needs to stay Jewish with the employment of these postmodernist literary narratives, hence the foregrounding of the realistic significance, the "minority" in the diasporic space which is merged with the "majority," the postmodernist literary narratives.

Conclusion

Cynthia Ozick, as a Jewish writer in Diaspora, has managed to give her literary power to highlight the minority, Jewishness, in the diasporic space she establishes in her fiction as is shown in the relationships between Jewishness and "literature as idol," Jewishness and history representation, and Jewishness and literary narrative. Likewise, as a Jewish woman writer in Diaspora, Ozick has foregrounded the dual minority of Jewishness and femininity in her Jewish feminine representation. The minorities have been constructed as the majority in her diasporic space as a result of the performance of her literary power.

Keenly aware of the tension as an observant Jew, a woman, and a writer in America, the three basic ingredients of the composition of her own identity in the diasporic context, and moreover, struggling to resolve the tension, Ozick explores the relationship between Judaism and imaginative writing and establishes diasporic space in her fiction, a paradoxical space, wherein the "minority" representing the homeland is morally adhered to and literally foregrounded.

Ozick has enriched the Jewishness of contemporary Jewish American fiction, for she has mingled and expanded the essential aspects featuring contemporary Jewishness, namely, moral ethos, Judaism engagement, and loyalty to fact in the Holocaust representation.

First, moral ethos is mingled with Judaism engagement in Ozick's literary representation of her primary Jewish insistence upon anti-idolatry in resolving the conflict between Judaic monotheism and literature as idol. The Jewish vision of idolatry resistance is foregrounded in her literary practice.

Second, moral ethos is foregrounded in Ozick's fictional construction and deconstruction of Jewish memories, in her efforts in balancing historicity and figuration in her Midrashic representation of the Holocaust, and in her advocacy of Jewish authenticity in the Post-Holocaust, pointing to her Jewish vision that history is judgment and interpretation.

Third, Judaism engagement is enriched with Ozick's moral judgment made of the prohibiting Orthodox Judaic gender law that results in her representation of Jewish femininity, highlighting "Eros of ideas."

Fourth, the scope of moral ethos is expanded in her employment of indeterminate postmodernist literary narrative to satisfy her determinate needs to be Jewish in endowing such postmodernist literary narrative as heteroglossia and polyphonic narrative, metafictional intrusion narrative, writing degree zero, and intertextuality with realistic significance to serve her needs to stay authentically Jewish.

The Jewishness in Ozick's fiction is characterized by the moral ethos that she has highlighted in the diasporic space, where the "minority" representing the homeland is merged with the "majority" representing the hostland and is eventually foregrounded as a result of the literary power she endows with her fiction imbued with moral weighing of the conflicts between the insistence upon Jewishness and "literature as idol," history representation, feminine representation, and literary narrative.

In "Toward a New Yiddish," Ozick advocates creation of an indigenous Jewish American literature in English, which is "centrally Jewish in its concerns" (174) and she has further defined "the Jewish writer" and "Jewish writing" as well.

She insists that "The Jewish writer, if he intends himself really to be a Jewish writer, is all alone, judging culture like mad, while the rest of culture just goes on being culture" (Ozick *Art & Ardor* 166). It is with the capacity to make judgments that Ozick comes to the decision to foreground the minorities in Diaspora and construct them as the majority with her literary power in her creation. Her practice is a testimony to her vision.

Emphasizing the significance of judgment-making to the Jewish writer, Ozick likewise highlights the significance of judgment to Jewish writing. She identifies Jewish writing as "literature which dared to introduce into the purely imaginative the elements of judgment and interpretation" (Ozick *Metaphor & Memory* 223), which is exactly what she herself has attempted in her literary practice.

In Ozick's judgment, no fiction produced by Jews in the Diaspora has had lasting value except that which is "centrally Jewish" (Ozick *Art & Ardor* 155). Her judgment, however, is in sharp contrast to the common practice of the Jewish writers who gained their predominance and significance at the expense of what is essentially Jewish.

The same is true of her insistence that "A writer is a writer" (Ozick *Art & Ardor* 285), and the idea that writers should not be separated by gender. In her judgment, the practice of basing literary judgment on gender is a "Great Multiple Lie," which takes for granted that women's imagination is sexually determined and that their gender "inherently circumscribed and defined and directed the writer's subject matter, perspective, and aspiration" (Ozick *Art & Ardor* 288-89).

Breaking through barriers of the conventional judgment, either in Jewishness or literary femininity, Ozick turns out to be a literary genius in a serious way, for she has put into practice what she herself defines as genius: "I think genius probably breaks through the barriers of all convention. That's special, that's genius. But then how could we talk about literature in a serious way without confronting genius...? Otherwise, it's simply writing" (Kauvar interview 1985 393). The barriers of convention, which Ozick has broken through, are not confined to the judgment of Jewishness and femininity. She challenges the conventional interpretation of imagination and introduces into the purely imaginative the elements of judgment and interpretation, which in turn reveals that Ozick's writing is Jewish.

Ozick is as committed as a Jew as she is a writer. Ideas, Jewish ideas, matter to her deeply (Pinsker 1987b 113). She means to "find out not what it is to be a Jew... but what it is to *think* as a Jew" (Ozick *Art & Ardor* 157).

It is with the capacity to make distinctions that Ozick comes to the realization of the existence of the conflicting claims. In "Bialik's Hint," she argues,

> The Jewish Idea, I believe, was characterized by two momentous standards. The first, the standard of anti-idolatry, led to the second, the standard of distinction-making—the understanding that the properties of one proposition are not the properties of another proposition. Together, these two ideals, in the form of urgencies, had created Jewish history. (Ozick *Metaphor & Memory* 224)

Distinction-making is related to the refusal to blur, which is incompatible with fusion, however, Ozick, while insisting upon making distinction, paradoxically advocates connection in claiming "I want to be a social writer. I want to write about, not about these walls as separation, but about connections" (Kauvar interview 1985 391). As a matter of fact, Ozick's intention to write about connections has seeped into her consciousness and serves as the guideline in her literary practice.

Therefore, there is a paradox between Ozick's insistence upon distinction-making and her practice in "the fusion of secular aesthetic culture with Jewish sensibility" (Ozick *Metaphor & Memory* 229), just like the diasporic space, which is paradoxically a non-space and a third space.

It is distinction-making that initiates her tension as a Jewish woman writer whereas it is the practice of fusing imagination with Jewish visions that has established her status as an acclaimed Jewish woman writer in America.

The paradox, however, is intrinsic in Jewish roots. As Leo Baeck, whom Cynthia Ozick has mentioned as one of her major influences, has pointed out in *The Essence of Judaism*, there is a "blend of tension and paradox prevalent in Jewish religiosity" (Baeck 150). As is argued by Baeck, Judaism is paradoxical concerning fear and love of God, free will and determinism, optimism and pessimism, revelation and commandment, significance and limitation, transcendence and immanence.

There is a paradox in Ozick's textual practice. In her literary insistence on anti-idolatry, for instance, in "The Pagan Rabbi, " which is concerned with idolatry and imagination, despite the differences in attitude to and capability of imagination, both Isaac and Sheindel are paradoxically characterized as having committed idolatry. In *The Messiah of Stockholm*, which focuses on idolatry and language worship, language is presented at once as both meaningful and destructive.

In her history representation, Ozick calls urgently for history and historicity, for she is entirely aware of historical discontinuity. In order to alleviate and resolve the strain of evoking memory where memories are scant, she paradoxically asserts the significance of the past through the past as fantastic invention. The problems with loss of memory and the possibilities and/or the impossibilities of repairing the loss are paradoxically foregrounded. Specifically speaking, it is Ozick who allows for Puttermesser's invention of Lower East Side origins, as is true with Kornfeld's reinvention of the biblical history and Lars's reinvention of his personal history, and it is Ozick as well who paradoxically instructs that all these inventions should be regarded as the protagonists' own fantasy. In addition, in pursuing a connection to the Jewish past, Ozick turns to the golem legend whereas the golem is characterized as representing appetite and hence lives exclusively in the present, distancing from the historical presence and the link to Jewish folklore and Jewish history. Finally, despite the actual recurrent subject of the Holocaust in her literary practice and her reputation as one of America's most accomplished novelists of the Holocaust, Ozick prohibits poeticizing the Holocaust. In representing the Holocaust, she seeks to dovetail historicity and figuration paradoxically.

In her feminine representation, Ozick has presented female protagonists who are both acquiescent to and rebellious against the Orthodox Judaic gender law. The Jewish mothering is superficially unmotherly. In the flights of imagination Ozick conjures for these female protagonists, there are ideas resulting from the act of purifying, while the conjuring and purifying aspects, as Ozick herself asserts, "are icily, elegiacally, at war" (Ozick *Art & Ardor* 198).

In her employment of literary narrative including heteroglossia and polyphonic narrative, metafictional intrusion narrative, writing degree zero, and intertextuality, the indeterminate postmodernist narratives are meant for a determinate need to be Jewish.

Ozick is as committed to her craft as she is to her faith: she carves out perfection in every single "comely and muscular" sentence (Ozick *Metaphor & Memory* 109). She contends that *"What literature means is meaning"* (247). All the judgment and interpretation she introduces into the purely imaginative result in meaning. She holds that *"Literature is for the sake of humanity"* (247). In an interview, John Updike says, "to be a person is to be in a situation of tension, is to be in a dialectical situation" (Upike 101). A similar view has been touched upon by Joyce Carol Oates who holds that "the spirit of contrariety lies at the heart of all passionate commitment" (ix). The tension Ozick encounters as a Jewish American woman writer is but the impetus of her creation.

Furthermore, Ozick insists that *"Literature is the recognition of the particular"* (Ozick *Art & Ardor* 248). It is out of this very insistence that her work is imbued with an authentically Jewish nature. Her celebrity status and the ample recognition of her belletristic reputation in the United States attest to her claim, "If we blow into the narrow end of the *shofar*, we will be heard far. But if we choose to be Mankind rather than Jewish and blow into the wider part, we will not be heard at all" (Ozick *Art & Ardor* 177).

Valued as Jewish merits, the capacities to make judgments and distinctions enable Ozick to come to the judgment and interpretation that she introduces into the purely imaginative, hence the insistence upon anti-idolatry, historicity and history as judgment and interpretation, "Eros of ideas" as the feminist mending of the prohibiting Judaic gender law, and the application of postmodernist literary narrative for realistic function in her literary practice. The paradox between Ozick's insistence upon distinction-making and her practice in "the fusion of secular aesthetic culture with Jewish sensibility" and moreover with Jewish visions, together with the paradox in her textual practice, further attests to her Jewish nature.

In a word, Cynthia Ozick is a committed Jewish woman writer and a literary genius in a serious way. Of abiding appeal in her fiction is the authentic Jewish nature, which has enriched the Jewishness of contemporary Jewish American fiction. Her fiction boasts of the power to elevate the "tribal" and the ethnical toward universal and timeless significance.

Works Cited

Primary Sources:

Ozick, Cynthia. "Bech, Passing." *Art &Ardor*. New York: E. P. Dutton, 1983.

—. "Bialik's Hint." *Metaphor &Memory*. New York: Alfred A. Knopf, 1989.

—. "Cynthia Ozick." *Publisher's Weekly* (Mar. 1987): 33-34.

—. "Innovation and Redemption: What Literature Means." *Art & Ardor*. New York: E. P. Dutton, 1983.

—. "Levitation." *Levitation*. New York: Alfred A. Knopf, 1982.

—. "Literature and the Politics of Sex: A Dissent." *Art &Ardor*. New York: E. P. Dutton, 1983.

—. "Literature as Idol: Harold Bloom." *Art &Ardor*. New York: E. P. Dutton, 1983.

—. "Puttermesser and Xanthippe." *Levitation*. New York: Alfred A. Knopf, 1982.

—. "Puttermesser: Her Work History, Her Ancestry, Her Afterlife." *Levitation*. New York: Alfred A. Knopf, 1982.

—. "Roundtable Discussion." Writing and the Holocaust Conference (State University of New York at Albany, 5- 7 April, 1987). *Writing and the Holocaust*, ed. Berel Lang. New York: Holmes & Meier, 1988.

—. "The Pagan Rabbi." *The Pagan Rabbi and Other Stories*. New York: Syracuse University Press, 1995.

—. "The Phantasmagoria of Bruno Schulz." *Art & Ardor*. New York: E. P. Dutton, 1983.

—. "The Riddle of the Ordinary." *Art &Ardor*. New York: E. P. Dutton, 1983.

—. "The Uses of Legend: Elie Wiesel as Tsaddik." *Congress Bi-Weekly* (9 June 1969): 19, qtd. by Amy Gottfried, 40.

—. "Towards a New Yiddish." *Art &Ardor*. New York: E. P. Dutton, 1983.

—. *The Cannibal Galaxy*. New York: E. P. Dutton, 1983.

—. *The Messiah of Stockholm.* New York: Vintage Books, 1988.

—. *The Shawl*. New York: Random House, 1990.

Secondary Sources:

Alexander, Edward. *The Resonance of Dust: Essays on Holocaust Literature and Jewish Fate*. Columbus: Ohio State University Press, 1979.

Alkana, Joseph. "'Do We Not Know the Meaning of Aesthetic Gratification?': Cynthia Ozick's *The Shawl*, The Akedah, and the Ethics of Holocaust Literary Aesthetics." *Modern Fiction Studies* 43.4 (1997): 963-90.

Alter, Robert. "Defenders of the Faith." *Commentary* (July 1987): 53-54.

Antler, Joyce. "Sleeping with the Other: The Problem of Gender in American-Jewish Literature." *Feminist Perspectives on Jewish Studies*. Ed. Lynn Davidman and Shelly Tenenbaum. New Haven: Yale University Press, 1994: 191-223.

Baeck, Leo. *The Essence of Judaism*. New York: Schocken Books, 1948.

Bakhtin, Mikhail. *The Dialogic Imagination: Four Essays*. Trans. Caryl Emerson and Michael Holquist. Austin: The University of Texas Press, 1981.

Bar-On, Dan. "Transgenerational After-Effects of the Holocaust in Israel: Three Generations." *Breaking Crystal: Writing and Memory after Auschwitz*, ed. Efrainm Sicher. Urbana-Champaign: University of Illinois Press, 1997.

Baskin, Judith R. "Women of the Word: An Introduction." *Women of the Word: Jewish Women and Jewish Writing*. Ed. Judith R. Baskin. Detroit: Wayne State University Press, 1994: 17-34.

Baumgarten, Murray. *City Scriptures*. Cambridge: Harvard University Press, 1982.

Bell, Pearl K. "New Jewish Voices." *Commentary*. June, 1981.

Berger, Alan L. "Jewish American Fiction." *Modern Judaism* 10 (1990): 221-41.

Bloom, Harold. ed. *Cynthia Ozick*. New York: Chelsea House, 1986.

Bogdanoff, Helene Rebecca. "Women in the Rabbinate and in American Fiction: A Literary and Ethnographic Study." M. A. thesis, North Carolina State University, 2006.

Boyarin, Daniel. *Intertextuality and the Reading of Midrash*. Bloomington: Indiana UP, 1990.

Brah, Avtar. *Cartographies of Diaspora: Contesting Identities*. New York: Routledge, 1996.

Brauner, David. *Post-War Jewish Fiction: Ambivalence, Self-Explanation and Transatlantic Connections*. New York: Palgrave, 2001.

Britannica Concise Encyclopedia. Shanghai: Encyclopedia Britannica, Inc. & Shanghai Foreign Language Education Press, 2006.

Brooks, Cleanth, R. W. B. Lewis, and Robert Penn Warren. *American Literature: The Makers and the Making*. New York: St. Martin's Press, 1973.

Brownstone, David M. *The Jewish-American Heritage*. New York: Facts On File Publications, 1988.

Butler, Kim D. "Defining Diaspora, Refining a Discourse." *Diaspora*. 10. 2 (2001): 189-219.

Cantor, Avia. *Jewish Women/Jewish Men: The Legacy of Patriarchy in Jewish Life*. New York: Harper, 1995.

Chodorow, Nancy J. *The Reproduction of Mothering*. Berkeley: University of California Press, 1978.

Clark, Tracy. "Cynthia Ozick: Overview." *Contemporary Popular Writers*. Ed. Dave Mote. Michigan: St. James Press, 1997.

Clifford, James. "Diasporas," *Cultural Anthropology*. 9. 3 (1994): 302-38.

Cohen, Arthur. *The Natural and Supernatural Jew*. New York: Berhman, 1979.

Cohen, Robin. *Global Diasporas: An Introduction*. London: UCL Press, 1997.

Cohen, Sarah Blacher. *Cynthia Ozick's Comic Art: From Levity to Liturgy*. Bloomington: Indiana University Press, 1994.

—. "The Jewish Literary Comediness." *Comic Relief*. Ed. Cohen. Champaign: University Illinois Press, 1978.

Cooper Janet L. "Triangles of History and the Slippery Slope of Jewish American Identity in Two Stories by Cynthia Ozick" *MELUS* 25. 1 (Spring 2000): 181-95.

Deleuze, Gilles, and Félix Guattari. *A Thousand Plateaus: Capitalism and Schizophrenia*, trans. Brian Massumi. Minneapolis, MN.: University of Minnesota Press, 1987.

Dickstein, Morris. "Ghost Stories: The New Wave of Jewish Writing." *Tikkun* 12, 6 November/December, 1987: 33-36.

Epstein, Joseph. "Cynthia Ozick, Jewish Writer." *Commentary*. March, 1984.

Eyer, Diane. *Motherguilt: How Our Culture Blames Mothers for What's Wrong with Society*. New York: Random House, 1996.

Finkelstein, Norman. *The Ritual of New Creation*. Albany: State University of

New York Press, 1992.

Fishbone, Carol A. "Transcending Stereotyped Motherhood." Dissertation. Drew University, 2007. UMI Number: 3284512.

Fishman, Sylvia Barack. *A Breath of Life: Feminism in the Jewish American Community*. New York: The Free Press, 1993.

Fleckenstein, Kristie S. "Resistance, Women, and Dismissing the 'I'." *Rhetoric Review* 17. 1 (Autumn 1998): 107-25.

Fuss, Diana. *Essentially Speaking*. New York: Routledge, 1989.

Galzer, Nathan. *American Judaism*. Chicago: University of Chicago Press, 1989.

Gilroy, Paul. *The Black Atlantic: Modernity and Double Consciousness*. Cambridge: Harvard University Press, 1993.

Glenn, Evelyn Nakano. "Social Constructions of Mothering: A Thematic Overview." *Mothering*. Eds. Evelyn Nakano Glenn, Grace Chang, and Linda Rennie Forcey. New York: Routledge, 1994: 1-29.

Goldsmith, Arnold. *The Golem Remembered. 1909-1980: Variations of a Jewish Legend*. Detroit: Wayne State University Press, 1981.

Gottfried, Amy. "Fragmented Art and The Liturgical Community of the Dead in Cynthia Ozick's *The Shawl*." *Studies in Jewish American Literature*, ser. 2. 13 (1994): 39-51.

Greenberg, Irving. "Polarity and Perfection." *Face to Face* 6. New York: Anti-Defamation League, 1979.

Greenburg, Blu. *On Women and Judaism: A View from Tradition*. Philadelphia: Jewish Publication Society, 1981.

Hartman, Geoffrey H., and Budick, Sanford, eds. *Midrash and Literature*. New Haven: Yale University Press, 1986.

Hays, Sharon. *The Cultural Contradictions of Motherhood*. New Haven: Yale University Press, 1996.

Heilman, Samuel C. *Portrait of American Jews: the Last Half of the 20th Century*. Seattle: University of Washington Press, 1995.

Hertzberg, Arthur. *The Jews in America: Four Centuries of an Uneasy Encounter: A History*. New York: Simon, 1989.

Heron, Kim. "'I Required a Dawning.'" *New York Times Book Review*. September 10, 1989.

The Holy Bible. New Jersey: International Bible Society, 1984.

Howe, Irving. *Jewish American Stories*. New York: New American Library, 1977.

Kakutani, Michiko. "Idol Worshipers." *New York Times* 28 Feb. 1987: A18.

Kauvar, Elaine M. The interview conducted by Elaine M. Kauvar in *Contemporary Literature* 26. 4 (Winter 1985): 358-94.

—. *Cynthia Ozick's Fiction: Tradition and Invention.* Bloomington: Indiana University Press, 1993.

Kielsky, Vera Emuna. *Inevitable Exiles: Cynthia Ozick's View of the Precariousness of Jewish Existence in a Gentile Society.* New York: Peter Lang, 1989.

Klingenstein, Suzanne. "Cynthia Ozick." *Contemporary Jewish-American Novelists: A Bio-Critical Sourcebook.* Ed. Joel Shatzky and Michael Taub. Westport, CT: Greenwood Press, 1997: 252-63.

Kremer, Lillian S. *Women's Holocaust Writing: Memory & Imagination.* Lincoln and London: University of Nebraska Press, 1999.

—. "Cynthia Ozick." *Jewish American Women Writers: A Bio-Bibliographical and Critical Sourcebook.* Ed. Ann R. Shapiro. Westport, CY: Greenwood Press, 1994: 265-77.

—. "Post-alienation: Recent Directions in Jewish-American Literature." *Contemporary Literature.* Vol. 34, No. 3, Special Issue: Contemporary Jewish American Literature. University of Wisconsin Press, Autumn, 1993: 571-91.

Krystal, Henry. "Integration and Self-Healing in Psychotraumatic States." *Psychoanalystic Reflections on the Holocaust,* ed. Luel and Marcus. New York: Ktav Publishing House, 1984.

Lehmann, Sophia. "'And Here [Their] Troubles Began': The Legacy of the Holocaust in the Writing of Cynthia Ozick, Art Spiegelman, and Philip Roth," *Clio* 28. 1(1998): 29-52.

Levinson, Julian Arnold. "'The Messiah is Uptown': Jewish Literary Practice in Postwar America." Dissertation. Columbia University, 2000. UMI Number: 9985920.

Lopate, Phillip. "Resistance to the Holocaust," *Portrait of My Body.* New York: Doubleday, 1996.

Lorde, Audre. "Uses of the Erotic: The Erotic as Power." *Sister Outsider.* Trumansburg: Crossing Press, 1984.

Lowin, Joseph. *Cynthia Ozick.* Boston: Twayne Publishers, 1988.

—. "Cynthia Ozick's Mimesis." *Jewish Book Annual*(1984-85): 79-90.

Lyons, Bonnie. "Cynthia Ozick as a Jewish Writer." *Studies in Jewish American Literature* 6 (1987): 13-23.

Merriam-Webster's Dictionary. 9th ed. 1989.

Mishra, Sudesh. *Diaspora Criticism*. Edinburgh: Edinburgh University Press, 2006.

Mishra, Vijay. "The Diasporic Imaginary: Theorising the Indian Diaspora." *Textual Practice* 10. 3(1996): 421-47.

Moelis, Joan M. "Writing Selves: Constructing Jewish American Feminine Literary Identity." Dissertation. University of Massachusetts at Amherst, 1996. UMI Number: 9709630.

Oates, Joyce Carol. *Contraries: Essays*. New York: Oxford Press, 1981.

Ofer, Dalia, and Lenore J. Weitzman. *Women in the Holocaust*. New Haven: Yale University Press, 1998.

Pappenheim, Bertha. "The Jewish Woman in Religious Life." *Four Centuries of Jewish Women's Spirituality*. Trans. Margery Bentwich. Eds. Ellen M. Umansky and Diane Ashton. Boston: Beacon Press, 1992: 148-52.

Parrish, Timothy L. "Creation's Covenant: The Art of Cynthia Ozick." *Texas Studies in Literature and Language*, Vol. 43, No. 4. Winter 2001.

Pinsker, Sanford. "Astrophysics, Assimilation, and Cynthia Ozick's *The Cannibal Galaxy*." *SAJL* 6 (1987): 75-87.

—. *The Uncompromising Fictions of Cynthia Ozick*. Columbia: University of Missouri Press, 1987.

Plaskow, Judith. *Standing Again at Sinai: Judaism from a Feminist Perspective*. San Francisco: Harper & Row, 1990.

Powers, Peter Kerry. "Disruptive Memories: Cynthia Ozick, Assimilation, and the Invented Past." *MELUS*, Volume 20, Number 3 (Fall 1995): 79-97.

—. *Recalling Religions: Resistance, Memory, and Cultural Revision in Ethnic Women's Literature*. Knoxvill: University of Tennessee Press, 2001.

Rich, Adrienne. *Of Woman Born: Motherhood as Experience and Institution*. New York: W. W. Norton and Co., 1995.

Rose, Elisabeth. "Cynthia Ozick's Liturgical Postmodernism: *The Messiah of Stockholm*." *Studies in Jewish American Literature*. Volume 9, No. 1 (1990): 93-107.

Rosen, Norma. *Accidents of Influence: Writing as a Woman and a Jew in America*. New York: State University of New York Press, 1992.

Rosenberg, Meisha. "Cynthia Ozick's Post-Holocaust Fiction: Narration and Morality in the Midrashic Mode." *Journal of the Short Story in English* 32 (Spring 1999): 113-27.

Rosenfeld, Alvin H. "Fiction and the Jewish Idea." *Midstream* 23. 7 (1977): 76-

81.

Roth, Philip. "Imagining Jews." *Reading Myself and Others*. New York: Simon and Schuster, 1985.

—. "Pictures of Malamud," *The New York Times*, April 20, 1986.

—. *The Counterlife*. New York: Penguin, 1986.

Ruddick, Sarah. "Maternal Thinking." *Mothering: Essays in Feminist Theory*. Ed. Joyce Trebilcot. New Jersey: Rowman & Allanheld, 1983: 213-30.

Schneider, Susan Weidman. *Jewish and Female: Choices and Changes In Our Lives Today*. New York: Simon and Schuster, 1984.

Scholem, Gershom G. "Isaac Luria: A Central Figure in Jewish Mysticism." *Bulletin of the American Academy of Arts and Sciences*. Vol. 29, No. 8 (May, 1976): 8-13.

—. *Major Trends in Jewish Mysticism*. New York: Marstin Press, 1946.

—. *On the Kabbalah and Its Symbolism*. Trans. Ralph Manheim. New York: Schocken Books, 1965.

Schulz, Max. *Radical Sophistication: Studies in Contemporary Jewish-American Novelists*. Athens: Ohio University Press, 1969.

Strandberg, Victor. *Greek Mind/Jewish Soul: The Conflicted Art of Cynthia Ozick*. Madison: University of Wisconsin Press, 1994.

Sungolowsky, Joseph. "The Relationship of Edmond Fleg and André Neher." *European Judaism* 35. 2 (Autumn 2002): 90-97.

Swidler, Leonard. *Women in Judaism: The Status of Women in Formative Judaism*. Metuchen, NJ: Scarecrow Press, 1976.

Teicholz, Tim. Interview with Cynthia Ozick. "The Art of Fiction" Series (XCV) of the *Paris Review* 29 (Spring 1987): 154-90.

Telushkin, Joseph. *Jewish Literacy*. New York: William Morrow, 1991.

Trepp, Leo. *The Complete Book of Jewish Observance: A Practical Manual for the Modern Jew*. New York: Behrman House, 1980.

Updike, John. Interview. *Paris Review* (Spring 1969): 101.

Walden, Daniel. "Cynthia Ozick's Classical Feminism." *Connections and Collisions: Identities in Contemporary Jewish-American Women's Writing*. Ed. Lois E. Rubin. Newark: University Press of Delaware, 2005: 35-44.

—. Rev. of *Greek Mind/Jewish Soul: The Conflicted Art of Cynthia Ozick* by Victor Strandberg. *American Literature* 67. 4 (Dec. 1995): 886-87.

—. Rev. of *The Messiah of Stockholm* by Cynthia Ozick, *Studies in Jewish American Literature* (1987).

Wiesel, Elie. *Night Dawn Day*. Trans. Anne Borchardt. New York: Aronson, 1985.

Wirth-Nesher, Hana, and Michael P. Kramer. "Introduction: Jewish American Literature in the Making." *The Cambridge Companion to Jewish American Literature*. Shanghai: Shanghai Foreign Language Education Press, 2004.

Wisse, Ruth. "Jewish American Writing, Act II." *Commentary* 61 (June 1976): 40-45.

Yaeger, Patricia. *Honey Mad Women: Emancipatory Strategies in Women's Writing*. New York: Columbia University Press, 1988.

Yalom, Marilyn. "Cynthia Ozick's Paradoxical Wisdom." *People of the Book: Thirty Scholars Reflect on Their Jewish Identity*. Ed. Jeffrey Rubin-Dorsky and Shelley Fisher Fishkin. Madison: The University of Wisconsin Press, 1996: 427-38.

Yerushalmi, Yosef Hayim. *Zakhor: Jewish History and Jewish Memory*. Philadelphia: Jewish Publication Society of America; Seattle: University of Washington Press, 1982.

Young, James. "Names of the Holocaust: Meaning and Consequences." *Writing and Rewriting the Holocaust*. Bloomington: Indiana UP, 1988.

Zhou, Nanyi. *Toward a New Utopia: A Study of the Novels by Saul Bellow, Bernard Malamud and Cynthia Ozick*. Xiamen: Xiamen University Press, 2005.

Liu, Wensong. 刘文松. 美国犹太大屠杀叙事再现和重构历史的方法 [J]. 英美文学研究论丛 (第十三辑). 上海: 上海外语教育出版社, 2010.

Qiao, Guoqiang. 乔国强. 美国犹太文学 [M]. 北京: 商务印书馆, 2008.

Wang, Shouren. 王守仁. 新编美国文学史(第四卷) [M]. 上海: 上海外语教育出版社, 2002.

Yang, Renjing. 杨仁敬. 20 世纪美国文学史 [M]. 青岛: 青岛出版社, 2003.

一. 美国文学简史 [M]. 上海: 上海外语教育出版社, 2008.

Internet resources:

Bolick, Katie. The interview "The Many Faces of Cynthia Ozick." May 15, 1997. http://www.theatlantic.com/past/docs/unbound/factfict/ozick.htm.

Chen, Xian. *The Jewish Memory and Literary Redemption: Cynthia Ozick's "Litrugical Literature"*. Dissertation. http://dlib.edu.cnki.net

Halperin Irving. http://www.complete-review.com/reviews/ozickc/shawl.htm

Holocaust Encyclopedia. http://www.ushmm.org/ wlc/en/article.php?ModuleId = 10005143

Li, Qiong. *Paul Auster's Quests: Finding One's Place in the Darkness*. Dissertation.
　　http://dlib. edu. cnki. net

Midrash. http://en. wikipedia. org/wiki/Midrash

Norwood, Stephen H. and Pollack, Eunice G. editors. *Encyclopedia of Jewish American History*. Santa Barbara: ABC-CLIO, 2008. http://www. abc-clio. com

Ozick, Cynthia. *Contemporary Authors Online*. 2003. http://infotrac. galegroup. com/itweb/bit?db = LitRC

The Columbia Encyclopedia, Sixth Edition, 2008. http://www. bartleby. com

Acknowledgements

It took seven years to complete the book and I would like to express my appreciation to the help that I have received from the people who were so important to me in the process.

My first and foremost gratitude goes to Professor Yang Renjing, my advisor, who made the nurturing years of the project wonderful, professionally and personally. It is he who initiated me into this challenging and rewarding project. It is he who exemplified to me the acme of a caring, inspiring and committed mentor. With his timely and insightful advice on the focus and outlining of the study, the project was rendered well-oriented and accessible. With his enlightening comments and probing questions, numerous doubts were clarified while the drafting was in progress. With his gentle trust that the direction I attempted to take the study would be worthwhile, the project was honored as one that authentically represents my vision, and even the most daunting days became gratifyingly productive. It is beyond me to express my gratitude with apt words and phrases.

My heartfelt gratitude also goes to Ms. Xu Baorui, wife of Prof. Yang, whose certitude that I would complete this project finally seeped into my consciousness, and I thank her for insisting that perseverance pays.

I would like to thank the members of my dissertation defense committee: Prof. Zhao Yifan at Chinese Academy of Social Sciences, Prof. Chen Shidan at Renmin University of China, Prof. Zhan Shukui, Prof. Zhou Yubei, Prof. Zhang Longhai, Prof. Li Meihua, and Prof. Liu Wensong at Xiamen University, for their rigorous reading of my dissertation, on which the book is based, and their incisive comments and suggestions, which have helped me immeasurably in the revision and optimization.

The project would not have been completed without the steady support from The School of Language, Literature and Law in Xi'an University of Architecture and Technology. I am indebted, in particular, to the coordinating efforts in the reduced teaching loads and administrative duties, which served as both an insurance of the project completion and a great source of motivation.

Grateful appreciation is extended to all those who have been a help during various stages of the project: to Prof. Du Ruiqing, for his generous gift of the book of *Diaspora Criticism*, which helped form the critical framework of the project; to Prof. Li Meihua who spared time to shower me with feminist literary criticism to consider; to Prof. Xu Delong, Prof. Yang Dafu, Prof. Gan Wenping, Wang Haiyan, Guo Shuqing, Dr. Zhang Yahui, Dr. Hu Yonghong, Dr. Wang Zuyou, Dr. Zhou Nanyi, Zhang Mingyan, Lin Xiaohui, and Ma Zheng, for their generosity and investment of time and energy in helping with the collection of valuable primary and secondary materials; to my doctorate classmates, Lin Li, Fan Xiaomei, and Jiang Chunlan, for their friendship; to Dr. Hu Xuan'en, Dr. Sun Jian, Dr. Qian Cheng, and Dr. Ye Dong, for their timely advice of various kinds; to Prof. Han Luhua, Prof. Zou Dening, Prof. Lu Li, Tang Yifan, and Wu Yu, for their patience in sharing over tea my joy and frustration as a book writer; to Lu Yan, for her encouragement and proof-reading of the body part of the book; to Prof. Liu Wensong and editor Wang Yangfan for their professionalism in making possible the publication of the book; and to Xu Jing, for her unflagging belief in me that the years have never failed to see.

I would like to acknowledge my gratitude to my parents and sister, for their genuine interest in and unconditional support for all of my endeavors.

Finally, I owe a debt of special thanks to my husband, Sun Jiwu, and our daughter, Sun Yiwei, for their empathy, forbearance, and love. To their kindness, I owe much more than I can repay.

图书在版编目(CIP)数据

在流散空间凸现道德意识:论辛西娅·欧芝克小说中的犹太性/肖飚著.
—厦门:厦门大学出版社,2012
(美国后现代小说论丛/杨仁敬主编)
ISBN 978-7-5615-4258-3

Ⅰ.①在… Ⅱ.①肖… Ⅲ.①欧芝克,C.—小说研究 Ⅳ.①I712.074

中国版本图书馆 CIP 数据核字(2012)第 075021 号

厦门大学出版社出版发行

(地址:厦门市软件园二期望海路 39 号 邮编:361008)

http://www.xmupress.com

xmup @ xmupress.com

沙县方圆印刷有限公司印刷

2012 年 3 月第 1 版 2012 年 3 月第 1 次印刷

开本:889×1240 1/32 印张:6.75

字数:200 千字 印数:1~1 100 册

定价:25.00 元

本书如有印装质量问题请直接寄承印厂调换